Not Forgotten

LESLEY ANN ANDERSON

Not Forgotten

Vanguard Press

VANGUARD PAPERBACK

© Copyright 2015
Lesley Ann Anderson

The right of Lesley Ann Anderson to be identified as author of
this work has been asserted by her in accordance with the
Copyright, Designs and Patents Act 1988.

A CIP catalogue record for this title is
available from the British Library.

ISBN 978 178465 057 5

*Vanguard Press is an imprint of
Pegasus Elliot MacKenzie Publishers Ltd.*
www.pegasuspublishers.com
First Published in 2015

**Vanguard Press
Sheraton House Castle Park
Cambridge England**

Printed & Bound in Great Britain

Der, Kris & Rach
Thank you
You are precious

Acknowledgements

I am indebted to:

Eileen McGill, Tommy Logan, Maureen Messer, Jim Messer, Steve Logan, Russell Logan, Meg Carroll, Dawn Hedderly, Shelagh Pearce, Angela Jones, Kath McKeane, Caroline Wood, Maureen Duncan, Adam Wood, Bernie Carroll, Derek Hedderly, Ian (Speedy) Walker, Ian Hill, Anne Hamilton, Sheila Latta, Sandra Brown OBE, Campbell Brady, Evelyn Douglas, Lynn Barlow, Mr O'Neill, Mr Hosny, & Mr Rainey.

You kept me alive with your guidance and advice, and have always believed in me.

Part One

I

Letter to Mum dated 10th April 1974. I found it with all the others today when I was packing up to move house. I wrote this letter twenty one years ago. It really is so sad, but it made me laugh too, it really did. I was only fourteen when I wrote it.

Right that's it Mum, I've had enough. I need to tell you this. I wish I could speak to you, tell you, I wish… I wish you were here. I am <u>not</u> going back, definitely <u>not</u> going back to church. That priest's a bloody idiot, he really is. Should've heard him, '… *that's virgin on profanity young lady*'. What the hell's profanity? And of course I'm a virgin I'm only bloody fourteen – idiot man.

He said I was '*decoratin*' your memory. Decoratin? What the hell is that? How do you 'decorate' a memory? He's a fucking idiot, honestly! Said I was '*sly*' and '*deceiving*'. He was raving that I wasn't to look at myself in the mirror again, **and** to make sure I was '*fully clothed*' when I did. He had slavers frothing up at the sides of his mouth. Bloody disgusting! You should've heard him shouting about '*sins o' the flesh!*'

Bloody hours I was there with my penance. Bloody shitty penance. What does he know anyway? Of course I look in the

11

mirror. Looking in the mirror at my bare naked body wasn't even my confession. I went 'cause I wore one of your bras to school last week. I never knew they were all different sizes. Honestly nobody tells me anything here.

Mum, seriously my boobs are there, and they're bloody agony. Robert punched me last week right on my chest. I thought I was absolutely, definitely, going to die with the pain. And I can't ask Dad, 'cause he just sits 'n bloody stares at the telly. Everybody was laughing at school – your bra was far too big. I never knew they were all different sizes.

Anyway when I was coming out of the church the priest was there and he was looking right at them, I swear he was. He's a bloody pervert. I'm not going back. I hate confession anyway. Dad went off his head when I told him. Said that was all <u>his</u> private stuff. He said I had no right and I was a stupid wee tart. I swear Mum everyday I hate him more and more. I wish he was the one that was dead. Why can you not come back, Mum? I wish you could come back and tell me about bras and all that stuff. I just wish you could come back.

Please, if there is a God, which there <u>absolutely bloody isn't</u>, you'd be able to read this from somewhere up there, or are your eyes painted on?

Oh shit, I hope there is a God.

If you're God then give this letter to my mum. Please. Tell her it's from Ruth. I'm Ruth Nairn, I live in Galashiels. Do you know where that is? I thought you could see everything? So if you can, then you can see me while you're floating about up there, and if you can see me then you will know who my mum is. So give her this please, and tell her it's from Ruth. Please.

July 1995

Ruth Nairn was now thirty-four years old, almost thirty-five. She was making important decisions, of which she was both certain, and hugely undecided; mature in her reasoning, yet she was approaching this day with the child-like essence of gay abandon. Reaching into her pocket for her keys, a nervous excitement began to erupt deep within her. It caught her breath. Her ears filled with the pounding of her heart. She checked her watch; just after half six. *A new day, a new start; oh my God please let this be the right thing to do. Bloody hell, what am I doing?* Easing her fingers from the letterbox, the keys to her now empty flat landed with a dull clink on the estate agent's floor. Ruth leaned forward, pressing her forehead against the cool glass of the estate agent's window. Each warm, exhaled breath generated a mist that descended slowly across the glass like a curtain call at the end of a show. With each long, certain yet fearful breath, the mist fell lower until the keys to her flat, the keys to her life as she knew it, were out of sight.

For a moment she considered breaking the glass with her bare hands and clawing them back. Then there it was again, that tight knot in her guts. It was as though she was responding to the tug of an invisible overstretched umbilical cord that had begun to spontaneously recoil.

Up until recently, Edinburgh had been her home; more than home, it had been her saviour. Edinburgh had been vitally important to her from the day she had arrived in the city from a sleepy Borders town over seventeen years ago. So it seemed a bit surreal that she should feel compelled to leave with no real idea of where she was going to end up. Whilst nervous, as she stood there she felt reassured when she remembered the very wise words of a former colleague, which she repeated to herself like a mantra as she pulled herself back from the door of the estate agents and turned towards The Meadows. *Wherever you want to go, you have no choice but to start from where you are. Wherever you want to go, you have no choice but to start from where you are. Wherever you want to go, you have no choice but to start from where you are. This is the right thing, this is the right thing, this is the right thing.* Before long, her uncertain step became a determined march, synchronising with the rhythm in her head, *this is the right thing to do, this is the right thing to do, this is the right thing to do.*

It was true there had been a time when Edinburgh had instantly seduced her.

Emerging tentatively, a somewhat shy, gawky and leggy teenager, from St. Andrew's bus station into St. Andrew's Square, she was taken in by the sheer size of the buildings. Looking around the square, she was impressed by the huge white stones built symmetrically into buildings that looked balanced; she liked that. Balanced. There were open spaces, cherry trees blossoming and sky to see. It wasn't what she imagined the city to be like. She expected to have the breath squashed out of her by over eager pedestrians, and the sky to disappear, squeezed out by the high, chaotic buildings. She had prepared herself to feel claustrophobic, prepared herself to feel afraid; but she wasn't. In fact she liked the uniformity of it. Turning left down South St. David's Street she became aware that as people hurried past her on her left and brushed by on her right, no-one looked at her, no-one nodded, no-one caught her eye with that 'There's Ruth, pity about her mum' look. No-one knew she was Poor Ruth. Poor Ruth was suddenly just another seventeen-year-old skipping school to hang out in Princes Street Gardens.

She could remember the noise of bagpipes that had drifted around her from a lone piper standing on the corner of Waverly Bridge. Crossing Princes Street to where the lone piper was stationed, her gaze fell upon the Walter Scott Monument. Looking up, shielding her eyes from the glare of the spring morning sun, she spotted movement at the top of the towering black spire. Straining her gaze against the sun she realised it was people, and what she could see was just their heads, shuttling back and forth around the top like small disembodied beads that had been cut loose from a thread. She'd never seen anything like this before. There were no towering awe-inspiring monuments in Galashiels. It seemed strange to her that people were up there. *What the hell are they doing up there? Are they stuck? Have they gone up on purpose? Everything's domes and spires around here,* she noticed as she walked onwards towards the Royal Infirmary along South Clerk Street, where the university dome is only just surpassed by the grand dome of Registrar House.

The bagpipes struck up again, interrupting her thoughts with the whine of the bag being filled before eventually infusing the air with the opening bars of *Cullen Bay*. Just then at seventeen years old, when it really does seem like the whole world is turning and moving wildly against and around you, Ruth realised she was the only one standing still. Everything around her was moving, some things fast; people, taxis, an ambulance, a cyclist, a bus. Others she noticed moved in huddled masses, necks strained and gazes aloft; namely tourists and groups of schoolchildren being herded along by fraught-looking teachers. Some meandered; students, window shoppers, and the couple that had just bought ice-creams who were looking for a quiet place to stretch out on the grassy bank of the Gardens. As she stood still, watching it all moving around her, she felt part of it all. She felt completely consumed by it all, and it felt nice. It felt right and it felt strange all at the same time.

She checked her map and started to move forward, stepping into the rhythm of the city centre. A rhythm that became less organised and less balanced as she wandered along Waverly Bridge. She was aware there was now an essence of chaos embedded in the narrow cobbled streets of the Old Town. Far from feeling afraid, she felt it all slowly and seductively engulf her as she made her way up Cockburn Street emerging onto The Royal Mile. Onwards she strode, absorbing it all as she made her way towards the Royal Infirmary for her interview.

Even now, in her mid-thirties, every detail of that first day in Edinburgh on her own in the city was rooted so deeply in her memories, it was like yesterday: the way the tips of her heels echoed as she sped nervously along the corridors of the Royal Infirmary to her interview; the overpowering smell of disinfectant wafting from invisible wards that were hidden behind red and black tiled corridors decorated with bronzed busts that seemed to make it look more like a museum than a hospital. It was all fresh. Just like yesterday.

In fact, Ruth had often marvelled at the way every insignificant minutia of those years between sixteen and twenty can be effortlessly recalled by a view, the first bars of an old song, or a hint of a scent. On her arrival in Edinburgh it was as though each of her senses had woken up after a long, long sleep. She could remember almost every outfit she had worn, every smile, every glimpse of an eye, every let down, every insult, every stumble, every sharp intake of breath, and every sigh of relief.

Yet now, she can hardly remember what she did last week. She was aware that over the past few years, most events had been rammed to the back of her brain, unexplored and largely misunderstood like unwelcome mail, to be opened and digested at a later date.

She paused on her way towards Lauriston Place to ask herself this – *What exactly I am leaving behind this time?* Her answer – *An empty flat and a nursing career that's turned out to be totally hopeless.* She could write a book on nursing. If she did it would be called *Nursing – My Psychological Death.* Then there was the issue of men. More so it was the issue of the random short and fragmented crappy relationships she had survived.

Inhaling the cool air of the early morning deeply, she conceded that the seventeen years she had spent in Edinburgh had been a seduction without substance. With that she felt the sharp intake of her breath sting the back of her throat. Thrusting her shoulders back, she marched with purpose towards her destination.

Wispy remnants of the early morning haar from the North Sea were still flirting with the edge of The Meadows as Ruth, with gaze firmly fixed ahead, made her way to the centre of Edinburgh. Her stride was sure, her poise erect, she did not turn back to look towards the Infirmary, or her flat beyond it in Beufort Road. She looked forward, towards Authur's Seat. She noticed the tips of the Crags managing to thrust defiantly through the sea mist that had silently invaded the city in the night. She realised that was just how she felt, like she was emerging from some kind of fog that had slowly and insidiously taken her hostage, a freezing fog that over the years had anaesthetised her sensibilities. Lifting her gaze upward, she noticed splinters of light cutting through, producing thin shafts of early morning sun that illuminated the dew on the grass ahead of her. It looked to her as though her path had become illuminated like some kind of celestial journey of self-discovery.

Led only by the strength of her instinct, Ruth was aware of a quickening in her stride, aware she was being pulled back to her roots like a floundering fish swimming against the tide, forcing her way forward, mentally leaping upriver like salmon returning to spawn. She felt it. She knew somewhere buried deep within the core of her soul there was a need for closure,

closure of a wound still raw, still open: a psychologically penetrating wound that had been left open and raw when she was sixteen, by Mick. Whenever she thought of home and her childhood, she thought of Mick. Not her dead mum and her almost dead dad. Always, always she thought of Mick Munroe. She was surprised to find her brother could also remember who he was, but for different reasons.

Ruth had phoned Robert the day before she left Edinburgh. She had purposefully left that call until the day before as she feared he might, with his inertly logical brain, talk her out of moving and taking what he would assume was a huge risk.

"Tomorrow, I mean tomorrow?" Robert was genuinely surprised. This was Ruth, safe Ruth. Ruth that didn't do spontaneity, Ruth that didn't take risks.

"Yeah, tomorrow." The doubt that had unwittingly crept into Robert's response didn't unsettle Ruth like it might normally have done.

"Why? What about your job?" Two questions there. Ruth chose to answer the second and ignore the first for the time being.

"I don't think I have ever liked my job."

"What? You do so. You've done it for years." It was as though telling her she liked her job would be enough to convince her she did.

"Doing it for years doesn't mean anything. Anyway I just kind of fell into nursing, or rather I crept into it. If I'm being honest I was kind of trying to find out how Mum died and I never did."

"But you know how she died." His tone was suddenly hushed. He was becoming a little impatient with Ruth.

"No, I don't. I know what she died of, but not actually how she died. And in all these years I have come to learn that people die differently every time. So I've never actually seen a person die, and then thought that's the one, that's how my mum would have done it."

"Jesus, Ruth, you can't keep going over that stuff." Robert had dealt with the aftermath of their mum's death, like he was sorting through 'stuff'. Like 'stuff' you might sort through for a jumble sale or a charity shop. It often seemed to Ruth that he had actually organised his emotions in quite a clinical and methodical fashion. So much so, she feared one day all the 'stuff' he had so cleverly sorted in his head would return disguised in some other huge, big, mixed up, unsorted pile of shite, and punch him squarely in the guts. Blow the wind right out of his sails. Not that she would ever wish that upon him. He was precious to her. She just knew that one day it would happen, and when it did, he would fold.

"I was curious, just curious. I was trying to see if I could get it right in my head. You know, find out answers and things like that."

"Answers? What answers? So does that mean your question would be, 'How did she actually draw her last breath?' For Christ's sake, Ruth."

"It was always all right for you, you got to go to the hospital."

"Do you seriously think that was a privilege? Or that I enjoyed that? That watching Mum die was a bloody privilege?

Or that all that made it better?" As it was, Robert's 'stuff' was actually quite easy to seek out, and mess up.

"No, no it's not that. It's just that I never got to say anything to her, or see her, or say bye or anything."

"It wasn't her though, Ruth. Really it wasn't in the end. We've gone over and over this." He wasn't annoyed by her remarks, just tired. Tired of trying to protect Ruth, and even more tired of keeping his sanity in check.

"I know. I know Rob. Please, don't be getting pissed off with me."

"I'm not, Jesus, no, I'm not… I'm just… I don't know. I suppose I wish I was you. I wish I hadn't seen her dying. I wish I wasn't the oldest. I wish I hadn't had to go and watch her drift away. Seriously every time I went I noticed something else about her had gone, disappeared. First her hair, then her eyes – there was just nothing there. Nothing. Her smile, her voice – everything. In the end absolutely everything had gone. Everything."

"Rob don't, don't. I'm sorry. Thing is, I'm not a nurse. I've never been a nurse, I've kind of been using the job and now I've stopped looking for Mum and how she died. I've stopped looking. I have. So I don't need to stay and work in there anymore."

"But Ruth… ?"

"There's no 'buts', Rob. I've already left and won't be going back. In fact it's a bloody relief to have left, should have done it years ago. There's been nothing for me here for a long time. Nothing. In fact, you know what? I do wish I was you. You've got Mark. I've got no-one. There's no-one here. I hate my flat now. I actually dread going through the front door. You know this, once I'm through that door, there's just me, only me, I'm just here myself, on my own. Myself... It's horrible here."

Ruth explained to Robert that she had spent months, if not years, wondering about relationships, love, lust and the like. She had watched couples as they came and went around her. She had often been intrigued as couples that were drawn together like magnets went on to form what seemed to be solid relationships. For the relationship then to explode and evaporate, like a chemistry experiment gone badly wrong.

She often considered this very strange. She thought that would never happen to her if she was ever drawn like a magnet to someone.

Whenever she thought of being drawn like a magnet, she thought of Mick. She knew it had been years, and wondered if it is actually possible to be in love with the memory of someone more than the actual person themselves. Could Ruth somehow be wrapped up in some kind of fantasy relationship with someone who she hadn't seen or spoken to for a very long time?

Indeed it seemed as though she was simply stuck like a magnet to the memory of him.

She would often bargain with her intangible purveyor of fate; *if I was ever to see Mick again, this time, this time...* Then as she imagined meeting him again, her head would spin, her heart would race and she could almost forget her name and date of birth. It struck her that thinking of Mick was like flirting with an all-consuming madness. She imagined what he would look like now. She imagined what their first meeting would be like. She imagined her pupils would dilate to the point she would have a stroke and be rendered speechless and salivating in front of him.

Lust-induced paralysis aside, meeting Mick was a scene she played over and over again, like a favourite record. It often made her wonder; what is that palpable thing that charges around in a person's veins and under their skin when two people meet? *What does this thing 'chemistry' amount to?* She deduced, in the absence of actually experiencing this, that the primary function of 'chemistry' lay in the preservation of the race – an instinct to breed.

To be honest these were all assumptions, as to date she had had only a few relationships. All superficial, not one of them ever stimulating her instinct to breed. Her lovers had come and gone just like the tide. None had seemed that interesting, none of them engaged her, or perplexed her the way her memory of Mick did. In reality, she and her lovers had simply been like pieces of driftwood all floating around, banging into one another in an indiscriminate fashion. Never connecting, not dovetailing together. Just bang, bang, bang into each other a few times and then drift away again, as though pulled apart by invisible undercurrents.

She was often envious of Rob and Mark. They had been together for eighteen years. They still had a palpable chemistry. Ruth had seen it – but they could never breed. So what of chemistry then? But there was a certain way they looked at each other when they thought no-one was looking at them. Those stolen little glances, the secret momentary touches that made Ruth feel like she was invading their privacy. Robert, she believed, was lucky: lucky to have Mark, lucky to have love, lucky to have affection.

It was frustrating because Ruth had in fact been in so many *right places* at supposedly *right times*, and was still on her own, that she had reached the conclusion that good relationships, with this elusive chemistry element, were down to some unimaginable force that went way beyond 'luck'.

"So, what's going to be so different back here then? Have you kept in touch with anyone here?" Robert hadn't been left assured that Ruth was going to find what she was looking for by returning home.

"No not really, but I just need to come home. I just need to come back home." She was trying hard not to sound desperate.

"Have you been in touch with Dad?"

"No, not yet".

"Well don't expect much. He's not spoken to me for years. It's that rampant homophobia of his. It gets the better of him. Anyhow, just watch out there. Don't be coming back for him."

"I'm not. I've actually been thinking about someone else for ages."

"Aye, have you? Who?"

"Mick Munroe – I just told you about him?"

"Yeah, but you did know he got that wee Polish girl pregnant, didn't you? Years ago."

"Did he?" Ruth remembered Martha Rosiewizck, walking home with Mick on the night of his twenty-first.

"Yeah, must have been a bloody quick one he gave her, 'cause her dad followed them about everywhere."

"Did he?" Ruth tried not to imagine the 'quick one'.

"They all did, did you never notice?"

"No." Ruth decided to side-swerve all this information. Mick, a dad? Not what she was imagining at all. So she changed the subject, before she could be told anything else about Mick, and what his real life might be right now.

"I found letters a few weeks ago."

"From him?"

"No, from me."

"To him?"

"No. To Mum."

"Mum?"

"Well I used to write to her. I used to leave them out on my bed and imagine that they would kind of be beamed up to her like a *Star Trek* thing."

"Oh my God. You poor thing."

"So, finding the letters has kind of given me a wee jolt, and I went to Mass a few weeks ago".

"You what?"

"Mass – Ash Wednesday."

"Seriously Ruth, I'm getting worried about you now. What on earth made you go to Mass?"

"I don't know. I was thinking about Mick, and I could remember seeing him watching us walk to church one Easter with those bloody ridiculous hats on our heads. The most bloody embarrassing thing I can ever remember. I was thinking about Easter, and when Mum died, so I went to Mass."

"And?"

"And there was nothing there really. Not really. It just made me want to come home, but I never felt anything being there, not really".

It wasn't a lie, just a half truth. She didn't want to sound like some silly airhead trying to describe this *thing* that was pulling her towards Galashiels, and that this *thing* had given her a tug when she was at Mass. It just sounded ridiculous and was just impossible to put into words. Well, logical kind of words that Rob would appreciate. He has difficulty with anything remotely abstract.

II

It's probably a good time right now to explain a bit more about the whole Mick and Ruth thing. To suggest that Ruth had grown up alongside Mick wouldn't be entirely accurate. It implies some kind of connection, some kind of similarity in their childhoods. Nothing could be further from the truth. Set apart by religion and financial wellbeing, they went to different schools. They mixed with different friends, and when, or if, they dared to look ahead, their gazes fell upon vastly disparate horizons. But their paths did cross a few times.

One of her first tangible memories of Mick was when she was around ten years old. He must have been around fifteen. It was an Easter Sunday, and he was sitting on his *Chopper*. It had a blue glitter seat with customised spokes, and multi-coloured lights. She noticed the bike also had the very enviable gear shift mechanism. It caught her eye immediately. It caught her eye more than Mick had done, because Robert, her brother, had wanted a bike just like that one, but their parents couldn't afford it. Where Ruth grew up, only a few hundred yards away from Mick, there was only one bike and one space-hopper to be shared around the cul-de-sac. Considering the bike had probably been stolen from the nearby estate, where

Mick lived, they were fairly fortunate to have had one to share at all.

Ruth remembers that every few weeks the shared bike would arrive in the car park. In those days the car park was a playground. It was mostly empty of cars as few families could afford one in the early seventies. When Ruth had worked out it was her turn to have a go on the bike, a bright orange-space hopper appeared that day too. So she had to choose. Ruth chose the space-hopper, and as a result never actually learned to ride a bike until she was seventeen, when she bought a second-hand one of her own to get around the city centre.

Back then though, when she was around ten, the excitement of the bike arriving in the empty car park was only ever surpassed by the news that a pram had been dumped on the old railway track behind the blocks of flats she grew up in. On hearing this, toddlers were plucked hastily from their door steps by panic-stricken mothers, as a frenzied stampede of young men hurtled past towards the old railway track. In the dusty scramble that followed, eyes were blackened, skin torn, wrists sprained, jaws dislocated. There really was a catalogue of minor injuries endured as all four wheels were wrenched from the pram frame.

Only those with the longest reach or strongest push would be lucky enough to grab a wheel for their bogey. This scramble meant that the wheels never went to the same person. Thus the art of bogey building, more-over bogey steering was a precarious one. Indeed the person to have a bogey with all four wheels matching was held in the highest esteem. A child's potential was all too often measured upon the calibre of their bogey. You could hear parents discreetly discuss who would make it in the wide world, and who wouldn't – the level of an individual's stamina and endurance being reflected in the condition of the bogey they produced. *'That's a fine bogey; he'll go far, that boy.'*

Ruth on the other hand, did not indulge in such fickle estimations of an individual's character or potential. No, she regarded everyone as equal, as primates. Indeed she often likened the art of watching people, which she regularly did, to that of pressing her face against the glass of the monkey enclosure at the zoo. Ruth has spent her lifetime to date watching everyone else, analysing everyone else, instead of listening to herself.

*

The morning she was returning home in 1995, the warm, awakening smell of fresh coffee drifted along flirtatiously towards Ruth as she neared the vendor at the top of The Mound. Emerging from George IV Bridge, Ruth surveyed the scene. She heard a siren in the distance. An ambulance came into view, hurtling along Princes Street with lights ablaze. Ruth wondered if it was a little person fighting to get into this world, or someone struggling to stay, that was being swept along to the Infirmary. She imagined the scene there. She followed the trail of the ambulance as it disappeared out of view along Lothian Road. The siren went on in the distance until it was silenced at the doors of A & E. Ruth sighed, almost regretfully, *not my problem any more.*

She looked along to the Walter Scott Monument in the distance on her right, and then felt strangely proud. George Miekle Kemp, its designer, had trained in her home town. Although many, many years before she was born, or even thought of, she felt as though this legacy indicated she could claim some form of ownership. Giggling inwardly at the absurdity of this, she kept up her pace and made her way along Princes Street Gardens to St. Andrews Square, where she would await the arrival of her bus home.

No stranger to getting up early, Ruth had given herself ample time. She was determined to get the first bus back to Galashiels that day. So with time to kill, she let herself drift off into one of her many day dreams, as the seven-fifteen to Corstorphine left the station concourse with a begrudging grunt at the release of its brakes.

Ruth drifted back to that Easter Sunday in 1970 when she first saw Mick – how her heart sank as she caught a glimpse of him – *what will he think of me?* Him, perched proudly on his *Chopper*, dressed in his *Birmingham Bags* and a most fashionable star-emblazoned tank top. Ruth remembers how they caught each others' eye, how Mick had started to smile, and how she had quickly lowered her head as she shuffled past – afraid he might have been laughing at her amidst the flurry of the Easter bonnet parade. This was a parade that was reluctantly, and yet proudly, conducted by the Catholic children on their way to Mass on Easter Sunday.

Now, when Ruth thought of this it seemed unbelievable. But it was believable. She had lived it. She lived through the humiliation of wearing an upturned lid taken from a cheese triangle box as a hat, with a few pieces of coloured paper glued in the middle, held on top of her head with a length of her dad's best waxed *GPO* string, cut to length by a swift swipe of his *Stanley* blade and then tied tightly under her chin, where it cut in until her skin bled. This was her Easter bonnet, and there on top of her head it stayed, with the string cutting into her chin until the end of the Easter Mass.

Ruth instinctively rubbed the underside of her chin as though the scars were still visible, still needing to be soothed. It was believable. Not just for Ruth, but for countless other Catholic children who endured the annual humiliation of wearing their decorated cheese triangle boxes on their heads from their home to the church, a journey of just over one mile on a corporative bus. God forbid that Easter Sunday should be a sunny day, for then, they would walk the mile, and thereby prolong the agony.

That was 1970. Here she was now, in her mid-thirties, moving back to her roots. In February she had gone to Mass on Ash Wednesday for the first time in twenty years. It stirred something within her when the priest smeared the palm ash across her forehead with the end of his thumb. Ruth realised then that there were certain elements of her childhood that were never going to go away, they were simply lying dormant. Whilst Ruth understood Easter to be the most important event in the Roman Catholic calendar, in her childhood calendar it meant a week of religious restraints. No playing out with friends for a week. Chapel every night, rubbing her rosary beads down to grains of sand, whilst trailing woefully around the Stations Of The Cross. Then the dark clouds of the crucifixion and Good Friday Mass arrived. All culminating on the Sunday in a parade of the most sorrowful Easter bonnets ever produced.

The saving grace on the Sunday was being able to indulge once again in whichever vice had been given up for Lent. In most cases for kids this was chocolate. Let's face it; it would never be cheese triangles, would it? They had to eat enough triangles in order to furnish the heads of every pupil in the primary school, so it goes without saying that the Catholic children of the sixties and seventies will have bones like iron girders, having had a yearly boost to their calcium intake throughout their primary school years.

There was a fairly novel mix of international pupils at Ruth's small R.C. primary school. Most of whom would never have come across processed cheese scrapings pressed into appetising little foil sealed triangles. Amongst this strong Catholic community there were Ukrainian, Polish and Italian families, who were second generation immigrants. The Polish soldiers had been stationed in the Borders during the war. The Ukrainians arrived after the Second World War, whilst the Italians originally arrived in the Borders as prisoners of war held by the British army during the Second World War.

Ruth often marvelled at the Ukrainian and Polish children in particular, who could already speak English as their second language. She remembers going along to a friend's house one afternoon and marvelling at her small friend talking fluently in Polish with her parents. As Ruth listened to them, and inhaled the appetising spice-filled air within their darkened home, she thought it was like peeping through a keyhole into another world.

Even today she often thought of this little doorway to Poland. As little snippets of these memories made their unannounced appearances within her consciousness, popping in and out of her thoughts and her dreams, Ruth was realising that there were some elements of her childhood that were quietly embedded and hadn't actually left her. Despite trying to convince herself they had. For example, the ritual of making a sacrifice for Lent seems to be a habit that becomes entrenched in a Catholic person's conscience. Even now, as an adult, Ruth still finds herself secretly making sacrifices for Lent – trying her hardest to make the forty day, forty night target.

During Lent in the most recent years she has tried to give up red wine. Usually within couple of days she realises this is an utterly futile ambition that she has little hope of achieving. More often after a stressful day in critical care, she would arrive home and uncork a bottle before her coat was off. That made it more acceptable back then, the stress relief element of drinking wine. Now she drank too much, and for no particular reason. In a turnaround, the alcohol she was drinking these days was causing her stress, not relieving it. As she waited on her bus she recalled her first encounter with the evils of alcohol.

When Ruth was sixteen, almost seventeen (the 'almost' giving her a licence, or so she thought, to go to a party without telling anyone) she had gone to a party in a block of flats near the flats she lived in. She had gone as Mick had asked her to come to his twenty-first birthday party. She had, at that point, been prone to drifting along immersed in hormone-propelled daydreams of him. Every daydream of Mick swirled around in her mind like an unpegged tent in a swift upward breeze.

Up until that night she had only visited these flats to play hide 'n seek in the stairwell. When playing games like hide 'n seek, or the more exciting version – kick-the-can, she usually hid in the second floor stairwell as the first floor stairwell had an old, well-stained double mattress tucked away in the corner. From an early age, Ruth had guessed this wasn't a provision made for the comfort of children playing a game of kick-the-can of an evening. She remembers being a bit surprised that he was having his party there. It wasn't the kind of place she had imagined Mick would live.

When Ruth arrived at the front door of the flat she could hear *Ballroom Blitz* was playing loudly and with too much treble. She knew more than most about music. It was one of her solitary pastimes after her mum died. Once inside the flat, she spotted the music was coming from an old turntable with a built-in speaker at the front. It was encased in a beige wicker-effect box, and it could stack three vinyl albums at once. It was the type that gave out a loud, mechanical click as each vinyl dropped onto the turntable, to the enormous glee of the glitter-clad audience who were strutting around on their platform shoes. Ruth was aware she was still wearing her school shoes.

She only ever had one of pair of shoes at any given time. With the bold efforts of her dad, the covert cobbler, footwear would often last for a year. If her bed was on a slant, Ruth knew her shoes were having their soles glued back onto the uppers. The broken shoe sealed up with a splodge of the finest *GPO* glue and placed under their collection of heavy encyclopaedias, or under the leg of the bed. A certain cure for any shoe that may lose its sole. The only drawback of this daring cobbling strategy was that it rendered the books unreadable for weeks at a time. When you consider that her brother's shoes were regularly being torn apart by playing football, encyclopaedias from A-G were often out of commission. Ask Ruth anything about a subject from H onwards, but A-G she's useless.

Then came the summer and the shoes would be fashioned into a pair of cunning peep-toe mules with a couple of swoops of her dad's *GPO Stanley* blade.

So there she stood, sixteen, almost seventeen, in her brother's brown duffle coat and her school shoes, which had been glued together at least twice that year already, awaiting the experience of her first illicit party, and more importantly, waiting for Mick.

On arrival she was given the choice of warm *Advocaat* and lemonade, a *Babycham* hi-ball or a mug of *Black Tower*. All were to be served in a thick-rimmed novelty mug, impregnated with tea and coffee stains, some bearing the words 'World's Best Dad'. Back then, working class homes didn't have wine racks well-stacked with wines from all corners of the globe, or display cabinets furnished with the finest of wine flutes and ornate cut glass crystal sherry glasses. Any glass tumblers that were available were usually reserved for bringing on the cuttings of a Bizzy Lizzy or a Wandering Sailor. After all, every home in the seventies had at least one window-ledge full of Bizzy Lizzy plants.

That night Ruth chose a *Babycham* hi-ball, having no idea what it actually was; it was just that the name seemed more appealing than *Advocaat*, which looked like milk gone off, or *Black Tower* which had a sinister connotation to its name, she thought. Three *Babychams* later, and a hefty dose of Showaddywaddy, Ruth was dizzy and Mick still hadn't arrived. She guessed she would never be '*Three Steps To Heaven*', feeling more like she was stuck at the bottom of a lift shaft with the up button out of order. At five years her senior, Mick Munroe seemed way out of reach. She guessed he was probably celebrating his twenty-first somewhere a bit more exciting than this. She realised it was too good to be true, he wasn't going to turn up. Thinking of Mick, with his tousled hair, and his guitar permanently strapped to his back, she imagined it would be somewhere where everyone smelt of patchouli, wore hair bands and Afghan coats. She imagined they would be spending the night dazed and confused on the floor with the likes of Crosby, Stills and Nash, Led Zeppelin and Pink Floyd buzzing away somewhere in their distant and detached psyche.

In his absence she felt her stomach heavy, like a hammock weighed down with a dozen boulders. Yet whenever she did see Mick Munroe, those rocks evaporated, popping wildly like a thousand bubbles inside her. She remembers standing on her own, willing him to arrive, waiting for that moment when the rocks in her gut would evaporate, but it never came. He didn't arrive. After a few drinks, the sharp symmetry of the orange and brown patterned wallpaper had begun to blur and Ruth realised then it was time to leave. She was, after all, just sixteen.

*

As she stepped on board the seven-thirty bus to Carlisle, Ruth realised how scarily long ago that party was, but felt she would soon travel towards some sort of resolve. Would it be too much to ask if the resolve she sought, and the instinct that was leading her, could be connected in some shape or form to Mick?

Don't think for one minute that Ruth was some sort of fickle-headed female who was living her life immersed in a notion that she was hopelessly in love with a person she never actually knew, wasting years and years absorbed in an imaginary romance. It wasn't like that at all. Ruth had tried beyond doubt to erase her memory of Mick. She has tried to ignore it, to deny it, to defy it, to pretend it wasn't there. But every time her guard is down, up he pops again, like a squatter in her head. A buoy anchored deep and firm in the bedrock of her soul. So, after all these years, she had given in to it and was heading back to find Mick Munroe.

As the bus slowly turned left from St. Andrew's Square and headed past the great dome of Registrar House towards The Bridges, Ruth sighed, realising she most likely wouldn't even recognise him if she met him now. This was probably just another of her unrealistic daydreams. She had a few of them. Some might call them delusions.

III

So what about this Mick Munroe then?

Well, if talking to oneself is a sign of madness then Mick has certainly been quite mad for as long as he can remember. Even now, at nearly forty years old, Mick often went out for a walk in order to talk directly to no-one but himself. It was something he did when he needed to think and get his head together. In fact, when he was young, around the age when memories are suddenly and magically accessible, that age when everything that's gone before is beyond recollection, unless placed under deep hypnosis, Mick remembers being warned by his gran not to talk to himself so much. She warned him that if he kept up this habit he would surely be whisked off in the dead of night in The Yellow Van (capital T, capital Y, capital V; it was much feared and much revered). Then he would spend the rest of his mortal days strapped into a straitjacket, beating his way haplessly around a padded cell, wetting and shitting himself. It was a common threat, and his gran did actually use the words 'shit' and 'shitting' when speaking to her young grandson.

As a result, even now, it trips off Mick's tongue as easy as a hello, or a thank you. Out it slips, 'shit' this and 'shit' that.

Furthermore, around the age of seven, Mick had already witnessed many adults muttering and mumbling incoherently to themselves, thus he imagined most of the adults in his life were living in a silent and constant terror of The Yellow Van. Every time he heard his mother speaking to herself, he imagined The Yellow Van careering along the rural roads in the Borders, tearing around the sharp bends on two wheels, making haste towards their home, straitjackets at the ready.

The Van, legend has it, scooped up all the maniacs, snatching them off the streets like stray dogs to be impounded in the local asylum. Sirens were often heard from the asylum high on a nearby hill to warn of inmates breaking loose. Mick grew up understanding that the siren warned the public to lock all doors. He harboured images of children and pets being whisked indoors with bolts and locks sliding and clanking securely into place. For some time Mick feared that the siren signalled that dangerous individuals were rampaging around the streets in a frenzy of incomprehensible babbling. And so for a long time he worried that adults who spoke to themselves may really be a danger to the public.

He had no idea then how misguided these casual threats of The Yellow Van were and how they were perpetuating stereotypical opinions of mental illness. He had no idea of the true horrors that surrounded the history of lunacy laws, or of the impounding of ordinary people: individuals who may have been locked away for simply being poor, or for suffering epilepsy, or having a baby out of wedlock.

Now, in clear defiance of The Yellow Van avoidance advice of his youth, at almost forty years old, Mick can often be heard talking to himself. You see, things have happened and now The Yellow Van, the memories of the siren, threats of the padded cell and the prospect of shitting and pissing himself for the remainder of his days, no longer score highly on his list of things that need to be worried about. So he talks to himself now, realising the only confinement he need be concerned about is that imposed by his own emotional straitjacket; the one that encases the seemingly impenetrable walls of his mind.

His seventeen-year-old daughter has just revealed that she floats out of her body at night. Mick has currently rated this as a number one worry. It had overtaken his long-term self-perpetuating anxiety of how to achieve being a mum and a dad at the same time, like some kind of chronic condition where he is required to be a double-gendered parent. Like a coin with two faces, that can be swiftly switched from Mum to Dad with the fleetest flip of a thumb on a forefinger. This was an all-time favourite self-indulgent worry. It had siphoned his energies and occupied the number one slot of all worries for as long as he could remember. Yes, it did seem as though he had been at war with himself, his life, and his responsibilities since soon after his birth.

At times like this he usually considered one of the three options. He considered that each of these options could be explored as possible cognitive escape routes. He coined that phrase himself *'cognitive escape routes'*. It's really a posh phrase for being screwed up.

That aside, these routes were as follows; Route No. 1 – to be opened up within a book, Route No. 2 – to be found within the lyrics of an all-time favourite song, Route No. 3 – go for a walk. There had at one time been an escape Route No. 4 – alcohol. However he soon realised that alcohol and grief did not mix well. He found that particular combination often gave birth to some form of grief-stricken alien being that was incapable of rational thinking. It was a metamorphosis that scared him, so he stopped drinking and hadn't touched alcohol for over a decade.

Whilst considering his choices of escape routes, Mick wondered if his daughter's confession of 'floating out of her body' was just the normal dreamy-headed stuff of teenagers, or had life screwed up his beautiful daughter's mind too? Ultimately he was anxious that Anna may be blighted by the same ruin as Rosalia, her great-grandmother. *'Bloody voodoo shit's back'*, he muttered under his breath, as he laced up his walking boots and checked his pockets for the keys before he left. Thus it was with a feeling of impending doom that he chose Cognitive Escape Route No. 3 that night.

You have to understand that these routes to spiritual wellbeing had not been patented or standardised at this point, there was no magic formula. These were simply his routes, which were time-consuming and often endless. The burning question that evening was: Would Route No. 3 provide the answer to Mick's current parenting dilemma? Could he, this time, somehow escape the shit-to-fan-at-high-speed scenario?

It was late May as he ambled high into the chequered fields. The sun had already begun to set ahead of him, the sky was clear, and the breeze still had enough of a chill to catch his breath every now and then. Especially when exerting himself on the steeper, incumbent areas of the hill. Littered with concealed burrows and hidden ditches, Mick was usually aware of the need to focus in order to avoid an ankle or knee injury. However that night he was distracted for a time, and could feel his joints jarring each time his feet struck the ground off-balance.

While he stumbled on in the dusky red-tinged light, he thought of Anna floating off into the night, as she described it, and he was aware of the air, the scent of the ferns and the nip of the nettles that grew in abundance around his ankles. Ahead he could see double-headed gorse that had burst into colour as though ablaze on the hillside, foreign – almost exotic in its smell, like coconut. As he walked and wondered about Anna, his beautiful daughter, he thought too about Martha, his love, her mother, his unbearable loss.

From the hillside, he turned back and looked over the town. He watched the traffic in the distance as it quietly shuttled left to right, right to left, and slid from the top to the bottom of his view. He thought about the drivers and the passengers, and wondered where they were in their lives. Did their daughters float? Had any of them lost their lover?

He stood still and listened as the town buzzed, the lights flickered, and he watched with a grumbling resentment as it all fitted together – the traffic, the lights, the buzz, the distant drone of farm animals. Whilst he remained still, looking ahead at his home town, it struck him that although it all came into view from different places, and it all moved out toward different places, it flowed, it did, it flowed with ease, like something natural, something expected, like water gushing unhindered from a tap. Mick thought: *If everything's moving with purpose, why do I feel like I can't get any further than the inside of my bloody head? And if everything's coming together so naturally out there, why am I still falling apart? It's shit, bloody shit.* His thoughts were accompanied by a resounding *"Everything's shit."* He spat the words out with certainty, into the early evening atmosphere.

The hawthorns ahead of him lined the outer boundaries of the brow of the hill. He stood and looked at the row of hawthorns for a while; their branches were bowed low, weighted down with bloom heavy like new snow. *That's just how I feel.* He felt burdened like each small, pleading twig drooping down before him. He thought of Anna, and believed himself to be hopelessly inadequate as a dad-forward-slash-mum.

It was no good, Route No. 3 wasn't helping – he wasn't escaping. Moreover, he was simply being reminded how detached he believed he was from, and ill-prepared he was for, the responsibilities of fatherhood, motherhood and above all widowhood. It had never entered his imagination that these roles would be packaged together and forced upon him in an all-in-one, a bulk buy. Mick wondered, could all this shit really be one of life's bargains in disguise?

Indeed it was ironic that while the world around him seemed synchronised and harmonious, Mick knew everything within him was most definitely unhinged. What good could he possibly be to Anna, his floating daughter, now?

He began to make his way back to the house. As he did so, he listened to the soil squelching satisfyingly underfoot. There had been heavy rain for almost three weeks. This wasn't unusual in Scotland. In fact, the reward for perseverance of the weather here in Scotland was the stunning lush scenery that Mick walked amid whenever he chose Route No. 3.

With his gaze unusually downward he watched his left foot as it bore down solidly in the mud, followed swiftly by his right foot, and his left, and his right, while his mind wandered off, trying to connect again to that seemingly remote and isolated place that allowed access to feelings. That place where his thoughts hammered relentlessly against the innermost corners of his skull. What had happened to the tiny little synapses whose job it was to usher along the feelings of excitement? He imagined these fatigued synapses; the ones that were supposed to transmit feelings of anticipation, feelings of being utterly alive, and deduced they must be fizzled out and singed and frayed at the ends, like fused wires at overloaded junction boxes. In his head he could see his exhausted little thoughts trying to repair these intricate little pathways in his brain, trying to restore the connection. *Connect to happiness, connect to contentment soon, please,* thought Mick, *make it happen soon.*

As he reached the edge of the field and swung the awkward farmer's gate round on its lopsided rusty hinges, he recalled how earlier that evening he had looked up and caught a solemn glimpse from his daughter. How at that moment, when he met Anna's intense glare, he had felt the infinite threads of his thoughts slip themselves into a tangle of knots and impassable junctions. It was the moment he had been dreading for years; the moment when all of his parental inadequacies would catch him up, and steam-roller over him. He feared it was the moment he would be exposed as a fraud of a parent.

Anna had gestured that her dad should sit down. Thereby, indicating the seriousness of her intent as she approached him. Mick was aware that whilst maintaining eye-contact with Anna and attempting to appear composed, his hands had begun to tremble. They were shaking so much he had even found it difficult to place his pen and invoice book squarely on his desk. As his ashen-faced daughter faced him, there was little stillness in his mind.

Anna found it equally difficult to decide what would be the best way of telling her dad. How would she tell him she could read his mind and often knew what he was about to say? How on earth could she explain to him she popped out of her body at night and floated around her room, or, that when she slept she seemed to be living out another life? Her dreams really were like a vivid living experience.

If Anna were to be honest, sleep was an exhausting, rarely refreshing experience. And it didn't stop there. Often she would be aware of people following her. Then just as they were about to approach her from the side, Anna would turn to say hello, and they'd have gone. It was like they had evaporated. This happened regularly, as regularly as the images that appeared like TV screens when she closed her eyes. Images appearing alongside names that float by in her consciousness like ticker tape in the breeze.

When names and images flashed up on her 'screen' she knew that she should expect it all to materialise in reality within a matter of days. Already at seventeen, Anna had learnt to trust this thing, this quality she couldn't define.

She did, however, fear the psychiatrists would be called in again. That unbearable procession of drooling, mild-mannered, inquisitive professionals, each of them sporting an intriguing display of facial hair; men and women alike. Indeed this was a matter that interested Anna greatly. In her mind it seemed that genders swapped over after a certain age. It had been an observation of hers, having seen middle-aged men with breasts and women who were clearly struggling to conceal the growth of a full beard.

With that aside it had been her experience that once the psychiatrists had liberally massaged their own egos with Freudian jargon they left and her mum was still gone. How could they make that better? She thought she had already worked out that if someone dies, then they don't come back. Well, not in the physical sense anyway. No amount of vaguely concerned, hairy-faced women and heavily breasted men, shamelessly wearing sandals with socks, could change that.

Mick had silently started a long list of 'if only' when Anna began to talk. She believed she knew exactly where to begin, until she saw the colour drain from her dad's face. Her starting point evaded her. Thoughts she had so well constructed and organised became fragmented. Her painfully well-practised calm composure was replaced by an overwhelming sense of urgency that tightened around her throat, as though she was being garrotted: *Get it all out*, she thought, *just spit it out*.

"Dad, I float!" She blurted.

"Anna?" His heart was racing furiously. He felt his legs weaken, as though the pressure of insufficient wisdom was bearing down heavily upon him. He focused, and as if finally defeated by the disembodied ravaging and plundering warriors of life, he quietly and calmly prepared himself to let his daughter down.

"I mean I hear stuff… 'n I see stuff… 'n when I say I float, I mean at night, I mean not through the day or anything like that."

"Oh good, Anna, night's good." He hesitated, confused, attempting to salvage himself.

"So that's okay?"

"Mm?" Mick was frantically searching for clues, anything in his daughter's expression that might give him an angle, an opening, ultimately a glimmer of hope that he might just be able to understand her or help her.

"Floating – it is okay, is it?" Anna was scrutinizing her dad's expression for reassurance and confirmation that she was normal.

"Well, I'm not sure, where do you float off to?"

Anna points up to the ceiling.

"How do you float?"

"I don't know. I'm just up there." She rolls her eyes to the ceiling. Mick follows her gaze upward. "Is it drugs?" *Logic, try and be logical;* he was coaching himself through this.

"No, no. Not drugs, it's nothing like that." She was very matter of fact.

"Not drugs?"

"No."

"Sure?"

"Yeah."

"Smokes?"

"No."

"Funny cakes, wild fungi?"

"No!"

"That's great." *Hoorah it's not drugs, we can cope with this,* Mick thought, trying to humour himself into believing this kind of behaviour was indeed normal.

"Great?" Anna was puzzled at her dad's response.

"So how do you do it, this floating thing?"

"I don't know. It's when I'm sleeping."

"So it's just a dream then?"

"No, no, 'cause I'm not actually sleeping."

"So you're awake?"

"No, I feel like I go off to sleep, but then I am kind of awake, wide awake, inside my head, but obviously asleep."

"Obviously?"

"And I'm seeing stuff, 'n doin' stuff, and I know I'm out of my body 'cause when I look down I can see myself in my bed. And I'm huge when I'm up there. I'm light, like a massive balloon, light, weightless, and I can touch the walls like this." Anna stretches her arms out. "But sometimes I'm a bit scared. What if I don't get back into myself again? Will I be stuck up there?"

"Have you been drinking?"

"No."

"So this just happens, and you're up there floating about?" Mick points to the ceiling now.

"Yeah. But will I?"

"Will you…?"

"Get stuck, up there, ever?"

"Shouldn't think so. Suppose plenty of folk float around at night. Probably quite a usual sort of thing." Realising this was strange and serious, Mick was trying to adopt the composed, sensible-with-humour approach to parenting. He did this whilst reminding himself that a chapter on floating children definitely wasn't in *Dr. Spock*.

"Kids do all kinds of funny stuff, don't they?" Mick thought back to his teenage years; to that menacing, murky and wholly misunderstood place – the mind of the pubescent alpha male. Was there any recollection of floating? No. Not really. Only when he believed he was in love; he felt like floating then. Each teenage crush lightening his step, dissolving his logic, weakening his will, whilst propelling him effortlessly into a breathless orbit of unconditional sexual self-satisfaction.

He would admit that his first crush was for a Tennents Lager model – Michelle. He reasoned now as an adult, that many a young impressionable boy must have fallen foul of the half-naked women that were draped around cans of Tennents Lager. There was an art, Mick could recall, of gently caressing the can of Tennents. Yes, fondly, and carefully, wrapping his hands around the cold naked waist of Michelle, slowly drawing her wantonly to his lips, whilst believing he was truly, slowly sucking in the very essence of her. Indeed in his precarious, self-perpetuating pubescent world, drinking a can of Tennents equalled kissing Michelle.

As Mick so painfully found out, kissing required further more extensive training. It came as a shock to discover that kissing and breathing at the same time wasn't a naturally occurring phenomena. In fact his memories of teenage kissing are of a cruel blend of oxygen deprivation and virtual asphyxiation. He remembers approaching any kiss as though embarking upon an endurance test; there was always the threat of failure, an eager sense of fear and worry, combined with the thrust of hormonal anticipation.

Oh, the humiliation of coughing and splurging to breathe half-way through the kiss, or that his tongue should wander aimlessly into her mouth, like an unwelcome intruder. He was mildly envious of friends who could hold their kiss for minutes without collapsing, or could find a comfortable place for their tongues, and gently fold together without breaking their noses, like pieces of Lego that fit together snugly.

Thus he concluded, when he pulled himself back from his momentary lapse in concentration, that his daughter must be in love.

"Have you met someone, Anna?"

"Met who?"

"Someone? Anyone?"

"Who?"

He had tried really hard to will Anna over each of the 'normal' psychological hurdles of growing up. He had attempted to explain things. Increasingly aware that most of her peers were boys, he talked awkwardly about relationship dynamics. He had drawn somewhat amusing pictures of sperm and eggs exploding into life. Never before had such a mockery been made of cell division. Above all, he worried that without the guidance of Martha, Anna's mother, he might just get the whole parenting thing wrong.

"You've met a boy?"

"Boy? What boy?

"You know, boyfriend stuff?"

"Forget it, Dad. You don't get it," Anna retreated, submitting. Submitting and dismissing the whole unbelievable concept that matter and life experience might exist in a place far beyond her human consciousness. Yet exist closely enough to pound her mind and make huge dents in her thoughts; to bombard her with tangible encounters that immerse her in touchable, breathable ordeals. For Anna, this would prove to be a constant and exhausting battle of mortal reasoning. This initial, painful revelation to her dad would be the first of many such encounters.

He couldn't make any sense of this. Mick started to make his way down the hill and home, where he thought he might find solace in escape Route No. 2 – music. He began to hum. As random lyrics tumbled around in his head, one line burst to the front: *Any minor world that breaks apart falls together again.* Steely Dan, he nodded approvingly to the imperceptible DJ that had slipped a tune onto the turntable of his mind. He continued to hum as he made his way home. He thought fondly of Anna, and wondered where she might be floating off to tonight, whilst the rest of the song played on in his mind; *You can try to run but you can't hide from what's inside of you.*

Mick found himself singing, 'yooo… ooh' out loud as he reached the edge of the town, just loud enough, he thought, to alert the forever faceless driver of The Yellow Van. Moreover, he managed to startle a lone pedestrian standing by his dog, which was adopting the crouched 'I'm just about to shit on the pavement' position. Confronting the pedestrian's nonchalant stare, Mick felt like he had been found out. Now it would become public knowledge that he spoke to himself and sung out loud whilst clinging ostentatiously, but aimlessly, to urban circumferences. *'Shit.'* The Yellow Van would no doubt, soon be coming for him.

*

IV

Then there's Martha, an only child. She was Mick's partner and Anna's mother. Most people found Martha a bit spooky; it was like she could read your mind, just by catching a glimpse of your eye.

When she was nineteen, she went along to the gypsies that arrive every year on the green at St. Boswells. They only stay for a week, and then disappear in the night. Like most visitors to the gypsies, Martha was looking for answers. Why did her mum leave her when she was a baby? Was her mum still alive? Why did her dad never meet anyone else? Why do her dreams come true? What should she do about this baby? She hadn't really intended to end up pregnant. It was just a couple of random dates with Mick Munroe. Oh, but she liked him, she liked him a lot. Trouble is so did lots of other young women.

Mick had some kind of extremely natural, unthreatening ability to turn women on. Not always in a sexual fashion. Just that he seemed to know where the 'on' switch was. It was in his eye contact, his words and his gentle approach to subjects no other men of his age, at twenty-one, would dare to let their conversation drift into. It's true there are men out there who can stop you in your tracks with their eyes, that fractionally longer gaze; not as long as a stare, but longer than a look. Then there are those that will stop you dead with their words. That's quite an exciting thing. But beware of the man who can knock you out with his eye contact and his words. That's a killer blow. Mick Munroe walked around delivering that killer blow in a fairly unsuspecting manner. It was that chemistry thing again. He seemed to ooze it like wild ether floating unchecked from a test tube. It was like every encounter he had with a woman was an unplanned experiment. The puzzle though, was that he was always genuinely shocked by the invisible explosions that occurred when he met a woman he liked, and he was genuinely shocked to learn that women found him attractive.

True to form, Martha chose the gypsy she would consult that day instinctively and impulsively. She had heard others who had been to the gypsies say that you should always go to the gypsy with the longest queue outside their caravan. Martha didn't check the queues that day, she just went to the first caravan she was drawn to on the Green. When she stepped inside she was slightly taken aback to find an elderly man sitting in front of her. She had imagined all fortune tellers were women.

The moment the psychic's eyes rested on Martha she felt uneasy, and yet excited. "I don't usually read for pregnant women." He was quite matter of fact. He was making a statement, not asking a question. In his mind there was little doubt of the condition of his customer. For a fleeting moment Martha wondered if he really could read her mind.

"Oh?" Martha's outstretched palm rested on her flat stomach. She knew it was too soon for anyone to know. She knew it would be a couple of months before her pregnancy would be confirmed. All the same, she just knew it was there. She could tell; she felt it in her instinct, with every breath, with every beat of her heart, within every chemical reaction in every cell of her body, she felt *it*.

For most girls in her position it could be months before they confirmed they were pregnant, often too late to do *anything* about *it*. To find you had missed a couple of periods and not be married was a bit of a scandal in the seventies, especially for a Catholic girl like Martha. But Martha knew. She knew within days, even hours; she had plenty of time to deal with *it*. Instead she chose to do and say nothing. What's more, Mick had no idea that he was destined to become a dad before he reached his twenty-second birthday.

At nineteen years old, Martha had a surety of mind that could sometimes come across as being a bit self-possessed. An only child of an unmarried Polish immigrant and local Catholic woman, Martha's upbringing had regularly come under scrutiny in Galashiels, especially so when her estranged mother, Catherine, left Henryk, when Martha was only two years old. The truth is she didn't just leave her family; she left the town, and never got in touch with anyone again. No forwarding address, no explanations. Henryk often thought it would have been easier if she had died, then he would have known it was definite, final. As it was, he watched the door, waited for mail, stared at the horizon, wondering when or if she would come back. It was precisely this uncertainty that surrounded much of her childhood that led Martha to behave impulsively.

"Sure 'bout this reading then?" The psychic searched for confirmation that she knew what he had sensed. Martha nodded, her palm resting outstretched on her stomach, pressing gently, feeling for the invisible little foetus that was quietly and cleverly taking form.

With his small bony hands, the psychic lit a small white candle and placed it in the centre of his little circular table that defined the physical boundary between them. Taking a deep breath, he closed his eyes briefly and appeared to pray, whilst inhaling deeply the thick cool air, heavily suffused with jasmine and patchouli incense. Martha relaxed a little and subconsciously tried to coax her heart to beat a little slower. As he sat with his eyes closed, she looked around his small room, as though with each fleeting angle of her glance she might somehow be invading his privacy. There were half-burnt candles on a mantle above a disused fireplace. One clear quartz crystal hung in the window, catching the light as it peered out beyond the November clouds, causing a spectrum of rainbow prisms to wander timelessly around the bare, pale yellow walls of the van. When he opened his eyes and raised them steadily towards her, Martha noticed how small, narrow, and screwed up they were, as though he was permanently trying to see through a fog. He caught her gaze and held it for a second.

"You have the gift." He nodded and grinned, exposing his gums; a toothless grin, which in itself told a story of neglect and hardship. He leaned back, nodded again and appeared almost gratified that Martha had chosen to come to him for a reading. He knew it could quite easily have been the other way around, for she too had the gift, he was certain of it. Martha watched tentatively as he swept up a pack of cards she recognised as *Rider-Waite,* and swiftly shuffled them. She could see each sinew and vein channelling deep gullies across the back of his white, withered hands. The transparency of his skin unnerved her. It was as though she could see right through each layer of his skin to the tendons and bones, to the bare mechanics of the hinge joints that allowed his fingers to move. She imagined he spent his days isolated in darkened rooms, throwing Runes and strange twigs onto the floor, reading the future from the configuration they landed in.

"Pick ten from the pack," he instructed Martha as he fanned the cards out face down on the table in front of her. "Place them here one on top of each other," he added, pointing to his side of the table as Martha's hand began to hover over the cards. It was as though she was waiting for an invisible magnetic connection to guide her towards the cards she was to pick. She wondered if he could read her mind right then, as though her forehead was suddenly made of glass and her thoughts tumbled around behind it, like random tickets in a tombola stall. She tried to concentrate on Mick, to send the old man Mick's name, test the psychic; see if he could get it. She noticed he seemed to drift off into a daze whilst she deliberated over her choice of cards. He began to hum, in a low tone, as one by one she teased each card out from the deck. The last two came out together. She didn't like that.

Carefully he counted them out, placing them in the order she had chosen them. Then he placed each card out on the table, flipping each over as he did so. He made faces, grimaced, smiled, even laughed out loud as one by one they were exposed.

Martha watched his every move, and wondered if he had a wife and a 'normal life'. She asked herself if this was his job, how detached did he have to be from 'normal' life, from mortal life, to do this properly and with integrity. *Where does all this stuff fit in to a mortal life? My normal life?*

Returning her attention to the reading she glanced down at the cards and scanned over her 'future' coldly laid out on the table in a Celtic cross formation, a spread that Martha knew well. She had often flirted with Tarot cards. She had a set of her own, much to her dad's disgust and Mick's distaste.

When the psychic began to talk she was aware of the light dimming as a wave of nausea washed over her. The cool air, heavy with incense, seemed to aggravate her lungs. Her dad had always warned her of a family weakness, with lungs and chest infections. She worried for a second that her lungs were going to cave in. It seemed to be hard for her to shift the air in and even harder for her to get the air back out again. She became conscious of a tightening in her chest, an extra effort in her breathing, and her heart pounding hard in her throat.

"A beautiful child," she heard as she willed her heart to slow down, "a child with your gift." The pounding in her chest continued tirelessly, she wondered how he could know this. "A gift she will not be so afraid to use as you are." Martha felt dizzy. She registered the '*she*'; *it* was a girl. But she was barely listening, her heart was now booming in her head.

"Although there will be many joyous times… " His words of prophecy fell upon the deafest of ears, her eyes had fixed upon *The Tower*, the card of havoc and unavoidable destruction. It was the last card, card ten; her future. That card, she recalled, had been stuck to the card she had wanted to choose. She had never really chosen it. It had, in fact, forced its way into her reading. She didn't like that.

"Now then, as I take a look at the future... mmm... interesting... " He paused and looked up at Martha. Martha was distant, preoccupied.

"Em ...... I think that's all fine then," he stammered, as she stared vacantly at the Tarot spread. With a sense of urgency, he swooped upon the spread, quickly lifting all the cards up into his hands, indicating the reading was over. Martha began to feel sick. The walls seemed to wax and wane like a tide. The pounding in her neck and her head faded away. The psychic dissolved into a blur. Then there was a dull thud as Martha's head bounced off the table, on her way to the floor.

"Ahhh... pregnant women," he sighed as he knelt down and cradled her head in his fine, bony hands until the colour returned to her face.

As he waited, he quietly acknowledged the cards had prophesised a terrible event. An unavoidable event. One the lay person would never normally notice. For sure, it had been the psychic's experience that the cards could readily imitate a surprise punch in the face if an individual wasn't ready for it. A punch he could normally shield his customer from. But she had the gift, he was sure of it, and she had seen her future. Once again his conscience was troubled, as it had been many times after a difficult reading.

As he watched the blood slowly return to Martha's cheeks, he was overcome by a feeling of inadequacy that he had been unable to protect this young woman from the brutality sometimes concealed within the Tarot spread. He hadn't been quick enough in removing the cards.

When Martha had recovered enough to leave the reading, the old psychic watched her, knowing that her thoughts had been hijacked, her head was heavy and would probably remain so, each step shackled down by the burden of foreboding truths. Silently he acknowledged the sleepless nights that were to come for Martha. He was getting too old for this, he thought, too old now to carry the secrets of the spirits around: Secrets that were never such an unbearable weight in his youth.

"May God bless you as you go," he whispered as she left.

God, thought Martha, had no place in all of this.

Martha would make a secret of this reading. She would not tell Mick. Secrets, Martha believed, were sometimes like heavy goods vehicles; there were just some bridges you could never take them across. She believed that if she thought of a bridge as an analogy of their relationship, it would be a temporary structure built hastily without much planning, and reliant upon materials and resources that were readily available at the time. Like one that's built during a crisis-type event, or life-threatening event. Like that built after a flood that has washed the previous solidly constructed bridge away. After all, that's what things have really been like for Martha for as long she can remember; as soon as she feels stable something comes along and sweeps everything she has away.

Some people who have their cards read shrug off the reading as a bit of fun, as something not that serious, and continue on with their normal life. Some wait for every turn of every card in their reading to come true. Martha was like this after that reading. She had been shocked to see *The Tower* in her spread. That's the thing with a Tarot reading, it's not really a 'fun' thing, it's a serious thing, and readers have responsibilities. Some of the older readers would say that if you are prepared to have one, you have to be prepared to take the good with the bad. Some are a bit kinder and do try to shield the customer from some of the harsher revelations that can emerge during a reading.

Although Martha's reader had tried to smudge the end of the reading, she knew the cards too well herself. As a result she did spend some days in silent turmoil, trusting the cards yet absorbing their information with utter disbelief: *Am I really going to die soon?*

As the sharp November winds pierced the crisp, golden air that day, unimaginable consequences had been mapped out coldly in front her. Martha recalled the old man's panic. She remembered how his fretted brow contorted, how his eyes narrowed, how he pulled his clothing tightly and securely around himself as the cards were revealed. She recalled how the look of regret had unfolded deep within his eyes, yielding for her a fleeting sympathy, as his outline blurred and the room spun. She can remember hearing the dull thud of her head on wood as she passed out. Somewhere in her consciousness, as she slid helplessly to the floor, she acknowledged he was right, pregnant women shouldn't have their cards read. That was simple reasoning, logic and common sense. It's stuff that exists in a mortal world. A world which seems far removed from the inexplicable psychic substance that was the foundation of her reasoning, and had been a conscious part of her world for as long as she could remember.

For days Martha reasoned with herself, she attempted to apply logic, and exhausted common sense. She desperately wanted to talk to Mick about it, but realised she had missed the window of opportunity. What they had wasn't exactly a relationship, more a collection of encounters.

It is also, after all, a short window between forgetfulness and concealment. Considering she had been with Mick twice since the reading it might have been easier to explain a lapse in memory, but not so easy to explain deliberately withholding information. Martha realised so many days had passed now that she was truly withholding information from him. She imagined his response to her confession; *Oh by the way Mick, sorry I've not seen you for a couple of weeks, but I couldn't shake my dad off my trail. Anyway, I've been to a fortune teller, terrible things will happen to us, I'll probably die, it's The Tower, shit really isn't it, just forgot to tell you, oh and I took our little foetus along too. 'When?'* he would shriek, *'why?'* he would beg, *'foetus!?'* He would suddenly realise.

Martha thought of the short, snatched times they had had together since the reading. Times when she had had the opportunity to divulge the information of her reading, but then decided to say nothing. Information that must now be re-branded, re-coded as a secret. Martha shuddered as she realised the reading would remain a secret from Mick. Her first secret; and she decided it would be her only secret. Now she would have to find the right time to tell him she was pregnant. Martha was unaware at that point that there was a certain element of history repeating itself.

Despite her disbelief of the old man's reading, she was determined to resume dialogue with the Tarot. This time it would be on her terms. Martha chose a day when she knew Mick would not be coming around, and a day when she was not being overwhelmed with placenta-induced nausea. She cleared a space on the floor in her bedroom and leant forward to light a small, white candle that she had placed on the floor in front of her. Beside her she placed an oil burner where a soft blend of geranium and sandalwood oils bubbled gently, bathing the room in a warm and rich quality that was somehow satisfying and comforting.

Removing the cards from their silk pouch, she drew a deep breath, composed her thoughts and began by shuffling the pack. The cards seemed stiff and uncooperative, as though conspiring against her. Her hands trembled as Martha split the Tarot pack and spread them out face down in front of her. She knew the cards well, but the old man's reading had troubled her, and she had been aware of his concealment. A cruel combination of cards had been spread out before her that day. Martha knew she was a skilled reader of the Tarot, but as she reached towards the cards she felt her confidence fade, like power draining from a battery.

Martha picked ten cards and arranged them face up on the table in front of her. There it was, now promoted in its importance, its immediate significance evermore apparent, now occupying the centre position – *The Tower*.

Martha's pregnancy passed uneventfully. Henryk's shock at the pregnancy was short-lived, and was swiftly usurped by his memories of his own relationship with Catherine. He knew he would be a hypocrite to criticise his daughter.

When baby Anna was born without complication, Martha dismissed *The Tower* and all its hellish implications. Having survived pregnancy, childbirth and a few clumsy mishaps along the way, Martha had now nurtured a sense of defiance, despite the words of her dad – *'These cards are bad, they bring you, me, your mother bad luck, they bring a curse'.*

He never liked the cards. He never liked Martha using them. Mick agreed with Henryk. Henryk liked that, it was something they agreed on, something they could try and bond over. He had not been especially welcoming to Mick on account of his daughter's pregnancy. In the beginning he had felt deceived and felt somewhat a failure as a father that he was unable to protect his daughter, and for a time he regarded Mick as something of a predator.

However, as Martha's pregnancy progressed, Henryk warmed to Mick. He could see Mick's genuine concern for Martha. He watched as Mick's love for her became more pronounced and committed. It was just so apparent in every way that Mick spoke to Martha, every way he held her, every smile he gave her. As Martha's bump grew for all to see, so too did Mick's deep love for her. Henryk felt reassured Mick would not abandon Martha, as Catherine had abandoned him. Before the baby was born Mick was granted permission to visit Martha freely. Henryk found himself toying with the idea that they really were all becoming a little family unit. He liked it, he liked this thought. He liked it so much that he invited Mick to come and live with them after Anna was born. He wanted them to have what he imagined was a normal family life. One that Henryk had never had himself. This was his chance; he was determined to make it work.

Both men agreed on one important thing, she should give the Tarot cards away. Henryk feared what he already knew about such things, whereas Mick feared anything he didn't know a whole lot about or remotely understand. Martha, tired of their objections, told them she had given them away. But they were stored, secretly in a silk cloth, beneath an old case she kept behind her wardrobe. She was never comfortable with this secret: secret number two.

There were countless moments where she came close to disclosing the reading she had had to Mick, each time pulling herself back from the confession at the last second. It was a confession that had been exhaustively rehearsed. Practised within a wide spectrum of possible confession situations, ranging from one made in a quiet moment of foreboding, to one made in a nonchalant, carefree manner. Sometimes she wished Mick was as good as her at tuning into vibes. Often she concentrated hard, sending the reading to the forefront of her mind in the hope that he might just latch on to it, in some form of magnetic telepathy, but he never did.

For five years, Martha attempted to manipulate the outcome of her Tarot prediction, and tried to diminish the odds that seemed stacked up against her by the appearance of *The Tower* in her spread.

In fact, it would be true to assume she had almost forgotten about *The Tower*, when one April afternoon as she walked into town with Anna (as indeed she had done almost daily), a car sped off the road. The driver was slumped at the wheel as it mounted the pavement. It careered hopelessly towards Martha and Anna. Martha took the full impact of the spinning car, whilst the young four-year-old was shunted gracefully to the side, where she landed on her bottom in the gravel. There she sat in a daze and stared in disbelief; a car on its roof, a dead man in the car, wheels spinning, smoke rising, her motionless mother on the pavement. There she sat, aware of an unpleasant smell, as petrol bled out onto the road. There she sat in the gravel, watching the upturned car haemorrhage onto the tarmac, as the last breath came and went from her mum.

The freak accident had not occurred far from their home. In rural areas word gets around fast, and it was only a short while before Mick arrived at the scene in a state of surreal panic and denial. He found Anna cradled in the arms of a sombre-faced police officer. Mick searched his daughter's expression, whilst feeling himself being pulled head first into a terrifying dark void of hopelessness. Trapped deep within the ravines of his young daughter's consciousness were new trespassers, ravagers of innocence. Cruel images and incomprehensible noises had now been permanently imprinted in the texture of her being, like the burn of a branding iron.

In the same instant, something bleak, something menacing and heavy, something sharp around the edges destroyed Mick. It seemed to slice cleanly, efficiently, effortlessly and invisibly through Mick's spinal cord, completely detaching his mind from his body. It was the moment he saw the bulk of a body under a cover at the roadside. Without being told, he knew it was Martha. He knew because he saw a mother's untimely death etched painfully deep within the face of his daughter. At that point he simply stopped feeling. It was a survival instinct. Mick knew that if at any point he were to acknowledge the stifling agony of this moment he would implode, and disintegrate into a smouldering mound of bubbling diffuse gases, and disconnected ions. What good would he be to Anna then?

V

Anna, Mick and Martha's daughter, well you see, she is psychic. It has taken her a long time to understand what this actually means. Even now it's mostly a puzzle.

The most vivid experiences she has are usually when she is falling asleep, or just before she wakes up. Sometimes the experiences are like premonitions, like this one that happened in May 1995.

Anna was unaware of time; she had relinquished all self-control by simply falling asleep. Her consciousness paralysed and mortal reasoning suspended, she had no power over her destination. Once asleep she was pulled by an inexplicable divine force like some sort of spiritual puppet; she had no control over when she would return, or indeed, as was her greatest fear, if she would return at all.

She was exhausted. She had been fairly busy lately. May, for a seventeen-year-old, means exams and lots of them; Anna was studying for her A-level exams. She was hoping to get into college to become a primary school teacher. She was determined to pass all five of her A-levels with straight As. This kind of ambition and determination wasn't unusual for Anna.

Mick had often marvelled at her perseverance. Take sport, for example. Anna was a keen young sportswoman, who enjoyed nothing more than a robust game of hockey or football, never afraid to go in for the tackle, win the ball. Mick, on the other hand, could think of nothing worse than hurtling aggressively towards a team of young hormonal women, bearing, what to all intents and purposes, were large wooden weapons, and where the risk of incurring some form of severe mutilation to the lower limbs was almost one hundred percent. Indeed, Mick could almost feel his shins spontaneously haemorrhage whenever he simply thought of a hockey stick or a high-speed hockey ball. He marvelled at Anna, who even when exhausted by her studies, still managed to get up early for a Saturday morning match. This was nothing more than lunacy to Mick, who had rarely emerged from his teenage bed before three in the afternoon at the weekend.

To become a teacher had been her intention from a very early age. She would often create her own class lessons, and mark the work completed by the imaginary class. She delighted in rewarding some of the imaginary pupils with gold stars, whilst chastising others with the words, 'please see me' written in the best ten-year-old's joined-up handwriting. So, in pursuit of her ambition it would be fair to say that May 1995 was a fairly stressful time. Getting to sleep wasn't always easy, as an accumulation of random notes for different subjects swam around in her mind like hyperactive goldfish in an ever-decreasing bowl.

That night, silently, and without conscious protest, Anna was aware she was light and was leaving her body. It's hard for her to put into words how that feels, being peeled out of her skin. Within a few seconds she was floating off towards a misty area. When the air cleared she found she was standing in front of a large, stone-built house. She was not aware if she was warm or cold, dressed or naked, as she stood there. The door to the house was closed. She didn't recognise the house, but did feel compelled to open the door and go in. The door was not locked, and did not emit a horror movie-type squeal when being set ajar. This action, entering an unknown house, was not something she would ever contemplate in her mortal 'normal' state of mind. Being safety conscious was something her dad had drummed into her from an early age, for obvious reasons.

She opened the door and stepped inside. The house was completely silent. She found herself standing in the middle of a long, narrow hallway that stretched as far as the eye could see to her left and also to her right. She was puzzled by this strange hallway which seemed to travel beyond the stone walls of the house she had moments before been standing in front of. She stood completely still.

After a while, she had no idea how long, a figure materialised on her left and drifted towards her. As it moved closer she could see it was a woman in a long robe of no particular colour or description. She moved gracefully but unnaturally, as though floating a few inches above the ground. The woman stared straight ahead as she drifted along. Anna glanced down at the cold slate floor. There was no sound of footsteps. The hallway was silent. She simply appeared and glided along towards Anna, and passed by her. Impulsively

Anna spoke. "Excuse me?" then hesitated. There was no reply. The woman kept going, moving away from her now. Anna raised her voice. "Excuse me, where am I?" The woman stopped; she looked at Anna in surprise, even amazement. "You can see me?" she asked in a gentle tone. Anna thought this was an entirely stupid question.

"Yes."

"Really, you can see me?" Anna could feel the woman was genuinely shocked by this. It seemed she had seen Anna, but had not expected that Anna could see her. She was quite obviously excited by Anna's response. "Well if you can see me then you must follow me, I've got some people waiting here for you to meet."

Without explaining where Anna was, she drifted off right down the hallway. Anna followed on foot. She was aware she was walking normally, not floating, like the woman, and Anna could see that although the woman looked human, she was different from her. She led Anna to a large sitting room, like a meeting room in a community centre. Sitting in the room were twelve elderly adults, male and female. They all turned and smiled at Anna as she was led in. She was not introduced to them, nor them to her, which Anna thought to be unusual since the woman had explained that these were people who would like to meet her, but she was not afraid. The woman then vanished, and Anna was left in the room with the twelve elderly adults.

One of the adults, a gentleman with a kind, square face, large brown eyes and a gentle, questioning expression, asked who she was and where she was from. They admitted they were not familiar with the Scottish Borders. Another man of roughly the same age began to talk. Anna thought he had a big bald head like a decorated egg, and she tried hard not to laugh. He explained they were all from the Bristol area. They were involved with the British Legion, and were waiting on their friends.

Without fear, Anna began to talk about her mother, Martha. She asked if they knew her, if they had come across her. It was as though something within Anna told her she was on the 'other' side, although she didn't consciously know this. She explained how her mum had died in 1982 when she was almost five years old as they had been walking together into town. She remembers they were on their way to buy a record. Anna explained that she remembers the music she and her mum had enjoyed, which was by *The Jam*. A song called *'A Town Called Malice'*. It was in the charts, they had listened to it on the Sunday evening previous. She recalled how she and Mum would often dance, no, leap around the living room to it. Anna, at the age of four, simply liked the beat. Music, it seemed, was in her soul.

She spoke calmly and coherently, without fear and anguish about the death of her mum. Something she could never normally do in the mortal world. They seemed genuinely sorry that they didn't know her mum, and repeated they were waiting on their friends from Bristol. They beckoned for her to sit with them. Anna remembers an elderly gentleman smiling as she went over to sit beside him. She has no recollection of ever reaching the chair.

Anna cannot remember when she left, how she got back or when she got back. She remembers waking at half-five, which was early even for her. Dreams like this one were so real she sometimes felt she was living life on two entirely separate and distinctly different levels. However, defining these levels was impossible for Anna. She had no idea she was psychic. She knew it was a strange experience; these people had seemed so real, *so alive*, but she couldn't interpret exactly what was happening to her. She simply added it to the list of all the other unusual experiences she was now encountering on a daily basis. At no point did she think, 'Hey get me, I'm psychic'. Well you wouldn't would you? Someone needs to explain this to you, and up until this day Anna hadn't spoken to anyone about these things. Not because she was afraid, but because she didn't understand it enough to question it with any sense of logic. All she knew was that these dreams, these experiences, were defying logic as she understood it at that time.

The following day in May, 1995, was an exam-free day. Anna lounged around, certain she had studied enough now for her Maths exam the next day. She knew her *sin*, *cos* and *tan* formulas, her algebraic equations and geometry calculations. In fact she surmised that should she open another book with numbers in it she may well render herself unable to add up one and one. Her brain was at saturation point. Thus she settled to watch some daytime television. This was not her usual routine, but it was one, for whatever reason, she settled into that day.

Just as the parade of daytime presenters was becoming unbearably ever more monotonous, the programmes were interrupted by a newsflash. It was two forty-five in the afternoon. A male newsreader broke the news that a tour bus carrying pensioners on an outing had crashed. There were reports of fatalities. Nothing more was said and programmes resumed, but something invisible had punched Anna hard in the middle of her chest. Her sternum ached and she gasped as she felt a strong, invisible force pull her out of her chair into a standing position. It was so strong she felt as though she had been physically grabbed by the front of her t-shirt and hauled to her feet. She was unsteady on her feet, her heart was racing, she had no idea what was happening.

The programme was interrupted again. The news that unfolded in the next bulletin paralysed Anna. The newsreader now explained that a tour bus carrying twenty-nine passengers from Bristol, on a British Legion day trip to Cardiff, had crashed. All passengers were elderly, and ten were killed at the scene. Two were taken to hospital. Anna's heart was pounding so hard she thought it might explode. *They were waiting for their friends*, she reminded herself. Instinctively, she knew then that the two in hospital would die. Twelve dead, twelve were waiting.

The force that had hauled Anna to her feet absolutely terrified her. It had followed a pattern of ever-increasing incidents that she could not explain. Anna was so disturbed by this prophetic dream, the first of its kind she had experienced, that she decided it was time to talk to someone about this stuff. There was only one person she trusted with this kind of information and that was her dad. Anna made her way hastily to his shop.

Mick owned and ran a small bookstore. The store occupied the corner building of two prominent streets in the town. It was on two floors, and could hold at full capacity just over one thousand books. It was a strangely shaped store, and stranger still were the collection of books he kept in stock. He had everything from John Irving's *World According To Garp,* to Homer's *Odyssey,* with a vast collection of poetry ranging from John Keats to Derek Walcott. Indeed, Mick was a keen collector of poetry, and most interested in post-colonial work, Amryl Johnson being amongst his favourites. He would often delight in reading *'Granny in de market place'* to Anna. He believed this to be a fine piece of work by Johnson, a piece so rhythmic and simply alive in Creole custom and tradition, rich in humour and authenticity, that Mick always found it refreshing, humbling and inspiring.

He felt he could relate to these women and their feelings of exclusion. He could relate to their losses and the losses of their ancestors, to their fight for identity and recognition of their historical baggage. Mick, in his lowest moments, would indulge in the analogy that his grieving process was similar in a way to The Middle Passage that these female slaves had endured. He recognised their pain at losing their identity, at being forcefully removed from their loved ones. He recognised their loss of language, their loss of communication and opportunities, as he felt his grief had deprived him of such things too.

As far as *Kubler-Ross'* theory on the stages of grief and grieving goes, Mick knew he was remaining in a perpetual state of denial. Even now, thirteen years later, acceptance of the bereavement was simply too painful to consider, because that would mean a new life, a different life and ultimately a life without Martha.

However, he would often rally himself with a quote he had come across from the great Greek philosopher, Plato – *"Every king springs from a race of slaves, and every slave has had a king among its ancestors"*. Thus Mick would conclude he would one day break free from the confines of the grief which presently enslaved him, and be liberated as a king amongst kings, as the father of all fathers.

Mick often felt that as a single parent he had become invisible, dissolving silently into a frantic social tapestry. He had spent so long concealed within the complicated weave of society he was now desperate to be noticed, to be heard, to force his way out, like a loose thread poking out. Searching for a keen eye, pleading to be plucked out and released.

Although not so keen a reader as Mick, Anna would tell you that when her dad read to her, these were her most favourite times, her most comforting times. She would listen and watch as, during his narration of a story or poem, her dad became animated, emotions surfaced, his eyes widened and facial expressions emerged like the sun rising again after prolonged darkness. As she grew older, she grew to understand how easy it was for him to come alive again when he was reading and immersing himself in the roles of the characters. It was easy for him to imagine that he and Anna existed in a different life within someone else's script, not the one that had been written for him; that script known by the names of destiny and fate.

Reading together was a precious past-time for them both as it was one of the few times Mick felt they connected as father and daughter, independent of the need for a mother. When she was ten years old, Mick read Harper Lee's *To Kill A Mockingbird* to Anna. Anna was a bright girl and could relate to the characters in the book. She drew certain parallels with the Finch family and her own. Namely there was no mother. Whilst she was too young to fully comprehend the complexities of some of the issues contained within the book, such as social injustice, prejudice, and preservation of moral integrity, she connected with the emotions these themes aroused in her dad's sensibilities. Sharing Harper Lee's work with her dad provided the beginnings of insight for Anna. It allowed her to understand the way his mind worked.

That afternoon, whilst she was confident he would understand her, she rehearsed what she would say on the way there to see him. She imagined his reaction as one of considered reasoning, followed by the imparting of a small nugget of wisdom. She was confident he would know what this was about.

She thought of him in his little world of books, his safe haven. It was a place where each new book that came into the shop offered another secret passage, another psychological escape route. However, she didn't realise that more often with the end of each book came yet another dead-end for Mick.

When Anna arrived at the book store, she must have looked so terrified and so agitated that she caught one look at her dad's expression and dissolved. Her heart was thumping forcefully, almost choking her, and as her throat tightened all that came out was:

"Dad, I float!"

VI

Prolonged thunder storms and torrential overnight rain gave way to unbroken sunshine, as Mick's cognitive escape Route No. 3 was once again being exploited. The early morning mist had evaporated and steam rose from the pavements, roads and stone dykes as though a giant labyrinth of underground geezers had been forced open by the turbulent and heavily charged night skies. Mick had taken to the hills early; it was half six. Two months had passed since his daughter revealed she floats out of her body at night.

Since that conversation he had been watching her a bit more closely than usual, watching for the warning signs of the late Rosalia, her great-grandmother. He made mental notes of her temperament, her appetite, her sleep pattern and how she coped with her exams. To date he had noted that her ability to communicate was now reduced to mono-syllables; that she had perfected the art of flying off the proverbial handle at the drop of a hat; she had stopped playing all sports; and was surviving on a diet of hot buttered toast and crisps, whilst also sleeping roughly twenty hours a day, emerging like a small nocturnal mammal for the bathroom and food only. He scrutinised her friends that came around, and noted the procession of young male friends arriving wearing more eyeliner and nail polish than the girls they were accompanying. He was relieved to deduce from his keen observations that things were all quite normal.

Thus he wondered if the floating episode was some kind of delayed, much delayed, response to losing her mother, and was not in the least bit connected with her great-grandmother, who he feared was hovering around in the ether somewhere, waiting for her chance to penetrate the mortal world once again.

He racked his brains for anyone else he knew that had lost their mother as a child, so that he could compare, perhaps measure his performance as a father against theirs. He found it almost impossible to gauge how he was doing, or if Anna's experiences were 'normal'. Everyone is quick to tell him that he's doing a great job, that Anna is lucky to have such a devoted dad. But it wasn't what he felt inside. *'My head's full of shit. It's all shit.'* He would often chastise himself. Inside he felt as though Anna had been cheated, and he wasn't able to redress this injustice in the way a dad should be able to. He was up against fate, destiny and history. The odds seemed stacked against him.

The only person he could recall having lost their mother as a child was a girl called Ruth Nairn. She was younger than him by about five years, and although they grew up near each other, she went to the Catholic School so they didn't have much to do with one another as children. Thinking of her made Mick smile; he remembered there was something different about her, something back then that he could not put his finger on. To be fair he had probably been too young and too inexperienced to appreciate the raw qualities of independent reasoning that estranged Ruth Nairn from the other kids.

He does remember that she often wandered along grinning and humming to herself, as though embraced in an unending daydream. When he heard her humming out loud, he worried about The Yellow Van. He worried about the secret maniac detectors that he had been warned about as a child. He noticed she wore the same things a lot: a Donny Osmond t-shirt (surely the sign of an undercover maniac, he thought), and boy's trousers that were often too short for her long legs, flaring out just above her skinny ankles. He could remember it seemed as though her family did not have a lot of money. He could tell by the home haircuts that left squint fringes on embarrassed faces, and by the battered ill-repaired shoes she wore.

When Mick was eighteen, he had overheard his mother talking about Ruth Nairn's mum. She had died the previous day. From what Mick could make out by eavesdropping, it had been a cancer of some sort. He presumed it must have been breast cancer as their voices dropped to a whisper at crucial points during their conversation about what had killed Doreen Nairn. He listened as they described how cancer will spread like feathers blown out in a wind if a person is opened up.

"Once the fresh air gets in that's it!" He had heard his mum exclaim.

"Those stupid doctors, if they had left her alone she'd still be here," the neighbour replied, and continued, "to think o' the fight she's pit up ower the last couple o' years! Bloody doctors."

Ruth had only been thirteen years old. "A bad age for a lassie to lose her mother," his mum said.

Mick recalled that hushed conservation and wondered if there was actually a good age for a daughter to lose her mother. He figured not, and wondered what had become of Ruth Nairn – last seen wandering in the dark, crying, dressed in her brother's coat and smelling of his aftershave. He remembered how he used to watch Ruth; there was something about her. He liked her, but didn't know why he liked her, they were poles apart. Not just by years but by cultures. Whilst he remembered they went off in separate directions every morning, he remembers once bumping into her at a youth club disco; she was just little, ten or eleven, still at primary school, but he remembers thinking she was nice. Who'd have thought then that her mum would be dead within in a couple of years?

He thought of Anna; was four a 'good' age to lose her mother? If he were to ask Anna she would probably be fairly indifferent, as apart from the actual day of the accident, Anna had no cohesive memories of her mum. Any memories she has have been constructed around photographs, and conversations with her dad. She imagined what her mum may have been like, more than she actually knew or could remember.

Mick had now been wandering around the hill for over an hour, with random thoughts applying an invisible pressure to the inside of his skull. He felt tense as every impatient thought was jostling for pole position, buzzing, fighting, poking and prodding at the front of his head. He imagined them chipping away until one day they would burst through the frontal bone of his skull and shoot off into the atmosphere, like the exit point of a bullet through his head. An outpouring of thoughts that he thought he might just die from if it was ever to happen. But he didn't want to stop all of these thoughts; he just wanted to arrange them into some sort of order. You see he found it hard, impossible, to weed them out and re-categorise them from random to organised: Anna, her mother Martha, Ruth – she was nice, what ever happened to her – Nairn, bad haircuts, old shoes, floating children, whilst all the time the fear of Rosalia's psychic legacy was fighting its way to the front, as though demanding some sort of acknowledgement.

Sometimes Mick became frustrated by all his thoughts, which he often regarded as devious and menacing, and independent from his sensibilities. He compared the art of reasoned thinking, that process of trying to carefully pluck out the right thought, as similar to fly fishing. If he wasn't quick enough to catch that important thought, the really relevant one when it bites, it's gone before he knows it. Whistled downstream into the great darkened pool of grey matter that was presently determining just how messed up he was.

The sun was now rising high in the cloudless sky, and he was aware of the skin on his face beginning to tingle with the exposure. It had been a long, hot summer. The grass all around him was dried out and brown, exposing parched soil and sharp edges of stones jutting dangerously out of the surface of the ground around him. There were only a few sporadic patches of colour, as wild poppies and wild daisies were managing to survive the dry, hot summer, growing in small clusters around rocks and boulders. Small, white butterflies fluttered around the flowers like confetti being tossed in the wind. The same breeze swooped the fluffy seed balls from the thistles and sent them bobbing off, high into the atmosphere. Mick imagined Anna must float off into the night like one of those fluffy seed balls, and he felt overwhelming pangs of guilt for not being able to stop this *thing* happening to her.

*

It was the summer holidays so Mick decided there was no need to wake Anna when he got back. That was what he normally did during term time. Then he would leave the house for an early morning walk, return around seven-thirty, wake up Anna for school, and then leave around eight-thirty to walk down to his beloved little book store, where he regarded the books as more of a personal collection than his stock. This morning he would leave Anna to sleep. He thought she needed sleep in view of all her recent studying. In fact, he had no idea just how disturbed her sleep actually was.

When Anna finally gave in to sleep it was like she was entering some kind of parallel universe. A universe where events played out as though they were surreal trailers for the mortal life she was living and breathing. When she awoke she often felt bewildered and absolutely drained.

She had also noticed over the past few weeks that something strange was happening to her in that split second, at that last conscious moment of submission before sleep, when she was only just aware that she was still awake; she had become aware of voices, lots of them, in the distance. It was as though she had inadvertently stumbled into a house where a party was being held. In an odd way it was as though the party had come to her, not that she had gone to it all. Whilst she could not clearly identify any one particular voice or hear with any clarity what was being said, she could tell the remote congregation of mutterings was being emitted by both men and women, as she could hear the different tones in the voices.

The first few times this happened, Anna shot out of her bed and switched on her light. The voices were still there. She dashed around her room pressing her ear against her stereo, then her television. She would eventually open her window to try and source where the voices were coming from. Each time the voices were still there, somewhere above, somewhere intangible, all around and beneath her. They never came any closer, got any clearer, or felt threatening. In the end – after the fourth or fifth night – Anna just got used to them being there, somewhere.

When she thought about her state of mind, she sometimes did become perplexed by it all. She had to remind herself she was normal, she had friends, she had laughs, and she did normal things that teenagers do. She experienced unearthly urges, like most teenagers, to take risks, test the boundaries like all kids do. For example, come in extraordinarily late once the search party has already been despatched, get drunk, ride in a fast car, maybe a body piercing, a tattoo, or a multi-coloured Mohican, and then there's sex; an even burden of excitement and embarrassment for most teenagers. Some of her urges would be seen to reality, some she would achieve, and some were best left where they belonged, within a daydream.

She also had normal everyday ambitions – she wanted to win when she played hockey, she wanted to pass her exams, she wanted, as she had always done so, to be a teacher. She often played that dream in her mind, standing in front of her own class; *'Good morning children'*, followed by a resounding *'Good morning, Miss Munroe.'* She imagined them sitting legs crossed, arms crossed, the way primary teachers always instruct the class to sit, in an effort to minimise disruption – trying to stop them fidgeting and prodding and poking at each other. She imagined she would maintain perfect control of the class; that they would hang upon her every word in a perfect classroom with perfect behaviour, their eyes constantly wide open, eager to learn, eager to know all about the world they were living in, and trusting that Miss Munroe would tell them everything there was to know.

Anna believed that this was exactly how it was when she went to primary school. That was how her memories had been banked – selectively.

VII

Letter written to Mum dated 10th Jan 1976, found April 1995 just before move. I was sixteen, still angry, apparently. Poor Robert, I just didn't understand what he was going through, he'd lost his mum too, and he had had to watch her get weaker and weaker on his privileged visits to the hospital. I used to be jealous of him, jealous that he got to visit and I didn't, but really I can see now that he had to watch her die. Having looked after so many people in their last few weeks, I can imagine now how she would have drifted further away on each visit. It's like trying to hold onto a handful of sand; grain by grain they slide away until there's nothing left, not even a grain, and then they're gone. I just couldn't see that at the time, I was just so consumed with my own broken heart. Poor Dad. Poor, poor Dad. Grief's a funny thing isn't it? Selfish isn't it?

Right then, Mum, I'm going to try again. The last time I wrote to you, it was absolutely ages ago, years, and I don't know if you got it. I left it out on my bed for God, that useless sod. Don't know what you bloody saw in him. He never took it; it was still there when I got home from school. Well maybe he gave it to you and then laid it back.

Anyway, I still miss you. I don't know what you think, but I still think this is rubbish. I never went back to church. I've got things sorted out with all that stuff now. But I still need to ask you about other stuff. Can you see me? I often wonder if you can, if you watch me. Do you watch me? Do you watch me all the time or just sometimes? I was looking at a photo the other day. It was you and me at Christmas. It seems like somebody else is in that picture, not you and me, not us. I've forgotten what it's like to sit and cuddle in with you like that. I've forgotten what you feel like. I've forgotten what you smell like. I can remember you used to spray stuff, but I can't find it anywhere, I think Dad must have thrown it out. I was looking for it. I went to a party. Did you see that? It was shite. I was supposed to meet Mick there. He never showed up. The bloody idiot asked me too, and then didn't bother coming. I imagine that you'll smell like peaches, but maybe that's just because you used to buy me peaches bubble bath from the *Avon* book. I can remember it came in a wee bottle shaped like a peach with two tiny wee leaves on the top. Christmas was last week. Oh yeah and you used to get Robert a soap-on-a-rope and beer shampoo from the *Avon* book too. It was shite. I didn't get any smelly stuff or anything like that last week.

Dad just sat still on Christmas day. I swear he looks more dead than you probably do. Seriously he is like a corpse. I wish I could see you. I swear he doesn't care about us. Sometimes I think I've forgotten what you look like. I keep that picture just in case. Dad doesn't know. He would take it off me. It's like you've never been here. He doesn't have any pictures of you anywhere. He doesn't even speak about you anymore. If I try he just gets up and walks away. It's the only time I can get him off his fat arse and away from the telly. I'm telling you Mum, mention you and up he gets.

Robert's just an absolute bastard. He's having it off with a bloke, I know he is. He sneaks him in when Dad's out. I can hear them. It's disgusting. And I can hear the toilet roll burring round in its holder when Robert sneaks along to the toilet for a wad of tissue. Honestly Mum. He's sick. Priest would have a bloody heart attack if Robert went to confession. He hasn't a clue. Anyway that's not why I am needing to write to you. Who cares if Robert fucks up? Not me, not Dad – the living corpse, nobody really. If you do watch me then you'll have seen why I'm writing. Have you seen him? Mick? Have you seen how he smiles at me, how he watches me? And I really like him. He's all I think about. All the time. Every day. I wish I was pretty, Mum. I wish my teeth were straight, I wish I had a nice wee pixie face, with the odd freckle, you know, a sun-kissed look, and little pert boobs. Why are mine like bloody udders. I swear one of your bras would be too small for me now, although I wouldn't do that again, honestly you'd think I'd bloody murdered someone. I wish I was as pretty as her. Oh God, God, God, God, sometimes I think you are an absolute utter bastard. Where have you put my mum? Why did you have to take my mum? She was helping me out with stuff. Are you completely blind? The least you can do now is make sure you tell her I'm writing to her, tell her I miss her, tell her I want her back here, tell her, tell her, tell her, and just tell her to come back. Tell her it's Ruth. Please!

*

When Ruth was sixteen, almost seventeen, and was making her way back home from the *ballroom blitz* party, she noticed a small group of people walking slowly towards her. It was roughly nine at night and she knew she was late; she quickened her step and pulled her brother's duffle coat tightly around her, checking each of the toggles were fastened, which they were, apart from the bottom one which had been pulled off during one of the many sibling battles that raged within Ruth's home. She and her brother fought more now than they ever had. They missed their mum.

Now it was late, she was slightly drunk and she was on her own in the dark. As the group got nearer and Ruth was able to make out their faces, she felt a stiff pain beneath her sternum. An unusual pain – so sharp she believed her heart might burst like a squashed over-ripe tomato.

Mick Munroe was with Martha Rosiewicz; Ruth recognised her from Sunday Mass. Martha was three years older than her and had already left school. As far as Ruth knew she didn't have a *proper* job yet. *Happy 21st Mick*, she thought. A few steps behind them walked Henryk Rosiewicz. Polish fathers were extremely protective of their teenage daughters, and often chaperoned them, especially if the Polish girls went along to a dance or a party. If the Scottish boys got too friendly, the Polish fathers would step inbetween, proclaiming 'too close'. Their English was limited. But they could say 'too close', 'step back', and 'no Scottish manners'.

Ruth watched as Martha was walked home by Mick, her daydream love. She could see that Mick and Martha tried to walk close enough together for their skin to touch, but without visibly holding hands; it would be Mr Rosiewicz's assumption that Mick had little or no Scottish manners – he believed he was walking too close to his daughter. Mick caught only the most fleeting of glimpses from Ruth as he and Martha passed by. Ruth inhaled the smell of Martha's perfume, she recognised it as *Charlie*. A lot of the girls at Ruth's age were wearing it. Ruth could never have afforded it; she had stolen a spray of her brother's *Brut* deodorant before sneaking out to the party.

As the group drifted by, Ruth had started to cry, the quick succession of *Babycham* hi-balls having rendered her defences useless. *'Shit,'* muttered Mick. He surprised himself with this reaction and hoped that Martha and her chaperone hadn't heard him swearing. Martha Rosiewicz noticed something fleeting had passed between Mick and Ruth, something very silent, very tenuous and very fragile all at the same time.

Martha had a good instinct. So good it made her nervous. Sometimes she had to pinch herself when people said exactly what she thought they would. Sometimes she really did wonder if she could read the minds of people around her; it was as though she could see straight through their skulls and into the mechanics of their brains. She was led to believe she had inherited this *'gift'* from her grandmother, Rosalia, a Polish Roma, a gypsy. Rosalia, or Rosa, as she was more commonly known, was Henryk's mother. It was widely claimed Rosa could see straight through the skin of people to their internal organs. She had travelled around the transient and much disputed border lands of what was to later become known as southern Poland, treating and supposedly curing the sick. She claimed she could see a broken body, as she called it, as to her eyes a person's skin became transparent, like glass, if disease was present. Compassionate to her core, the young Rosa would do whatever she deemed to be in her powers to help an individual to heal. She used water mixed with rock salt brought to her from the nearby Salt Mines of Wieliczka to make healing brine. She would receive a handful of salt in exchange for healing. Salt was currency in those days, and with the brine she made, she doused around the aura of anyone who came to see her with their various ailments.

In the late autumnal months of 1918, Rosa was approached by a young man called Leon, who worked in the Salt Mines of Wieliczka. 'I cannot breathe,' he told her. He was young – possibly in his twenties, she estimated by the lack of deep lines on his face, and the fact that he still had his teeth and hair. It was the same way she estimated her own age, as she did not know exactly how old she was. She just knew she had a full head of wild dark hair, all her own teeth, her joints didn't ache that much that she had to walk like she was folded over, and her eyes could still burst open in the morning like a flame had been ignited. Despite her estimation of her age, she couldn't say exactly which nationality she was. Born in a time where there was no independent Poland, she guessed she may be either Romanian, Hungarian, or Polish, but couldn't be sure. Rosa had no documented record of her date or place of birth. In her heart though, she *felt* Polish.

"I cannot understand," the young man explained. "I work in the salt mines, it should be good for my breathing." With this, he stretched his arms out towards Rosa. She glanced down at the groves on his upward-turned palms. She gently grasped his wrists and examined each little pathway of his life furrowed deep within the skin of his palms. His skin was hard, broken and pale beneath the grasp of her swarthy warm fingers. She sat down in front of him, and softly rested his hands on her knees. As he knelt in front of her she took his face in her hands. His white skin was grey, his lips and under his nose were tinged with blue. As she passed the palm of her hand gently across his cheeks, the skin that stretched across his bony face felt cold and clammy. He looked just like a plant that had been kept in the dark. More worryingly, under her scrutiny his skin was like glass. His body seemed too broken to mend. Despite this, Rosa found something completely entrancing in his deeply pleading pond-like eyes. It quickened her heart like a horse to a gallop.

"Please, heal me. Please, I cannot die."

"I don't know if I am the right person to help you." Rosa was ever mindful of the criticism her practice invited. God forbid there should be a death on her doorstep. Yet that was the only outcome she could foresee for this young man. Despite this she could not send him away.

"I am desperate. My mother is desperate. I am all she has." He looked over to his mother, who held her head in her hands. She was muttering, praying quietly to herself.

"For how long has your breathing been so bad?" Rosa was puzzled as to why such a young man should be so unwell.

"A long time – months. I have been afraid. I am very afraid now. This is why I come to you now."

Rosa took his cold grey face in her hands. "I fear too. I fear for you."

"Look at my mother, she prays all day long."

"What is your name?"

"Leon."

Rosa took Leon's hands and, standing up she gently helped him to his feet. As they stood facing each other, their eyes met and a small electrical charge was silently exchanged. For a moment Rosa forgot his mother was in the room. For a fraction of a moment she forgot he was desperately unwell. For a split second she had to steel herself. Compose herself – this had never happened to her before.

"Leon, you must stay here with me, if we are to have any chance." She looked over to Leon's mother to see if this could be possible. His mother nodded. She had resigned herself to the fact that she was now handing the fate of her son over from God to the gypsy in the woods. She was desperate. Her beautiful, precious boy was dying before her eyes; she would have left her son hanging by the ankles over a cliff edge if she thought it would cure him.

Rosa stayed with him day and night for three weeks. Twice a day she soaked his naked body in warm brine, hoping, praying she could wash away the disease that was consuming him day by day. In the beginning her work was almost clinical. Back and forth she washed, up and down she bathed him. Careful to cover every part of his body. As the days passed, she became evermore careful to control the urges that rose up within her. An urge to linger with her touch, an urge to breathe too close to him, an urge to take him in. Take all of him in.

The warm, salt water was strangely soothing for him. He watched her move swiftly across his body, her light, tender touch easing the pain in his joints. Her warm, soft hands easing the tension in his body, relaxing him. Relaxing him enough to allow his mind to wander from his fear of death. Relaxing him enough to feel alive, to feel energised.

Day in, day out, she felt a want gather momentum within her. With each healing wash, she became aware of something in his response, in the way he drew each breath deeper, in the way he held her gaze longer, in the way he would momentarily take her hand and hold it – just for a second – stop her from washing. Stop her from working so clinically. Make her stop and look at him – take him in. Take him all in. Each time it became more and more difficult for her to deny this overwhelming desire for him. With each wash, Leon found it more difficult to control the life that was suddenly surging around in his veins.

Some days she worked in silence. On others their conversation was animated, even excited. On days such as this Leon told Rosa about the Salt Mines. Rosa had heard much talk of their wonder, and often held the salt in her own hands, but she had never been down to see for herself. She was suspicious of places like the mines, where hoards of people gathered and where there were regular reports of death; miners perishing whilst struggling to bring salt to the surface from what was really just a hot, dark, deep hole in the ground. It scared Rosa and seemed to her like it might just be a slippery walkway straight to hell.

She would be the first to admit she never really embraced the world around her. Instead, she waited until it came to her; and it did in all shapes and forms, with warts, with leg pains, stomach pains, head pains; anything that could physically have a pain arrived at Rosa's door, along with poor vision, bad hearing, sore teeth, bad skin; the list was endless. Despite a never-ending flow of afflicted visitors to Rosa for her healing powers, she was rarely welcomed in any community. In fact, she was often persecuted and humiliated for merely trying to help people. Any help she gave, she offered with honesty, with the entirety of her sensibilities, and fullness of her soul, but this was always overshadowed by a menacing fear of the unknown. The fear drove individuals to threaten and intimidate her. One man promised to gouge her eyes out with hot blacksmiths' nails if she ever went near his wife again. What he couldn't grasp was that his wife had gone to Rosa, not the other way around. So unlike most of the people around Wieliczka, she hadn't gone along to gaze open-mouthed at the wonders of the Salt Mines. It wasn't a choice of ignorance or arrogance, it was her need to survive that kept her away.

"They have ballrooms the size of a field carved from salt, where orchestras can play, and chandeliers all carved out of salt by the miners," he marvelled. "It's my job to take the tourists around." Leon explained how he played the violin in the Miners Band. Twice a week he would join the band members at the railway station and meet the tourists. "Important people are coming to the mines now, royalty even!" he boasted to Rosa.

For two weeks he related a story of grandeur and beauty beyond belief. He explained that a breathtaking chapel was taking shape, with plans to carve out an altar, a pulpit and wall plaques depicting biblical scenes. He was excited to report that work on the carvings the full length of the right hand of the chapel were almost finished and included a magnificent sculpture of the Virgin Mary, which had just been finished. All carved from salt, all hidden four hundred feet deep underground. "These miners don't just dig, this is art and it is beautiful beyond your imagination. When I am better, when I can breathe easier, I will take you down, and then, my word, I can assure you, your breath will be taken away with surprise!" Something in the way he said this made her lean forward and kiss him gently. Very gently. It was though she was saying thank you. *Thank you for considering that I might be part of your future. Your futile future.* Then with what she considered might be a fit of madness, she kissed him again. Time was running out for both of them. They knew it, and something in that moment that spoke of desperation, of impending loss, pulled them wildly together.

That was the last time Rosa saw Leon smile. They lay there together for a long time, both completely surprised by the sheer strength of the desires that had overwhelmed them. Yet, as they lay there together, both were quietly despairing at the hopelessness of it all.

Within days he had drifted into a sleep that he could not be roused from. Three weeks after their meeting, despite Rosa's best and exhaustive efforts, Leon died.

On the day Rosa first ushered a tired and breathless Leon into her kitchen, Leon's mother, Jogoda, had been surprised and somewhat puzzled when she first saw Rosa. It's hard not to imagine what a person might look like when their reputation precedes them. Rosa's reputation was so powerful, and for some, induced such fear, that Jogoda had expected an aged, stooped woman with a heavily lined face and a bristled chin. She had imagined Rosa would be a woman who would examine anyone who arrived at her door with narrowed eyes that warned of perpetual danger. She had certainly not expected to be met by a young, fresh-faced woman, whose deep, eager eyes glowed with anticipation, and whose reassuring smile was simply captivating.

Once Rosa had agreed that she would help Leon, Jogoda smiled and quickly wrapped her arms tightly around Rosa. It was a fleeting embrace, but it carried with it a lifetime of compassion. It took Rosa completely by surprise, as it seemed this desperately worried mother had nothing but kindness and respect for Rosa. She helped Rosa, bringing salt from the mines for the warm brine that Rosa bathed and soothed Leon with. She spent time with Rosa when Leon slept, and when he had died, she helped Rosa to understand him; she filled in the gaps, told Rosa everything there was to know about Leon.

Jogoda had recognised the connection between her fragile son and Rosa; however brief, it had been tangible, and it was somehow ironically exciting that at his weakest moments,

Leon seemed to be alive with anticipation when he had been bathed and attended to by Rosa.

She explained to Rosa how her precious son had been a very sick child, always troubled with chest problems and breathing difficulties. Born too quickly, before his time, and to a mother whose soul had just been ripped out, she had feared he was too weak to live more than a few days, and she was too weak to nurse him.

When he did live she worried about how he would run with the other children in the street. When he did she worried of the day he would ask how his father had died. What will she tell him? When he did and she had provided a carefully constructed explanation, how would he manage to work? How could he possibly make his way in this world and survive when his lungs were so weak? When he did, she finally thought of herself. What happened to Jogoda, the prophet? Jogoda, the joker? The answer: Jogoda was murdered along with her husband.

The night Leon died and Rosa and Jogoda had washed his mottled cold body and wrapped in him freshly washed cotton sheets, Jogoda told Rosa of the time when she was heavily pregnant that her husband, Leon's father, a member of the Peasant Party, was captured and mutilated by the Russians. It was an episode in Jogoda's life that she had never spoken of until that night.

She explained to Rosa that when she was pregnant with Leon, but not at full term, there was a group of around twenty Russians that had set up camp nearby whilst working on the Silesia Line. Some thought this new railway was a life-line connecting Krakow to Warsaw. Whilst others, like Leon's father who was part of a peasant co-operative, opposed this expansion in the Polish State Railway. He believed the new line would merely provide these impostors with an easier route into the guts of Poland, and once there they would tear what remained of Poland's heart right out.

As a keen activist of the Peasant Party, he spoke out against the Russian and Hungarian troops that had been living like parasites now around Wieliczka for almost sixty years. He was silenced though, and when his beheaded and skinned body was tossed at Jogoda's feet, the sight induced fierce uterine contractions that led to Leon's premature arrival. Despite this obvious trauma, she had actually blamed herself for Leon's condition, believing she had held her breath for so long that day when staring down upon her husband's raw remains on the gravel, that she had damaged Leon's little lungs.

When Henryk Rosiewicz, Jogoda's grandson, was born in the late summer of 1919 in the small farm outbuilding, Jogoda believed that her prayers had been answered. Her son had lived on. He lived on in the blood and flesh of this beautiful and more importantly, strong little baba, whose loud, wailing lungs brought tears of joy to Jogoda. "Listen to him! He has the strongest lungs ever!" she proclaimed, as she helped lift him onto Rosa's breast. And with the boundaries of Poland now reinstated, she could proudly boast of her Polish grandson.

Rosa was forever thankful she had been helped at the birth by Jogoda. For at that time, Rosa had been disowned by her own family, as having clearly lost her virginity when not yet married, she had broken a strict rule of the Roma. In stark contrast she had been embraced by Jogoda, a tall, round-faced Rubenesque woman, who, once introduced to Rosa, displayed an unfaltering loyalty.

It was true that initially Rosa was uncomfortable with Jogoda's attention. She would examine every glance and every twitch of Jogoda's expressions trying to decode every tensed muscle, every relaxed muscle, every non-verbal clue in Jogoda's vivid responses, searching for that familiar hint of mistrust or a glint of disbelief, fearing that perhaps soon she would be the victim of an exploited opportunity for ridicule; as was Rosa's usual experience when confronted with members of the public. This time it was different. She was never confronted with any of these when in contact with Jogoda. Indeed when talking with Jogoda she was aware of eye contact, something not many individuals indulged in when in Rosa's company. Always they would avert their eyes, for fear of what she might see in their tortured or guilty souls. Jogoda seemed to have no fears and nothing to hide; and when engaged in their many conversations, what Rosa could see was the face of a deeply warm and compassionate woman, whose soul was full of humour and boundless imagination. She had wide, dark eyes that seemed to deflect the trials of life like light bouncing off the dark glass-like surface of a bottomless lake. A surface that, even in the sharpest light, seems impenetrable, until you simply dip your toes in. Then the ripples release a soft, radiating energy and the lake opens up. That was how Rosa came to understand Jogoda. Whilst some might have found her obstinate ability to absorb disaster without evidence slightly intimidating, Rosa found it intriguing, even inviting, and wholly enviable.

When Henryk was five, Jogoda died suddenly but quietly, whilst sleeping in her armchair. It was though she had been stolen in the night, and Rosa felt as though she had lost her own mother, she felt as though she had been abandoned and orphaned for a second unbearable time. Rosa had never considered there would be a day when Jogoda wouldn't be there giving her strength and providing protection by simply believing in her; believing in her not just as a healer, but as a mother. Whenever Rosa felt down or betrayed and misunderstood, and yearned to have a normal life, wishing for a little piece of the ordinary, Jogoda would take her quietly aside and spend time with her.

There was an occasion shortly before she died when Jogoda found Rosa tearful and exhausted after a particularly difficult spell of criticism from a group of people from Wieliczka. She held Rosa gently in her arms and told her, "Remember this, Rosalia; all your life is, all that your life amounts to is what you are right now. Not what you have or haven't had. Not what you wish you were, or want to be, or want Henryk to be. Because one has already occurred, and one might never happen. And what you are right now is a beautiful, gifted young mother who wants to do her best for anyone who comes to see her. What can possibly be so wrong with that? And who in their right mind would ever want to change that?"

Henryk was a resilient and intelligent little boy who had always been strong, both physically and mentally. Some he had inherited, some he had learnt from watching his mother and grandmother. These traits were to save his life as a young adult.

When he was twenty years old, Henryk was forced to flee Wieliczka, after Rosa was accused of killing a peasant woman while attempting to remove what she described as a 'broken baba'. The 'surgery' was desperately but crudely carried out on a stone slab laid over the kitchen table, after the peasant woman had collapsed on her doorstep. "She bleeds too much!" Rosa had protested frantically, as the peasant drifted into unconsciousness and bled to death. Rosa was deemed by the German authorities to be a murdering fraud, regardless of the fact that the woman would have died anyway. Despite protesting the desperation of the situation and the integrity of her intentions, she was dragged from her home and shot in the head by the German army.

Lucky for Henryk, she was accused of killing a peasant, lucky for him she got shot, and lucky for him he was forced to flee Wieliczka. For within a year of this incident, Henryk would surely have perished in the 'Silent Holocaust' of Birkenau and Auschwitz. Gypsies were, after all, one of the non-Jewish communities who were included in Hitler's mass extermination plans, and were amongst the first prisoners to arrive at Auschwitz in June 1940.

*

And so it was always with the sternest of warnings that Martha was informed of her supposed psychic inheritance by her dad,

Henryk. In fact once, when Martha was thirteen, Henryk found her notebook. Recorded in the notebook were records of Martha's dreams and the following related events. Martha had kept the notebook updated diligently. She had been aware for some time that she was dreaming of events before they happened, and was often intrigued by their accuracy. Sometimes they were so vivid and so clear, it was like setting an event alarm clock buzzing in her mind. "You bring such bad luck to you, to me, to your mother – wherever on this God's earth she might be! To write these things? We might as well be cursed. Is bad! So very bad!" Henryk raged. As he thumbed through her dream diary he was consumed with fear for his daughter. He told her it was useless trying to make sense of them. He said they were like broken puzzles. "Lots of damaged parts, bits missing, never be in one piece, never make you any sensible thing, look what happen to Rosa, this a curse, no a gift, you no listen to this dreamy stuff no more!" With that he took away her dream diary and set fire to it in the garden.

As her precious notes disappeared in flames, Martha watched her father weep quietly in the garden by the fire. When he returned to the house he was silent. His silence lasted for almost three days. From the day she watched the charred remains of her notes drift high into the sky, and her father's tears dripping quietly from the end of his nose, Martha feared the dreams, she feared the voices she heard, and many times before her untimely death she feared she may be cursed.

VIII

Just as Anna knew little of her mother, Martha, except that which her dad and Papa Henryk had told her, she knew nothing of her great-grandmother Rosalia, as neither of them had told her about Rosalia. It may have helped Anna to understand the phantom voices and the evanescent images in her mind if they had, not to mention the premonition dreams that regularly disturb her nights. But they were struck dumb by the notion that Anna had somehow inherited this so called 'gift'. Indeed it filled both men with terror. For sure, Henryk had lost both his mother and his daughter within an impenetrable haze of supernatural mystic dabbling. So it's no surprise that Henryk was having trouble taking in what Mick was telling him.

"What can this floating be she does in the night?"

"I don't know, Papa, she just says she floats. She comes out of her body, 'n flies off." Mick flailed his arms in an upward motion, as though to demonstrate the fine art of achieving an out-of-body experience. Anna hadn't gotten round to telling her dad all the rest. He knew nothing of the voices, the images, the people she felt all around her, not to mention the premonition dreams.

"Is she eat all right?" Henryk has always placed a great deal of importance on food. Whilst his fatherless childhood was often blighted by harassment and anxiety, there was always ample to eat. Quite simply food was currency and the afflicted were often indebted to Rosa. As a result, food and the love of it was in his blood; in fact there's an old Polish saying he still often referred to; *eat, drink and loosen your belt.*

Mick nodded. He explained she ate as well as the average teenager would. Henryk was unimpressed. Where was the evidence she was eating cereal, fruit, meat? He decided from Mick's reply that he would make her his favourite dish, Klopsy.

"She needs meat for her body, no toast with this 'n toast with that, 'n toast with the next thing, 'n crisps, 'n all that gas she drinks; one day she float all right, when she explodes!" Although perplexed, Henryk was careful not to be too harsh. He tried to lighten up the conversation. "She'll eat my Klopsy; just tell her she need it, especially if she need to grow wings!" He had a dry sense of humour, too.

The two stood momentarily in silence as though considering Anna's fate; will she explode under the pressure of carbonated drinks or will she float off one night and not manage to come back?

"Is she got boy beside her in the day?" Henryk was keen to get to the bottom of this. He remembered how Martha had seemed detached and lighter in step after she had met Mick.

Mick nodded. "Lots, they're her friends."

"Are you watching by her?" He meant was Mick following her the way he used to follow Mick and Martha.

"No Papa, it's not like that these days; if I followed her around with her pals, I'd get arrested." Mick laughed.

"Okay, okay now, is she take any of the alcohol?" He said it as though 'The Alcohol' was just one big brand.

"Some," Mick nodded. No more than the usual seventeen-year-old, he thought. "She's nearly eighteen, Papa; didn't you drink alcohol when you were that age?"

Henryk nodded. "Just a wee little bit, we no had bars here, 'n there, so we can only sip at what we can make. Pwaaa, it was strong stuff, just a wee little bit all you need." He laughed in his hybrid Polish come Scottish accent. Henryk chuckled as he remembered happier times as a youth, when his mother was still alive, especially the autumns when much time was spent collecting berries for brewing gin.

Mick had left his beloved little book shop for the afternoon in order to talk to Henryk about Anna. He had left Anna in charge. Not something he made a habit of, but he had no choice. Mick was aware that Henryk applied a great deal of importance to the responsibility and privilege of fatherhood. Not only had he been denied a father, the sudden loss of Martha had denied him the opportunity to fully redress the balance. He hadn't been allowed the opportunity to see Martha grow into an independent young woman. So the honour of fatherhood now lay with Mick. Basically in Henryk's eyes, Mick was occupying an enviable role that he was bereft of.

Mick had told Anna he was going to look at a new book outlet, maybe buy in some new stock. Anna had no idea he had gone to discuss her with Papa Henryk. As she wandered around the shop, she considered there was hardly room for a magazine on the shelves, never mind more books, and wondered if her dad was wasting his time sourcing even more stock. As she wandered around she ran her hands along the spines of the books that were stacked at her shoulder level, wondering where on earth he would put any additional stock. They resonated with a dull thud, thud, thud, and thud as she wandered up and down the shop, tapping the spine of each book as she went. It was quiet, not just the shop, but the town centre; a lot of people had left for their summer holidays. Anna surveyed the shop, paying particular attention at how her dad had organised the shelving; there was too much of it, she surmised. In her opinion, her dad's little corner of worldly treasures had 'this shop belongs to a man' written all over it. He may as well douse it daily in *Old Spice,* she thought. If it was her shop she would have it organised very differently – she would brighten the place up a bit first, make room for a chair, where people can come in, have a seat and browse through the pages of the books before they decided which one to buy. She would take away the high shelving that met the ceiling. Who can see up there anyway, she thought, wondering all the time if this is where her dad keeps the books he didn't want to sell. His favourites, not really part of the stock, more they were part of his personal collection. She looked along the shelves at eye level for some of her old favourites, the ones her dad had read to her. She found Harper Lee and then a few stops along in the alphabet, Muriel Spark. In the *Penguin Classics* she found D. H. Lawrence. She had only just finished Sons & Lovers. It was given to her by her English teacher. "Read this," he'd said, "you'll enjoy it." She scanned the Lawrence collection that took up almost all of 'L' on that part of the shelf of 'Classics'. She recalled how a couple of weeks ago she had watched her very favourite English teacher meander around the desks, cradling a large pile of books for summer reading. She remembered the thick, stifling air of the classroom, where every now and then a draft from the open window shunted the heavy, stale pubescent air from one end of the room to the other; a putrid kind of sticky smell that gathered un-wanton force as the day wore on. She remembered how slowly he moved around the room, as though the atmosphere was acting like a kind of glue, suspended in the air, sticking to everything. She watched him as he moved from desk to desk, and how with every tenacious step he siphoned off the wafer thin novellas, and how her heart had sunk when the doorstopper at the bottom of the pile came crashing down on her desk for summer holiday reading. In spite of herself, something within her and the words of D. H. Lawrence connected and for two weeks she was immersed in the world of *Paul Morel*. Lawrence had found his way into her mind and deepest thoughts. She imagined how hellish her life might have been if she had had a dad like *Paul Morel's*. Just as she was considering this, the shop door opened tentatively. A young woman came in. Anna strolled out from behind the bookshelves and smiled. The woman smiled. Anna wondered for a moment where the woman's friend had disappeared to; she was sure she had seen two people coming in. She watched as the woman walked around the shop scanning the shelves. She stopped in the poetry section and stood still. Anna watched, only the woman's head was moving, side to side, up and down. Then the woman raised her right hand and traversed the spines of the books with her index finger. She shook her head a little and walked towards Anna. Anna was unnerved as she was certain she had seen two people come into the shop, but only one, this woman, was there.

"Can I help you?" Anna asked.

"I was looking for…" The woman hesitated and didn't finish that sentence. Instead, she drifted off amongst the books again. She found herself another set of shelves and went through the same procedure. She stood still, moving only her head, side to side, nodding as she scanned the higher and lower shelves. Anna wondered if there was such as thing as a book shop inspector, as this woman seemed to be inspecting the stock. Inspecting the light, sniffing and inspecting the air, inspecting the wood, inspecting the floors, and as they exchanged fleeting glances, Anna worried this woman was inspecting her – a secret shopper, trading standards. Anna's imagination was slowly uncoiling as the woman moved towards where she was standing. Anna shifted uneasily from side to side as she became aware of a shapeless presence drifting along beside the woman. Anna gradually worked her way to behind the desk. Once behind the old maple desk, with its dented, worn table top, she felt safer. This desk was originally her papa Henryk's; it would protect her, she thought as she held onto the corner of the desk. Protect her from this woman and protect her from the ghostly image that was following this woman around the shop. Making contact with the wood, the wood her papa had many times leaned upon to write his letters, his notes and memorandums, made Anna feel instantly secure.

"I was looking for a small book of poetry." The woman managed to finish her sentence as she stood directly in front of Anna. Her shrouded companion floated around and behind her. Anna found it difficult not to look beyond the woman, as the grey mist around her kept drifting around.

Anna had never heard of the author before. She asked the woman to write it down, along with her name and contact number, explaining that her father would get in touch as he knew every book on the shelves.

"Okay." The woman wrote down her name and telephone number on the back of an old envelope she had dug out from the bottom of her shoulder bag, along with a pen that had a wrapper glued to it with the melted remainder of a sweetie. She handed Anna the envelope, tore off the old wrapper, popped the pen in her bag and smiled at Anna. As she smiled at Anna, she kept eye contact momentarily, only fractionally too long, but long enough to unnerve Anna, and then she left, taking her ghostly companion with her.

*

Letter to Mum dated April 4th 1983. Found with all the others just before move back in May '95. Some days I'm just so, so sad. Not every day, just some days. This was one of those days. I was a bit mixed up too, about men mostly I think. Men in general have been a problem for me, that's definitely true.

Wish I had an answer for that one. Maybe going home will help.

Mum, I can't believe it you've been away for ten years today. That has to be the longest ten years of my whole life. A decade. Bloody hell. I miss you so, so, so much. Sometimes if I think about you too much I worry that the huge lump in my throat might choke me to death. But sometimes I think I have actually died too for a time, 'n if I let myself start to cry I think there's a danger I could possibly wash half of Edinburgh away. I think I came to live here to feel closer to you, but I'm not sure it's working. I wish I could meet someone. I'm trying not to be homesick, because there's nothing to be homesick for. Dad's lost his job now, after he was caught drinking at work. That was a matter of time. He's stopped speaking to me and Robert. Robert seems okay though. He's been with Mark for a long time now, they are so sorted. Dad's a bloody fool; he won't speak to Robert because he's gay. For Christ sake, he's such a bloody old dinosaur. I haven't been with anybody. I mean *really* been with anybody.

I still have that Christmas photo of us; you, me and Robert. You managed to squash us both on your knee, despite the fact Robert was already nearly ten feet tall, 'n he must only be about nine. Sometimes when I'm in Boots, or recently I was in John Lewis's in Edinburgh (your favourite shop), and I just stood totally still at the perfume counter. Someone had just sprayed a Nina Ricci perfume, and it just smelled of you. Sometimes I think if I close my eyes and reach into the thin air I might just touch you. I wish I knew where you were. I wish I could be like you and believe in God, and know that's who is looking after you now. But I don't believe in him, 'cause he's never looked after us has he?

I know this is embarrassing, but I have to tell you, but then you probably already know. Anyway, what's wrong with me? I'm twenty-three years old and I've still not done it. You know – IT. I've been away from home, was that home? I'm not sure; anyway I've been away from there for nearly six years. Six years, that's nearly as long as you've been away. I just keep thinking that you're watching me. Maybe you're the wee star I can see from my window, gleaming, with the perseverance of the very strongest star that exploded into life sixty-eight thousand years ago. Then I suppose like these stars I imagine you will probably be quite fragile like the very end of the taper on a long-burning candle that's almost burnt out, 'n if there was a storm in space, a huge puff of wind could put you out totally, then I wouldn't be able to see you up there anymore. I've always been worried you would lose sight of me. Whenever it gets to this time of year there are certain things that take me back to when you died like it just was five minutes ago; as soon as Easter eggs appear in the shops, or if I smell fresh cut grass, or squash soft, summer fruit between my fingers, I can hear Dad telling me as clear as though he was speaking to me right now, that you're away, away to heaven and you wouldn't be coming back.

I used to hear him crying in his bed, when he thought we were asleep. He must have kept it in all day, and then he howled at night – sometimes he sounded like some sort of weird animal. It was a horrible noise. I hated it, it really scared me.

113

Oh, God, you're a selfish sod, keeping her tucked away up there. Could I just have five minutes with her? Even just one. Just one, please?

I love you, Mum. Ruth X

July '95

Few things unsettled the murky sediments of Ruth's memory more than the smell of blackberries. Even the mention of blackberries was enough. It stems from a time when she was around ten years old when she spent her summer holidays berry-picking with a few other kids from school. It was an early start, the orchard was four miles away, and they had to catch the eight a.m. bus. The orchard was in a secluded spot halfway up a steep hill on the way to the local psychiatric hospital. Ruth often looked out for The Yellow Van, the van renowned for scooping up anyone who may appear to be a danger to the public, and whisking them off behind closed doors. She had been warned about this van by her parents, and lived in fear of being passed by it, the same way kids are superstitious about being passed by an ambulance or a hearse. Ruth used to say *'touch my head and touch my toes, hope I never have to go in one of those'* whilst frantically touching her head and her toes if a van of any description, or any colour, passed them on their journey to the orchard.

To a ten-year-old, the orchard seemed vast. There were apple trees, gooseberry bushes, plum trees, strawberries and blackberries. The boys always managed to hike up the hill first and book their spot under the apple trees. For obvious reasons it was easier to make money filling punnets with apples than it was filling punnets with blackberries. Quite simply blackberries occupied the bottom slot of the fruit picking pecking order. Ruth and her friend at that time, Mary, were the youngest and were last up the hill, thus they were banished to pick the blackberries. They picked all day until their fingers were raw and stained with the green and black sour juices of the fruit, and the sap from the branches and leaves. If they were lucky they managed to fill maybe two punnets a day, earning them a pittance, unlike the boys who were making a small fortune filling punnet after punnet with apples. Soon the girls figured if they just picked enough fruit to earn their bus fare home and return fare the next day, they could then eat and chat all day. This proved more fun and they were never halted by hunger pains.

So there they lay, under the high summer sun, eating blackberries and sometimes gooseberries until their bellies ached, and until it was time to race down the hill to be the first on the back seat of the bus home.

Ruth can remember lying under the blackberry bushes, her face tingling with the heat from the sun, chatting and giggling the way young girls do. That summer when they were chatting about boys, namely young priests they had met on a visit to the local college for priests, Ruth admitted she had seen a boy she thought was beautiful. Mary lay on her back, staring into a cloudless sky, listening as Ruth described every imaginary sinew of the boy she had fallen in love with. His name was Mick Munroe.

"No! He was never one of the priests, was he?" gasped Mary.

"No, no, I saw him at the community centre last week. He was there." Ruth explained that as their junior youth club had come to an end, and the older kids had arrived for their disco, Ruth had spotted a young lad who had ambled in on his own. He had long, wild-looking dark brown hair and a deep wanton look in his eyes. He looked at Ruth and said, "Hi."

"He said *'Hi'* to me, to me, actually to me." Ruth had been amazed by this. Amazed that someone had actually said, *'Hi.'* Someone had actually taken notice of her.

"He said, *'Hi'*?" Mary answered in amazement.

'Yeah, *'Hi'*, that's what he said." There they lay silent, dumbfounded and awestruck; Mick had said *'Hi'*. Ruth loved this tiny little snippet-like memory of Mick.

She remembers just lying there, in the orchard in the sun. It was the first time she had seen strawberries growing out of straw. That summer when she was ten, was also the last summer Ruth's mum was well. Well enough to see her on the bus in the morning. Well enough to hear about the antics of the day when she got back. Blackberries equalled that summer, which equalled the start of her mum being ill.

She remembered one afternoon she had come home from berry picking, and from talking tirelessly about Mick Munroe all afternoon, and had stumbled upon what should have been a very private conversation. It had happened when her mum had come home from hospital after her mastectomy. Ruth, aware of a tension of some sort in their voices, had quietly positioned herself near the top of the stairs in the hallway. She had sat very still and silently and listened as her mum was trying to explain things to her dad. She heard them both talk about her operation and what it meant for her. For a time it had seemed like a matter of fact kind of conversation. Like, this is what's wrong and this is what has been done, and this is what still needs to be done, and Ruth remembers actually feeling reassured by that. Not worried at all, it was as though they had all aspects covered, sorted, and that they were in control. Then she remembers her mum's tone changing;

"Say it, Bruce." Ruth listened as her mum raised her voice and had seemed to become angry. Ruth had found this very unusual. She could never remember her raising her voice.

"Say what?" Her dad had seemed nervous. Ruth had never heard him sounding nervous and vulnerable before. She remembers how it made her stomach feel like a large knot had developed in it.

"You keep avoidin' it. You've never said anything about it since I got home. Say it." Her mum was insistent.

"What? Say what?" Ruth remembered hearing her dad's voice hesitate. She remembers thinking he must be trying to eat something while they are talking, as it sounded like he had something stuck in his throat.

"One breast. Your wife has only got one left now. 'N then there's the cancer – you've never said that word either."

"Do I have to?" She remembered that he didn't sound defiant, he sounded scared.

"Yes, yes you do." And she sounded angry.

"But how can that make any difference to all this?"

"Because it makes it all real. You have to feel those words leave your mouth. I need you to say it. I need you to see what those words feel like. I swear, Bruce, every time I say it it's like a metal shredder, tearing at the root of my tongue: one breast. Cancer." Her mum started to cry. Ruth considered running away so as not to hear any more, but she was paralysed with fear. Immobile, she listened further as her dad was trying to reassure her mum. But his voice was like someone who had forgotten how to speak. Like every word was an effort.

"C'mon hen, you heard the nurse, you're her star."

"'N that's great. A great nurse. A super nurse. But I'm not married to her, am I? I wish you would say 'cancer', 'n just talk about it." The last few words led into a whisper, as though her mum had just lost power, or been unplugged from her energy source.

"But there's nothing to talk about. Your breast's off. It's all away."

Ruth physically jumped and thought her heart might have stopped as her mum shouted.

"It. It. IT! Cancer! Stop calling my cancer 'it', 'n it's like my breast being taken off is like… is like the rubbish getting put out, the way you talk."

"For Christ sake, Doreen, give me a break." He couldn't shout. He could hardly hold himself up.

"You've never looked at me, look at me, Bruce. Look at me!"

"I have, I am."

"Look right at me though, look at this, and see what I have to see." Ruth couldn't see, but Doreen was unbuttoning her blouse revealing the scar of her mastectomy.

"Doreen, Doreen, stop hen, not here, not now, Ruth's in now, I heard the door, she's went upstairs."

"I have to look at this every day."

Ruth heard crying and couldn't make out if it was her mum or dad, until her dad tried to speak, and she knew it was him.

"Please hen, please no, don't do this to yourself."

"This is not just about me, and myself, this is about you, about you and me, look, look, please just look at me, look at this."

Ruth couldn't tell from the silence if her dad was looking or not. She was trying to imagine what her mum wanted him to look at. The breast that was there or the breast that had gone. She was finding it all a bit hard to understand. She was only ten.

"Please, please don't you cry, Doreen, I just thought, you maybe didn't want me to see," her Dad pleaded.

"I'm not ashamed. But I would be lying if I said I wasn't embarrassed to show you this. But really it doesn't matter a bugger how I feel, because the thing is I've not got the luxury of choosing how I might or might not want to feel. It's like this; keep the breast and die, get rid of it and live. That's how I'm breaking this down, Bruce. Live or die."

The word 'die' hit Ruth like a hard-fisted punch in the stomach. Jumping to her feet, she ran to her bedroom where she sat in silence for what seemed like an eternity, terrified by the thought that by the end of that day her mum would be dead. As it was she wasn't far wrong.

Doreen Nairn survived only a further three years. During that time the cancer slowly consumed her, spreading to her liver, bones and her brain. She spent long periods in hospital, that remote, almost imaginary place that Ruth was rarely allowed to visit. In the end, Ruth's mother's demise was conducted entirely within the realms of Ruth's imagination. Ruth knew that Robert had been allowed to visit. He was older and deemed 'adult' enough to cope. But he never spoke to Ruth about his visits.

It was most likely this exclusion from these hospital visits that led to Ruth's fascination with hospitals and her eventual career in nursing. She started her training at the Royal Infirmary Edinburgh six months after her first visit to Edinburgh when she had gone for her interview in the late spring of 1977. Over the years she had worked in a variety of wards, never quite finding her niche, an area of specialist care that might inspire her. It took a long time for her to realise she wasn't looking for inspiration in this career, she was simply trying to find the answer to why her mum had died, as she knew she would never stop wondering just what happened to her as she was dying. After a few months in the job, she realised there were so many different ways that a person could die, she was never going to find out for sure just what happened. Neither her dad, nor Robert could ever, or would ever fill in these gaps. Ruth realised this after returning home in May 1995 when she went to visit her dad.

"Oh, bloody hell, you're never Ruth, are you?" Laced with sarcasm, her unannounced arrival clearly surprised and annoyed her dad. Ruth had felt overwhelmed with anxiety, the tone of his welcome making her think she might throw up with the tension of it all. It was not exactly how she imagined her first meeting with her dad in over ten years might be.

"Dad?" Ruth barely recognised him. *That is my own father, Jesus Christ, what has happened to him? That is my flesh and blood.*

She was struggling to define what 'that' meant as she leant forward to give him a hug. He staggered backwards before they made contact. Bearing in mind they hadn't seen or spoken to each other for over ten years, they were acting like opposing ends of two magnets repelling each other.

Ruth had been back in Galashiels for almost a week. It had only taken a couple of days to track down where her dad was living now. However, having had no contact at all for such a long time, it took her a few days to summon the courage to visit him. On account of both parties, there had been more than one too many forgotten birthdays and Christmases. In fact the first time Ruth had heard her dad say, '*Sorry I forgot,*' was her twenty-first birthday. She waited for his card for two weeks before eventually phoning to remind him. "Sorry I forgot," was all he said. On that day Ruth deduced that singularly, these three words were utterly harmless, but string them together and they become probably the most damaging phrase ever spoken. She had heard it before; 'Sorry I forgot your mum had died,' had been a common one. Ruth thought about this phrase a lot – '*Sorry I forgot,*' and came to the conclusion it was the ultimate insult, the ultimate lack of respect, and complete lack of understanding. '*Sorry I didn't realise,*' now that was different. There was margin for forgiveness. Not knowing, and knowing and forgetting are two different things. '*How could he forget my twenty-first, how could he?*' But then he wouldn't get away with saying, '*sorry I didn't realise it was your twenty-first,*' either. He was in a no-win situation there.

"What you doin' here?"

"I've left Edinburgh to… "

"Hah! Fucking city of dreams!"

"Dad I just wanted to... " He cut her off again.

"To what? What? Fucking what?" He staggered through to his kitchen. "Yah bastard! Again ya wee bastard!" Ruth leant forward into a position where she could see her dad in his kitchen. She watched him slowly removing a slither of glass from the ball of his foot. Fully anaesthetised by alcohol, it seemed to be a well-practised procedure. The floor was littered with empty bottles and broken glass. "What do you want, Ruth?"

'*I want to tell you your house stinks of piss, and you look like you've been dead and decomposing for years; you're a selfish, pathetic old bastard. Why do you never keep in touch? Why did you forget about me? She was my mum, my bloody mum, not just your wife,*' but of course, she never said any of these things.

She wanted to tell him he was barely recognisable and that he was desperately in need of help, but realised she had relinquished that right when she left home at seventeen, leaving only a short letter of explanation with a forwarding address. At the point she left home she firmly believed she was

122

the only one that was hurting, that no-one else felt the intense pain she did. Hers was the only measurable devastation. That's what grief does. It's selfishly all encompassing, a selfish vacuum of endless self-pity.

"I want to say hello, 'Hello, Dad.'"

"So what do you want?" He staggered back through to the living room and sat down in his threadbare chair in front of her. He never offered her a seat, and Ruth never sat down.

"How's Robert, I've been trying to… " He cut her off again.

"That fucking queer! He's a poof, did you know that…? Fucking queero wee git!"

Ruth considered this and concluded that Robert was in fact the only one of them who had found some kind of solace. He had found more comfort and commitment in his long-term relationship with Mark, than Ruth had ever found in her short-lived, perplexing heterosexual encounters.

She watched her dad, as he made every effort not to give her eye contact. She knelt down beside him, as he defiantly stared ahead, glass of liquid therapy in hand. Overcome with a sense of profound compassion and love for him and without fully appreciating what she was about to do, she instinctively wrapped her arms round him. All was silent. He never altered his gaze and did not put down his glass. He stared ahead as Ruth held on. She held on tightly like she was clinging to a life raft. But he never moved – he was rooted to the spot with rage. He's been angry for years, angry at life, angry at everything in life. The thing with some anger is that it moves like a thick sludge, suffocating the rational parts of the brain, blocking out reasoning and sense. Once that sludge gets right inside your head, like old oil, it's hard to rinse out completely. Ruth wondered if her dad's brain had been sapped up by an angry sludge. It was like he had seized up, incapable of thinking anything much other than how bad things were for himself. So she let go of him, realising her embrace was not going to be reciprocated.

As a result, her visit was short. Shorter than she had planned or expected it to be, so she went for a walk along the main street in the town centre she remembers as home. She thought about what had just happened there with her dad. It had been a harrowing and exhausting visit, that although had not lasted long, had left her smarting deeply from his determined rejection.

She noticed as she walked along that the town had changed dramatically, but only at eye-level. As Ruth raised her gaze upwards, she recognised the architecture of the upper floors of the buildings that lined the main street. She recognised the intricate grey stone carvings that decorated the high, triangular out-shots of the roof tops that somehow harnessed the town to its roots. The lower floors and shop fronts had been systematically bulldozed a dozen times to accommodate changing retailers, especially during the eighties, when shop fronts changed at an alarming speed as the lucky traders boomed and the unlucky went bust. She looked around for any originals; *Woolworths*, *WH Smith* and one local café were the only ones still in the same place, but nothing else. Ruth stopped at the window of a shoe shop. She would be the first to admit she had never formed a relationship with shoes in the same way it seemed all other women had. The efforts of her dad – the covert cobbler – had had a lasting effect. Ruth, to this day, bought a maximum of two pairs of shoes a year; one for summer, one for winter. She could never bring herself to indulge in a pair just because the heel was higher, lower, narrower, or because the toe was square, pointed, or, God help, peep toe. That just brought too many memories of the swift summer manoeuvres of the covert cobbler's *Stanley* blade. Most of all, Ruth detested patent leather shoes. That stemmed from her dad too, and his enduring competitive streak, which led him to adopt a cobbling strategy that would win Ruth the shiny shoe prize every week at school. He achieved this by applying a couple of coats of clear varnish to the uppers of her shoes on a Sunday afternoon after they had returned home from Mass. Therefore no matter how much glue was holding the uppers to the soles, the uppers always shone as though they had been polished by a member of the Royal Marines.

Despite herself, Ruth smirked as she thought of her dad. As she walked on along the street, she noticed how quiet it was. She didn't recognise any of the few people who were scuttling along with their shopping lists rolling around in their heads. She was starting to feel like a stranger in her own town when she came across a small book shop straddling the corner of the two main streets. Above the door was written 'Books'; there was no name, no known proprietor, just a black sign with white writing – Books. Despite the lack of imagination in the shop name, Ruth felt compelled to go in. She had been looking for a book of poetry for some time, but had not been able to find it yet. Ruth often read poetry; it stemmed from a desire she had to write. Whenever she tried to write, it had always fallen out onto the page as either a letter or a poem. It was not how she imagined she would write her memoirs. But the more she tried, the more poems and letters she penned. She joined a writing circle in Edinburgh and had access to all kinds of poetry by authors old and new, published and unpublished. Ruth made a lot of friends in that writing circle, but it dissolved after one of the main members died following a routine operation to remove varicose veins. Ruth was devastated. He was an inspiration to her, an older man of wisdom and profound unalterable integrity. She considered him to be her patriarch. The void she felt was shared amongst the group, and soon after his death the group disbanded. As she stepped into the book shop that day and scanned around the overwhelming display of books, each of them a product of an individual's blood and sweat, she thought of Brian; he was writing a novel when he died. It struck her as unfair that his would never be on these shelves. Oh how much she missed his wit and his astute observations on life and the living. With this thought, she reminded herself that that was another reason to leave the city; there was nothing, absolutely nothing, left there for her anymore.

At the same time she considered how her dad had been with her earlier that day, and she wondered if there was actually anything here, now, in her home town for her. As a heaviness formed and sank within her, a young girl stepped out from behind one of the long bookshelves.

There was no-one else in the shop, which had two long islands, shelved to the ceiling on each side with books. Three walls were also shelved to the ceiling. The only wall without a book shelf stacked to the hilt was the one with the door in and out. An old maple desk stood to the right of the door. It had seen better days, thought Ruth. It was an imposing, musty atmosphere in the shop and Ruth wondered if it was a little neglected. She began to feel slightly uncomfortable. She waited momentarily as her eyes took a second to adjust to the sudden reduction in daylight. Once they did, she surveyed the shelves for the poetry section. She worked her way along the alphabet to S. It wasn't there. She heaved a sigh and walked around the end of one of the islands. The young girl asked if she needed any help. When she spoke, something about the curl of the girl's narrow upper lip, the glance of her dark brown eyes, and awkward shift in her gait unsettled Ruth. She looked familiar. Brown eyes, long, dark tousled hair. The way she smiled, the way she shifted in behind the old desk. *'I know her,'* Ruth was thinking. *'I know her, for definite.'* But yet she knew she couldn't know her; she had been away for too long a time, and this girl wasn't old enough for Ruth to have known her as a young adult before she left.

"Can I help?" The girl said. Ruth couldn't answer. She was aware of a quickening within her, she felt as though she was suddenly too desperate to connect to something, anything from her past; she stuttered and hesitated and just couldn't answer. She felt such a fool. Her tongue froze and she couldn't speak. She pretended she was concentrating hard on finding a book, and slipped in behind a bookcase again until she gathered her thoughts into some kind of logical order. She felt like her brain had just completely seized. For a moment she just stood there staring. It felt like she was trying to scrape a thick plaque off from behind the edges of her skull to free up her brain and get her memory back. She kept digging deep into her memory, and kept reaching the same conclusion; *'I know her, I definitely know this girl.'* Up until then this girl, who was actually too young to have known before she left, was in fact the only person that had seemed familiar to Ruth that day. Ruth took a deep breath and reminded herself why she was doing this. Why she had chosen to step out of every comfort zone she had quite comfortably slipped into in the past seventeen years. It was lost love. It was lost childhood, and lost opportunities. Ruth left the girl her name, contact number and the name of the book she was looking for and left. When she stepped out into the daylight and fresh air she felt stirred up inside. *'Something happened in there,'* she thought, and she wondered whether that was a connection. *'Was that instinct or imagination?'* Ruth mulled this over as she went off along the street in pursuit of clues to her abandoned childhood. She had no idea she had just handed her name and phone number to Mick Munroe's daughter.

*

Mick was relieved when he returned to his precious little shop. He and Henryk had exhausted themselves, and were no further forward. Both were terrified and extremely worried about Anna.

"Busy?" He asked Anna, already suspecting what the answer might be.

"No, just one woman looking for poetry of some sort." Anna was desperate to tell her dad about the thing that came and went with that woman, more than she was to tell him there was a customer. She wanted to tell her dad about the bulky shadow, the feeling of being chilled by a stiff winter breeze, the feeling of someone sneaking up behind her; that it had made her heart race and her head spin. She wanted to tell her dad what she had seen and what she felt, but knew it was too abstract to explain; part of her wondered if she was just being stupid.

"What poetry? Did she say? Did she look around here?" he asked, scuttling off behind the book shelves, avoiding eye contact with Anna, as though she might suspect that he and her papa had been talking about her.

"Yeah, sounded like sofa, or sofo or something like that." With that, Anna decided once again to keep these thoughts and this questioning of mortal boundaries to herself for a while longer.

"Sappho?"

"Yeah that was it, I think that was what she said."

"Someone was in here looking for that?"

"I don't know, it sounded like... she was a bit weird. Anyway, here, she wrote it down along with her name." Anna lifted the note from the desk and handed it to her dad. "I don't know the author... thought her, the woman's name, was Doreen or something like that."

"Sappho." Mick looked puzzled and wandered off without taking the note from Anna. "That's incredible. No one around here asks for that. Was she young? Student type? Must be.

Doreen?" He muttered to himself as he pulled out his step ladders, and from the top shelf of the farthest away stack of books, he pulled out a small book from the Everyman Collection.

"Here we are. I knew I had it up here," he assured himself. "There." He gestured to Anna, *"Sappho Collected Poems."* He climbed down from the ladder and thrust the little book at Anna in an excited almost animated fashion. Anna looked startled.

"What's the deal, Dad?"

"This is the earliest recorded female poet. Old, old, hundreds of years before Christ."

"Hardly any of them are finished," Anna tutted as she thumbed through the book in an entirely unimpressed fashion.

"No. I know. They are called 'fragments' officially, it's just what they've managed to save and to decipher, and she didn't write in English, she was Greek. Who was looking for this?"

Anna handed her dad the piece of paper. He was aware that he had actually stopped breathing as he read the name – Ruth Nairn. As he contemplated the name in a state of apnoea, CO_2 in his blood rose sufficiently high enough for him to breathe again without any conscious effort.

Rooted to the spot, he wondered then, how on earth did Anna know about Doreen? This thought troubled Mick more than the name that was written down on the paper in front of him. For all he knew this could be any Ruth Nairn. *There's bound to be hundreds of women with that name.* Whilst logic lead him to believe it would have to be a hell of a coincidence for this to be *the* Ruth Nairn he remembers from more twenty years ago, he was perplexed by Anna's assumption that her name was Doreen.

Mick knew that this was the name of Ruth's dead mother.

IX

July 1995

In those fragile, disconnecting moments just before falling asleep, Anna had become aware of a regular visitor to her bedside. When it first started to happen she could sense someone was in the room with her, but that was all, just quite simply a feeling of not being alone. It was like being silently and invisibly enveloped by a low voltage current. It made the hairs on the back of her neck, and along her forearms stand erect. Each time this happened, something within her responded to the invisible magnetic surge surrounding her. Goose bumps would burst out rapidly across her body, as though her subconscious was now being plugged in to some sort of ethereal electrical port. Whenever it happened Anna would consciously summon every cell of her senses, trying to hear anything different, taste anything different, smell anything different. Then, on one occasion when she felt especially fearless, she peeled back her covers just enough to expose her forehead and eyes. When she opened her eyes, Anna was astonished to see a pair of feet standing beside her bed. Two smallish bare feet, with neatly trimmed toenails, pointing towards her, level with her shoulders. Anna could tell by the position of the feet that whoever or whatever it was, they were now standing over her, watching her. Quickly she pulled the covers back over her head. There she hid, breathing quietly, all the while deafened by the overwhelming rush of her heartbeat, waiting for the moment to pass, for the disembodied feet to evaporate and disappear. Twice now, she had also felt the bed depress as though this ghostly visitor was actually sitting down on her bed next to her in that little nook created when lying on your side with your knees bent, like a foetus in utero. The person, the thing, found that little nook, and sat in it, comfortably and quite naturally. Anna was aware that this thing was heavy, and was able to balance its weight like a real person. It was happening often enough for Anna to be certain she had felt the weight of a body, like an actual person with substance sitting down carefully beside her. She knew it was a woman, as on another occasion when she became aware of the weight of the person sitting down on her bed, she felt further compelled, inquisitive and brave enough to pull herself out from beneath her covers to sit up and have a look. When she looked she was stunned to find that her eyes met with the searching eyes of a young woman. The woman smiled. Anna nervously smiled back and thought: *Are you a real person? Is this what a ghost actually looks like? Are you my mum?* Fleeting, transient thoughts spun around in her head, and she began to feel dizzy, as though something was sucking the oxygen from her brain. The moment that their eyes met seemed protracted. It was as if normal time had ceased to lapse, and they had both entered some sort of hiatus, where the substance of both their minds had been momentarily coupled together, allowing a charge to pass between them and through them as though a pin had been pressed into a socket. Before Anna could bury herself back beneath the covers, she was aware that something even stranger was beginning to take shape. The corner of her room seemed to be changing. The walls were moving like fluid being swirled around by an invisible whisk. Anna watched open-mouthed as the spinning column of fluid worked its way up from its starting point on the floor, stretching up until it met the ceiling where a colourful hole began to appear. It looked just like the base of a kaleidoscope was being carved out.

Anna shook her head, hoping this would return her to her senses. As she did the woman drifted from her bed into the vortex and disappeared out of sight through the hole in the ceiling.

Anna gasped as the woman she wondered may have been her mum vanished into the kaleidoscope. Wide awake and now far from the submission of sleep, Anna sat up, kicked off her covers and swung her legs over the side of the bed. Tentatively she walked over to the corner where the walls had become flaccid and the ceiling had somehow appeared to melt and expose an opening. Anna was perplexed to find that there wasn't a mark, not a trace of what had happened there. *That did happen. I know that happened there. A woman arrived from somewhere and then disappeared through my ceiling. To where? Where the hell has she gone? Why me? Why is she sitting on my bed? Was that my mum?*

As she stood and wondered about what had just happened in front of her, she became aware of low level vibrations buzzing beneath the soles of her feet. It was coming from the sitting room below. She pressed her bare feet firmly to the ground as the resonance of loud music came seeping through the solid joists of the flooring beneath her. Immediately she knew this had nothing to do with the mystery surrounding her eerie visitor. It reminded her quite literally her feet were on the ground, reassurance that she hadn't been sucked into some kind of obscure kaleidoscopic parallel universe.

Downstairs, Mick was currently pursuing Cognitive Escape Route No. 2. *Supertramp's* 1971 chart hit, *Dreamer*, was emerging with such palpable volume from his much treasured *Jamo D 266s*, that it was putting their three-way bass reflex tweeter protection configuration system through its paces. As for *Supertramp,* he still had it on vinyl on his old turntable despite the recent CD explosion. He had refrained from dashing out and replacing all his vinyl with CDs. Maybe he was old-fashioned, but he liked the noise of the needle scratching its way around the vinyl, and he still laughed out loud if he played a 33 at 45 or 78 revolutions per minute. He liked the hypnotic effect induced by watching the vinyl spin, especially when he played a limited edition album pressed onto coloured vinyl. He had a couple of good ones for that; Cheap Trick live at The Budokan, that was bright yellow, and his much prized limited edition Scorpions album, pressed in bright green. Mick still remembers that tingle in his belly induced by the anticipation of a new release. Waiting for new music to arrive discharged an excitement deep within him that uncoiled like the spring of a flintlock, stimulating a sprint-like run into town to get his newly-released album as it came into his favourite record store. When he was young, Mick's favourite record store was a small, independently run shop, owned by an elderly man called Tommy. Tommy had clearly spent his lifetime behind the counter of this shop, immersed in a world of Elvis-induced rock 'n' roll. He still tried to sweep his thin grey hair into a teddy boy point at the front, and like a slave to the beats of the vinyl, he shuffled around the shop as though his feet were loosely manacled together. But he looked fragile. He was thin and pale, as though he was rarely exposed to sunlight.

Tommy had a system where the vinyls were stored in their inner sleeves behind the counter, with only the empty outer sleeves on show in the front of the shop. In Mick's favourite record shop there were only three categories for the records. These were 1950s, 1960s, and Modern. That was it. When Tommy opened his shop in 1957, Bill Hailey had already topped the charts with Rock Around The Clock, Shake Rattle n Roll and See You Later Alligator. Tommy liked Bill Hailey. In fact, he liked rock and roll so much it was as though he was trapped in some kind of time warp. He had taken little notice of any other bands or musicians since the 1950s. Stacks and stacks of albums in their inner sleeves were filed on shelves in order of their age, not alphabetically or in association with their genre; with most importance being given to the 1950s section. In his little time warped shop, Tommy played music from musicians he defined as legends – Bill Hailey, Bo Diddley and Elvis to name only a few. Tommy had absolutely no interest in what he defined as 'modern' music. Modern being anything from 1969 onwards. Thus all the music Mick was looking for as a teenager in Tommy's shop, was modern, and, according to Tommy was Shite, with a capital S. He once tried to get Mick to listen to Gene Vincent. Mick was unimpressed, he had gone in for 10cc. Tommy just didn't get it.

"10cc? Who is it?"

"It's not a 'who', it's a what," Mick replied.

"Well then, what kind of crap name is that for a 'what'?" Tommy retorted.

"And just what kind of crap name is Bo bloody Diddley, then?" Mick always had Bo Diddley up his sleeve as ammunition.

Most, if not all, of the bands Mick asked for, Tommy had never heard of. In fact if you went in for a record and asked for it by artist, and did not know exactly what year it was released, you could expect to be there for a very, very long time. Some of the vinyls in his stock had been there so long the inner sleeves had changed from white to brown. The paper sleeves perishing in time, exposed to the damp, musky, patchouli-laced thick air that clung like glue to the dark maroon-painted walls of the shop.

As you can imagine, in this environment, managing to secure ownership of coloured vinyl, which was like a right of passage for any music fan in the seventies, could only be compared to a miracle. Tommy receiving a batch of coloured vinyl was sheer luck. He had no idea just what they symbolised to the young music fans who were loyal to his shop. He knew nothing of the way they were polished and admired like trophies, and how they represented high currency for any young music fan building up a much coveted collection. But Mick trusted Tommy. If Mick asked for a record that he knew was being released soon, he knew Tommy would get it in. No question, even if he did think it was Shite. You see Tommy had one basic thing in common with Mick; he knew what it was like to get excited about music.

Now more than twenty years later, Mick was having to rethink the importance he placed upon, and his indulgence in, such possessions. Each of these possessions being weighted down with the responsibility of having to endorse Mick. Each saying, I am a part of Mick, I have contributed to Mick as we know him. So Mick clung to his possessions like life-belts, like he might just dissolve if they weren't there. What if one day, all of these possessions were gone? What would give credibility to his past experiences, other than his word for it? These possessions provided proof he was a sociable person. He did have a life. He did engage with society on an emotional level. He did, it was just that he feared no-one would believe him now. Hoarding all these tangible relics of the past were his proof.

Whilst they might have kept him attached to his past life, they gave no indication of what he was now, or more importantly, what he might be. This current state of self-questioning and self-interrogation had been brought about by his recent cognitive journeys down Escape Route No. 1, which have taken him into the realms of Tibetan theories of how to live well in order to die well. Only yesterday he had read the words of Bhudda; they informed him that "What you are is what you have been, what you will be is what you are now."

This troubled Mick. *What I will be is what I am now... What am I now? What am I? Shit. What the hell am I?* Mick deduced he was a variety of different things. He was a father. *That's good, yeah, responsibility, that's a good one.* He was a shop owner. *Also good, yeah, good one that.* He liked books: *that's okay, books are good, reading's good.* He loved music: *well, what can I say, it keeps me sane, and I'd be completely fucked up if I didn't have music.* He liked to walk, to be outdoors whenever possible: *What else, what else, what else? Shit, what else am I?* So far he had identified essentially solitary pursuits. Even being a shop owner was a solitary pursuit for Mick. It wasn't that his shop wasn't busy, it was at times; it was just that he never really struck up a conversation with any of his customers. Ironically he believed it was they who were not willing to interact with him. He was often intrigued at the way they just bought their books and left, without a word about the book or the author they were spending money on. Mick found this strange as he often marvelled at the skill of writers and how they made words work on paper; for example, he would marvel at the way John Irving finds humour in emotionally sensitive situations, or the way D.H. Lawrence can make a ploughed field sound like the second coming of Christ.

Truth is, the customers did want to speak, but Mick found eye contact anxiety-provoking and so avoided all the natural cues to engage in dialogue. Indeed it seemed as though he had actually forgotten how to orchestrate the art of conversation. Mick wasn't always like this. He can remember being drawn into fierce debates with Tommy regarding lyrics of songs. Disputes would often rage between them regarding the dubious merits of Be-Bop-a-Lula, versus Ziggy Stardust. If he was honest he no longer knew how to talk about the books, how to share the feelings he had about the work he was selling, as it had been so long since he had shared anything with anyone other than his daughter. Mick was trying to confirm when he lost his sensibilities. *It was after Martha.* He knew Martha's death had been like a watershed. Everything Mick was now, bore little or no resemblance to Mick before Martha, and as a result Mick was truly struggling with the current task of identifying what he was, in order to get some kind of a handle on what he will be. The words of Bhudda had gotten under his skin. That was the difference with this book. It was as though invisible tentacles were wriggling out from every page, searching, reaching out, penetrating areas in his head that had been long since sealed off. Books in the past had never come remotely close to stirring up his memories the way that this one was. *The Tibetan Book of Living and Dying* had appeared amongst the books delivered with Mick's order from the wholesalers last month. Whilst he couldn't remember ordering it, he made a conscious decision to keep it, and immediately assumed ownership of this book. He considered it his own. It was not for sale. It would not become part of the stock.

For over a week he surveyed it carefully, dipped into bits here, and small extracts there, as though he were tentatively building up a relationship of trust between himself and the text of the book. After each dip in, he laid the book down in a preoccupied manner. He realised after only a couple of dips into the book that it was going to be difficult to read. It was like trying to get into a bath that was constantly too hot. He was afraid that reading this book would cause him pain. Cause him pain because he would have to acknowledge the fact that death is a certainty no matter what. As such, he would have to examine why he clutches to the confines of an over-stretched bereavement. Could it be it has become a comfort, a safe place to be? By constantly refusing to accept Martha's sudden death was he allowing himself a get-out clause for actually living himself? He could easily turn down relationships, offers of companionship, because he was still bereft.

Ultimately he was afraid this book would prize open his mind like a blade twisting open the shell of a tightly locked mussel. This was different from the other 'healing' books he had so often come across and dived into, expecting to find the answers to his questions, only to dismiss after a few pages as being unable to answer his questions: Why him? Why Martha?

This book was different. He sensed that answers were about to emerge from the print on each page. Each turn of every page inviting him to live, to get out there and live, embrace the here and now. Thus he should not be clutching onto his coloured vinyls, or polishing his Jamo D266s, or marvelling at the capacity of his tweeters.

In the past, when Mick was aware that a cordoned off area of his brain was at risk of being breached and unlocked, he simply slapped the book shut, went for a walk, and dismissed it as another dead end meander down Escape Route No. 1. He thought that was the only way to survive.

This time, however he didn't slap the book shut, he didn't give in and give up, he kept going over and over; *What else, what else? Well, that can't be it. What does that mean? What will I be? "What you will be is what you are now," what the hell will I be?* As Supertramp's "Dreamer" stopped spinning at 45 on his turntable and the needle arm clicked into its hold, his mind had also clicked into a stall mode. *Shit, shit… right then;* a change of tack; *what am I not? What am I not going to be… I am not anyone's partner… I am not anyone's friend.* He paused for thought… *I've been forgotten.*

Mick shot to his feet, searching his pockets for the torn corner of paper with Ruth's name and phone number on it; it wasn't there. An unexpected wave of panic and confusion washed over him. *Where the hell is it? Why is it important?* It was the first time for years he had felt a sense of urgency about something, anything, and he spun around the room looking frantically for Ruth's number. He couldn't find it. Keys, a handful of copper coins, a pen, remnants of a washed out tissue and his little piece of amethyst that he carried everywhere, were amongst the items turned out of jeans and jacket pockets. *Where the hell is it?* He darted up the stairs to his bedroom, to where he had changed his jeans. There in the pocket of his jeans that he had thrown on the floor was the torn corner of an envelope with Ruth Nairn's phone number on it. *Is it her, though? If it is, will she remember me? What if it is her? She's probably married with kids of her own now.* Mick's thoughts were tumbling wildly around his head. He unravelled the paper and there it was; Ruth Nairn 0778965556, Sappho – collected poems. Please call if you have anything by Sappho in stock. Thank you.

Do I chat? Ask her how she is? What if it's not her? What if it is her? Forget it, just leave a message to come and collect the book. But what if she comes to collect the book? Of course she's going to come and collect the book, she asked for the bloody book... So what if she comes and recognises me? What if she remembers me asking her to my twenty-first? Which she never showed up to, but she was out that night because I passed her on her way home... Bloody hell that was my first date with Martha. Why did Ruth not show up to my party? What if she had, would I have ended up with her? Probably... Then I wouldn't have Anna, so that's a stupid thought... wonder what she looks like now? Better haircut I hope... Huh! Who the fuck do I think I am? Look at me, bloody brain-dead. What would I say?

"Dad?" Anna interrupted his thoughts, thoughts he'd inadvertently started to have out loud.

"Huh?"

"You're speaking to yourself again." She walked away shaking her head, "There's nothing wrong with your hair, Dad."

"Mm?"

"Well at least you've got some." Anna turned round and faced her dad. She wanted to tell him about the person who had appeared in her room. "I need to tell you something, Dad."

Mick tightened his grip on the piece of paper he had in his hand. It would have to wait. At moments like this, whenever he looked at his daughter, really looked at her, he saw Martha.

143

My God, she gets more like her mother every day. She has the same deep dark eyes, thick dark hair with a natural wave, and she had been lucky as a teenager with hardly a blemish, in fact her skin glowed and she looked sun-kissed all year round. *It's the gypsy blood*, that's what Martha would say whenever anyone commented on her suntanned skin tone.

"The thing is, Dad, there's a woman keeps appearing in my bedroom, and before you say anything, I know it's a ghost."

X

"Right then, Henryk, your ECG looks fine, and your chest sounds clear."

"Aye, aye, my mother always say my lungs is like a magic balloon, never go down, always full with air!" Henryk chortled.

"And your blood pressure's good," the GP continued, smiling warmly at Henryk and his balloon lungs. "Probably better than mine in fact!"

"This is good, Doctor. Good. So you think it's gonna be okay?"

"Indeed, I don't see any reason why you can't fly."

"Good. So, what about this insurance for the flying person? What do I need for that?"

"You need this." Henryk's GP smiled at the image of 'The Flying Person'. He handed Henryk a letter confirming his fitness, at approximately seventy-six years old, to fly as a passenger on an airplane, and confirmed that any other form of human air travel would be rendered uninsurable in Henryk's case. Henryk liked this, it made him laugh.

"Did I hear you right there, Henryk, this is your first time flying?"

"Yes, yes it is, Doctor." Henryk had known his GP for over fifteen years and still insisted on the 'Doctor' element of his 'address' to his GP.

"Can I ask, how long have you been in Scotland?"

"Oh now that is an easy question for me to get you the right answer. It was fifty-six years ago. Mind, I'm no sure o' my right age, exact, when I come, but I can count the years since."

"So how did you travel when you came here all those years ago?"

"Oh my word, Doctor, you no realise the way from my little Poland to here; it was difficult, on foot mostly, of course no across the water o' the Channel, no on foot then! Hah! No even a good swim!"

"Incredible!"

"Well you know I was no alone, maybe you no remember, Doctor, they have a name for our arrival here."

"They do?"

"Yeah, they say it was the peaceful invasion."

Henryk's GP appeared genuinely intrigued.

"No you too young, 'n you no get history of Poland at your doctor school I no suppose." Henryk chuckled as he lifted his certificate of fitness to fly, albeit as an airline passenger, from the doctor's desk.

In truth, Henryk's arrival in Scotland was far from 'peaceful', it was in fact the culmination of a horrendous journey that began at the farm where he had grown up, on the southern outskirts of Wieliczka. It was around mid-September 1939, just past the time when his twentieth birthday would have been, although like his mother, he was never sure of his date of birth.

Once started, his journey was one he made over a period of around one year whilst in a constant state of terror, juxtaposed with an inert desire for revenge. Throughout this time, whilst he knew what he was fleeing from, he had no idea where he was fleeing to. He had never heard of Scotland – his destination.

Within hours of the German army murdering his mother, Henryk had run deep into the void of the bleak and deathly silent Polish countryside. He had scrambled across fields and along narrow dirt tracks, winding his way through the Wisla Valley. He skirted around a series of small, shallow lakes, with each frantic breath being expelled from his lungs like an urgently freed hostage, his eyes stinging as though they were being sprayed with acid.

When he first stopped to catch his breath and checked his compass, he realised he was travelling north to north west. It wasn't a conscious decision to run in that direction, but as fate would have it he realised he was heading in the direction of Krakow. He knew this as when he was around twelve, or eight summers earlier (Henryk measures time in seasons changing), he was taken to Krakow by Rosa for the national census. There, in the shadow of St Mary's Basilica, he and his mother were officially recorded as Polish Gypsy peasants. They had no papers to offer in confirmation of their nationality, but he remembers his mother telling them he was Polish, that he was definitely born in Poland, just as he heard the hourly bugle call from the spires of the Basilica. He remembers his mother describing his place of birth: their farm near Wieliczka, within the Polish borders, and her proud insistence, "My son is Polish." He remembers squinting into the sun, trying to see where the bugle call was coming from and wondering quite why his mother was making such a fuss, and holding up the line of hungry, dishevelled individuals who had also travelled by foot to register in the census. It was all a bit of a puzzle to his young mind. But her pleas were not in vain and they were both recorded then as Polish. It was the first time in Rosa's life that she had been officially recorded as Polish. She felt it was the proudest day for her and her son, despite being recorded as a peasant; she was a Polish peasant, and she seemed to walk taller for it as they embarked upon their return journey across the Visla River and then across the fields back to their farm near Wieliczka.

Continuing north-west towards Krakow, he flipped the little lid of his compass shut and gripped it tightly in his hand, realising it was now the only tangible object he had that linked him to both his mother and father. It had been given to Henryk by his grandmother, Jogoda. She explained it had been Leon's, and how he had been given it by a miner in the salt mines. The salt miner had confessed he had taken a fancy to his mother Jogoda. Quite how the Polish salt miner came to own a British pocket compass was a mystery. But in an effort to impress her, the miner had spun an enchanting yarn of being a world-wide traveller, with memories and sketches from his travels inspiring his carvings in the mines. Whilst

Jogoda had liked the little compass, she had cared little for the miner and his fertile imagination and made no return gesture. Leon on the other hand, had been impressed by the salt miner, his tales of other lands and the compass with its finely engraved nickel brass case. Even today, despite a small indentation on the outer side of the lid, the manufacturer's inscription was still clearly visible: 'Clement Clarke Ltd. London VI 1918'. He remembered clearly the day he was given it by his grandmother. He would be around four years old when Jogoda called him to come in for something to eat. Chewing on his Kielbasa and pickled beetroot, a particular favourite of his back then, Jogoda explained that she had a special gift for him. She had noticed how he was wandering further afield from the farm when he was out. Handing him the compass, she explained that when he had learned how to use it properly, it would always guide him home.

When he first peeled back the frayed felt-like cloth that had encased the compass since Leon's untimely death, and held the compass in his hand, Henryk's eyes had widened like saucers. At that moment he did wonder if he might be grasping a small, cold nugget of gold. He listened intently as she explained how Leon had been given it by an admirer of hers in an effort to win her affections. Young Henryk could easily imagine this as he believed his grandmother was utterly beautiful.

From then, whenever he had wandered off the beaten track, he had always used the compass to navigate himself back to the farm. He grew used to carrying it in his pocket; like a young boy might carry a small pocket watch, Henryk carried his compass, his dad's compass. It was small enough to sit comfortably in the palm of his hand. When he held it securely in his little hand it was like his comfort blanket. Whenever he flipped open the little nickel brass lid he would watch the little pointed arms spin momentarily around the cardinal points. Sometimes when the compass stopped, he would wonder how far he could walk in the direction north before he might run out of land. Jogoda had passed on the miner's tall tales about the supposed huge expanses of water that separated vast areas of land; but he had believed he would probably never see this in his lifetime, unless he left his mother, and left Wieliczka. That thought was unimaginable.

Now with Rosa dead, he fled Wieliczka. With his compass firmly in his grasp his pace fluctuated, sometimes walking, sometimes running, but always, always hearing his mother's screams as she was torn away from the house and dragged into the dark by three men in grey-green suits. He could barely see them from his crouched position amidst the trees that surrounded the north side of their farmhouse, but he could hear them shrieking. All of them shouting; a strange accent with harsh, throttled vowels that stuck to the sharp consonants like an acrid glue. They were words belonging to a language that Henryk had never heard before. But Rosa had, and he heard her shout out, "*Germans, thieving Germans!*" He watched as though his eyelids had been completely peeled off. She screamed in terror, her eyes wide with fear, her startled expression an urgent warning to her precious boy, Henryk, to stay out of sight, to stay hidden, to live.

He had often heard his mother speak of the Germans, along with the Prussians, Russians and Austrians. She said they had stolen her country, that they had partitioned Poland and deprived her of her true Polish identity. Whilst Henryk listened and absorbed this information, he had believed that these tales of his mother's were firmly stored in the history books. He never for a moment feared that he might come face to face with the Thieves of Poland, as she had christened them. Indeed, immersed in his youthful naivety, he felt strangely detached from the events that had constructed Rosalia's fate as a single mother; marginalised by the judgmental public, she was disenfranchised by an absent national identity.

Rosa, on the other hand, believed she was not alone. She knew it had been the same for hundreds of years, where thousands and thousands of others had been born into a country with no borders, as thieving neighbours grabbed at Poland and claimed ownership. She believed she could feel the weight of persistent injustice as something palpable, something enormously burdensome that dragged its way along every street, and into the heavy hearts and minds of every displaced and dishonoured Polish person. Thus, over the years Henryk had often heard her muttering on about The Greedy Thieves of Poland. Little did he know that these Greedy Thieves had surreptitiously leeched their way into the Wieliczka community the previous month, with the sole intention of rooting out members of the community who might just get in the way of Germany's plans to clean up Europe.

These members of the German Minority had heard about the young woman who had bled to death in the outlying farm buildings belonging to the peasant gypsy. They immediately added the details of the peasant gypsy to their list of undesirable individuals. Rosalia was now appearing on a list along with many prominent names of Wieliczka. The Orthodox Priest, the Rabbi, a bank manager, a local accountant – a self-made man, the head of town planning, and two lawyers. At any other moment in history, should she have appeared on a list with these individuals she may well have felt honoured, but this was 'Operation Tannenberg', and each list submitted by the German minority provided a role call for the systematic execution of important Polish citizens.

That evening Rosa had reached the top of their list. The Greedy Thieves spat in her face and hauled her by her hair until she fell onto her bare knees on the stones of the track that led to the abandoned farm they had long since made their home. It was remote, it was dark, and no one would hear her screams. Only an individual with purpose made their way to the farm. It was usually someone who had heard of Rosa's incredible gift for healing, a gift now re-branded by the invading Germans as murderous intent.

Burning pains ripped through her legs, the skin shearing from her knees and shins as she was hauled out onto the rubble. When she looked up, one of the men pointed a pistol at her head and pulled the trigger. Over and over this image tumbled around in Henryk's mind. His mother's terrified face. It was the face of a vulnerable woman who had feared the persecuting cynical masses throughout her life, her eyes now wide open with a realisation of her impending execution, and then her screams silenced. The bullet, dispatched by a simple click of the trigger, hit her square between the eyes. Her body sagged and folded over without resistance.

Nausea frequently overwhelmed him as he thought of her slumped in the dirt, bleeding, with her brains oozing onto the rubble of the roadside. He was left gasping, choking, and helpless with utter disbelief that he had silently witnessed the murder of his mother.

Ordered by Hitler to 'kill without pity or mercy', they laughed as they kicked Rosa over onto her back and checked she was dead. As the smoke from the pistol drifted silently into the air, they mounted a truck and sped off. Paralysed with a strangulating belief that his silence might somehow have been an accomplice to her death, Henryk had been unable to get to his feet. With the acrid fumes of the truck's diesel hanging like an ethereal shroud in the dark, night air around him, he crawled over to where Rosa was lying. Gently, as though he feared he might hurt her further, he lifted her head and held her close to him, as though he may be able to mend her. He carefully cradled and soothed her punctured head as it lay motionless on his shoulder.

In his mind, at that point, this terrifying experience seemed completely surreal. It was as though animated characters from history had leapt out of the dark night from the pages of a book, destroyed his mother and then disappeared again, returning cloaked in mystery to the confines of a country's archives.

Having lived their lives cut off from the town and its people, he had no idea of the German invasion of Krakow, and the German minority that had quietly seeped into the darkest corners of the community, like a leaking drain from a sewer. He had no idea of the state of terror the townspeople of Krakow were enduring at that point.

As Rosa's flaccid body grew heavy in his arms, he began to think of how vulnerable they had always had been; how, viewed as gypsy peasants, they were often subjected to eager ridicule and persecution.

Oh how, as a child, he would often protest at not getting the freedom to venture to Wieliczka. He had wanted to visit the Salt Mines. He longed to stand with the band that welcomed the visitors and be part of the wonder and excitement. He wanted to listen to the band his father had been part of, to stand where Leon had once stood. Indeed he felt so impassioned by his desire to get to the Salt Mines, he often imagined he could taste salt on lips and in his breath whenever he spoke about it. Rosa had talked often of Leon, and Henryk was desperate to connect with this man, to feel a sense of belonging to a man he knew was his father, but who had died before he was born. Now he realised she wasn't concealing anything, she had simply been protecting him. How utterly ignorant he had been to think that in all these years she was just venting her spleen and getting in his way, that her ranting was without substance, that her constant fears were misguided. He should have been able to protect her; he should have been able to shield her. He should have listened and been ready, prepared. She had always warned him to be on his guard.

When he placed her body into a shallow grave by the old farm house he ached with a guilty realisation that he might have let her down, with the worst possible consequences.

Stooping over the freshly dug earth, he reached in and tenderly covered her face with a cloth before covering her with the cold, wet soil. With anger rising like thick burning oil in his blood, hungry for revenge, Henryk believed he knew what he was running from but he had no idea what he was running to. In his mind, numbed after a night clambering around in a sleep-deprived haze in the swampy Polish lowlands, he believed he would hunt down the truck and its three occupants and kill them, squeezing the life out of them with his bare hands. He had no idea that they were three within an occupying force of almost two hundred thousand.

When daylight broke, Henryk thought he could hear running water, and wondered if he must be nearing the Visla River, believing then he must be nearing Krakow. Preoccupied with thirst, hunger and excruciating pains in his cold wet feet, Henryk pressed on, certain the soldiers would have travelled to Krakow. He had deduced that trucks like that aren't seen commonly in the countryside, and would more often be seen in the city. Inhaling deeply as he neared the lights of the urban outskirts, he was convinced he could smell the truck in the air.

In fact, he was still some distance from Krakow, nearing a small village of Worbela. As he got nearer the outskirts of the village, he realised then it wasn't Krakow. From what he could remember this was too small. His heart sank as he considered running on into the village, its occupants still asleep, and screaming 'Wake up, they've murdered my mother'. He wanted everyone to know there was an enemy in their midst. He hadn't realised they knew this already.

Suddenly he didn't feel brave enough. Lack of food and water left him weak and dizzy, and he ran around the circumference of the village until he came to the stream. Kneeling down he immersed his head, responding to the chill of the water with a sharp intake of breath. Just then he considered it might be just as well to draw water rapidly into his lungs until he drowned, and for a moment an overwhelming desire to die usurped his desire to survive.

XI

July 1995

Mick opened his front door to find shoes of various sizes and styles piled up in front of him. Anna had friends over.

'Shit,' he sighed. It was difficult to know what that shit/sigh represented. He scanned the pile of untidy, unpaired shoes for Erin – can I empty your fridge? – Bower's boots and sniffed the air in an effort to track down the acrid fumes of James – mind if I shag your daughter? – Hamilton's trainers. They weren't there. Was it a sigh of relief then?

If truth be told it was a mixture of things. His home was under siege just when he was hoping the house would be empty when he got home. He had been planning to give himself some time to contemplate the phone call he was intending to make to Ruth Nairn. The name on the piece of paper he been carrying around all day. He kicked his shoes off, with a silent 'bugger it', propelling them onto the mountain of indiscriminate unpaired shoes that had bred in his hallway since he had left for work that morning.

From the sitting room, Mick could hear something familiar. He felt his chest tighten. Subconsciously he was reacting as though he had found a trespasser on his precious Escape Route No. 2. It was as though one of his private psychological hiding places had now been found and exposed.

Senses have that unforgiving capability of prodding at those carefully concealed corners of our brains. Music and smells are like sensory master keys, sometimes even unlocking what we believe are our most secure secrets or acting like a form of time travel, instantly transporting us to a previous time and place. For example, the smell of cut grass in late spring will always remind Mick of the day Martha was killed by the drunk driver. Weddings too; on his way to the accident he had stumbled across a group of excited young children scrambling around the road chasing copper coins as they bounced and clattered along the tarmac, finding their way into the cracks by the kerb, and the dips around the drains. A handful of coppers that had been thrown only a moment earlier by a bride's father were causing squeals of excitement as an orange Avenger Princess, with ribbons flapping from its wing mirrors, trundled off around the corner and made its way down Melrose Road to the town centre. Since then, spring weddings have always reminded him of the day Martha died.

The Rain Song had been played at her funeral. It was torture. It was like a never-ending song, it seemed to go on for hours, but it was Martha's favourite song at the time so it was played for her. In fact the whole *'Houses of The Holy'* album was her favourite. Hardly a day went by that she hadn't listened to Led Zeppelin. She had the same passion for music as Mick. But whilst he would sample almost anything with a drum and bass beat, Martha was a bit more blinkered. She listened to

Led Zep and Rush, and that was almost it, other than a slight divergence into Level 42, when their very first album was released; she liked the jazzy stuff on that. So it was doubly ironic that she was killed going into town to buy a record recorded by The Jam, a band she had rarely given any time to, regarding them as fake, marginalized punk and way too commercial. Mick used to think it might have been slightly more justified if she had been going into town to buy *Moving Pictures* – it had been by released by Rush a couple of months previous but they had never had the spare cash to buy it. That's what happens when a baby is born. The baby takes priority. Suddenly it's not a world of music; it's a world of nappies and nipple shields. Then when they did have spare cash she's killed heading to town to buy a record for a band she didn't even really know enough to like or dislike. It always pissed Mick off.

Hearing Led Zeppelin for a few bars as he came home that night turned his stomach; it made him angry, sad, desperate, excited and wildly euphoric all at the same time. Thoughts were spinning around his head like they were trapped in a giant vat of oil and water.

"Anna?" He crept into the sitting room as though he might be interrupting something.

"Dad?"

"You okay?"

"Yeah?"

"Hi folks." Mick gestured a wave and a smile to Anna's friends.

"Hi, Mick." A collective welcome. They liked him. They liked him a lot. Especially Zoe; she would regularly remind

Anna that her dad was 'actually cool', a sentiment that quite literally horrified Anna.

Mick smiled and retreated, his head was spinning. What he wanted to say was, *How can you be 'okay' for Christ sake? That's your Mum's song, for fuck sake. How can you sit there and just say 'Hey Dad'? What the hell?* Then he remembered how little she was when Martha was killed. How would she know? Of all the records he had, why was she playing that one? When did she find it? He kept all the old vinyls in his room in a chest-like box that made them look extremely important, like secret government documents. *Did she go looking for it? Has she been going through my things? Did someone bring it?* He decided to wait. Leave the questioning until later, when everyone had gone.

"Papa's coming over shortly." He interjected.

"Yeah?" Anna never looked up.

"Yeah, he wants to see you." Mick was trying to make eye contact with her, straining his neck like a heron fishing.

"Me?" Still no eye contact.

"Yes, you." Mick was staring at her.

"Why?" Still looking at her feet.

"Something to do with your birthday coming up." Mick turned and made to leave the room.

"Really?"

"Yeah, really," he said impassively, submission in his tone. Task: to make eye contact whilst communicating with teenage offspring. Result: fail.

"Me?"

"Yeah!" His voice was raised, but only because he had left the room and was heading to the kitchen.

"Why?"

"Don't know, he didn't say, just said he was coming over, it sounds important."

"Important?"

"Yes!" He was definitely shouting now.

"When?" Anna suddenly raising her voice too, realising she has to keep the dialogue with her dad going if she wants to find out what her papa is planning.

"When what?" Mick continued to shout. The monosyllabic language of teenagers, accompanied by an aversion to maintain even the slightest of eye contact, often left Mick exasperated. Shouting from a distance was almost like an acceptable retaliation.

"When's he coming over?"

"Em soon I think, tonight. I can't tell you anything else, he wants to surprise you." Mick plucked some cheese and a tomato from the fridge and started to prepare himself a snack. He wasn't really feeling hungry enough for a meal. For almost twenty-four hours now, he had been carrying around the notepaper with the number of some unknown female that coincidentally had the same name as a girl he knew, and it was making his stomach churn. Anna and her friends shrieked and laughed at the possibilities of her papa's surprise. Mick stayed in the kitchen; he was needing a bit of quiet, time to think about what to say when he phoned this woman back. If he was being logical it wasn't really such a big deal, all he had to say was that he had the book she wanted in stock. Usually it was such an ordinary routine phone call, but Mick was aware it was now starting to seem ridiculously like he was about to embark upon one the most important conversations of his life.

Back in the sitting room the excitement was building in anticipation of Anna's papa visiting.

"Wow Anna, what's your papa got you? A car maybe?" Zoe, Anna's life-long friend was intrigued and bewildered all at the same time. That was something that happened to Zoe quite frequently.

"Don't be stupid, I can't drive."

"Oh, yeah, right. What then?" You could almost see the cogs of Zoe's brain turning. You could really, because she had shaved her head only just three days previously, much to the amusement of Anna, and horror of her parents, who were recently despairing of their precious daughter. Zoe's parents were generally acting a bit weird right now. Recently they had actually revealed themselves as being a couple who envied Mick and Anna. They regarded Mick as a dad who seemed to have a secure handle on the whole complex parenting thing. However, whilst they were trying to tell Mick this and heap praise upon him, they were also the type that would openly pity Mick in an almost patronising way, stating Anna was 'really quite well adjusted… considering'. Mick wanted to tell them to fuck off. And then there was the look he saw in Zoe's mother's eyes; it scared him, he considered her something of a predator. He believed her to be completely transparent, in that it was quite obvious she fancied Mick. But he didn't fancy her. Not so much that she was already married. It was more the fact that in Mick's eyes she was perhaps the least attractive woman he could imagine. She was clearly defined by unadulterated materialism and self-righteous prattling. It made his toes curl and he made every effort to avoid her.

At the same time, you have to realise that those little chemistry explosions that Mick delivered daily as a teenager, have stood the test of time and tragedy. It's fair to say he is still capable, as a single middle-aged dad, of sending women careering sideways with just a look or a few indiscriminate words. The thing is, he is no more aware of the effect he has on women now, than he was then. What made it worse was it was difficult to avoid Zoe's mother as Zoe seemed to spend twenty-four hours a day in Anna's company.

To be honest the surreptitious attention from Zoe's mother had caught Mick off guard. Whilst he had surprised himself that he had actually noticed her attentions, anything further than that involving Zoe's mother made him physically recoil. This wasn't the case when he held onto that torn piece of notepaper that Anna had given him the previous day with Ruth Nairn's number on it. The idea that it might be *the* Ruth Nairn made his head spin. Could it really be her? Ruth from years ago; Ruth that just seemed to disappear; Ruth that made him turn around; Ruth that smiled a huge brimming smile whenever she saw him; Ruth that never showed up at his twenty-first after him finally summoning up the courage to ask her. He remembers that because she was a lot younger than him and it took him ages to pluck up the courage to ask her. Then she never appeared. Then he passed her when he was walking Martha home, holding her hand, and Ruth was crying. It was strange because as she passed them by, she smelt really strongly of aftershave, and he worried that Ruth might have been taken advantage of, and that the criminal had left the scent of his cheap aftershave upon her. At that point he remembers being really confused, because although he felt guilty at being with Martha, he had also felt a moment of relief; relief as he had an alibi, and he couldn't be blamed for taking advantage of Ruth Nairn, if that's what had happened, because he wasn't with her.

Now the idea that she might somehow have returned and left her number with his daughter all seemed a bit unbelievable, and *it* stirred something. He could feel *it*. *It* was registering as something palpable, something he could feel as a momentary quickening in his heartbeat, or with the stifling of his breath whenever he stole himself to imagine it might actually be her. He swung from feeling riddled with guilt that he hadn't helped her – what if something had happened to her? He should have stopped to help; she was crying after all – to feeling astonished and perhaps maybe even excited. He was also mindful of the fact that he had been a feeble, selfish young man that had been too busy worrying about himself and what the repercussions might be for him, than checking if she was actually okay. He considered though, that he was young, immature and not quite the man of the world he had believed himself to be, and he hoped if this was *the* Ruth Nairn, he would get a chance at some point to explain and to redeem himself.

At the same time he had fleeting moments where he felt overwhelmed, and yes he was definitely excited that he might actually just see Ruth Nairn again. Just as he registered that he was excited, he would feel guilty for allowing himself to feel excited like that, especially when he thought about Martha and Anna.

Oh God, if he could just silence his mind, keep it still for just a minute, he thought, he might then be able to untangle it all.

Then he would think *if I could just get the phone call over with first; it might not even be her.* But it did strike him as strange that a small piece of paper with that name written upon it had opened some sort of floodgates – a dam had burst, and part of him wanted to hold it back but a huge part of him wanted to be washed clean away with it all. During this time, part of him was starting to realise that if it wasn't her, he would be properly disappointed. That's the funny thing with the past – with one hand it can push you forward, but with the other it can hold you right back. Truth is, life has been the same for Mick for thirteen years and maybe it was time now for him to realise that this thing referred to in the *Tibetan Book of Living and Dying* as *impermanence* was really his ally, and not his enemy at all. He knew he was desperately needing to change, but he had no idea things were about to change so dramatically.

Part Two

I

Anna's Story

When I was asked a few years ago to describe what it's like to be psychic I laughed and heaved simultaneously. Not a proper hearty laugh or a proper heave that might have emptied my stomach contents out onto the pavement. It was more of a nervous, half-choked, half-baulked, spluttering effort. My instant verbal reaction could really have been many things, but in the end was simply '*Why? Why have you asked that question? Why is it important for you to know?*'

I remember that despite having experienced quite a lot of weird things as a teenager, at nineteen I was only just getting used the idea that I might be 'psychic' myself. My papa was the first person to use the term with direct reference to me and what was happening to me. It was still all a bit surreal and I found it hard to believe back then that anyone would take what I had to say seriously, on any subject, let alone this one. Current events however, are forcing me to revisit this question, and try and find an answer for it.

My beloved papa is dying, and I am asking myself, if I was truly psychic then I would know when his last breath was going to be, and I would know where he was going to go to, wouldn't I?

Today I have already spent four hours just sitting by his bedside watching his chest rise and fall, and other than that constant movement, there are now no other signs of life. Even his skin is grey and waxy, and looks and feels like it died days ago. He hasn't opened his eyes for two days. He hasn't eaten anything or drunk anything for a lot longer than that, and I am puzzled as to how he is still alive, even if barely so. I wonder also why *it* is taking so long for him. Why does he have to be forced to try so hard to do the one thing that should be natural to us all? I mean for some people it's simple, they just drop down dead, no warning and more importantly, no pain. My papa has been in pain. Take yesterday, he was rolling around the bed from side to side, groaning. As far as I am concerned that was the most thoroughly hellish experience of my life to date. I thought my head was going to explode with the frustration and the utterly helpless lack of control I had had over it all yesterday. My dad had to leave the room, it sounded like he was choking when he went. He hasn't come back. He says he finds the whole death and dying thing about life unbearable. He should come back in now though because my papa is better. Yes, he is, you see he's hitched up to drugs now, and so is hopefully floating along towards *'the light'* on an opiate-induced high.

So here I am sitting at his bedside with nothing to think about but death, and what or who might be waiting for Papa when he does finally leave this world and move onto the next, and I have been thinking about when I was asked to describe what it's like to be psychic. At the time I didn't really take the question very seriously. You see I have been so used to being ridiculed about lots of things (children are cruel and not having a mum made me an easy target to some) that I was really quite taken aback. What made it more difficult was the fact that it was my so-called friends at the time who were subjecting me to the serious questioning. Although I felt I could trust them, I found their animated questioning at the time awkward. It had taken me almost a year after my papa told me I was most likely psychic to finally divulge the information to them. It felt a bit like a 'coming out'. I don't know what kind of reaction I expected, but the one I got, I felt was a bit indulgent and intrusive. I think I naively expected them just to listen and not to ask.

At the time I couldn't give them an answer, because I really truly didn't know how to describe what it's like, as I didn't really understand it. I just knew it was something that 'happens' to me, and for the time being, my papa had given it a name. I've never actually thought about 'what it's like to be psychic' or actually being 'psychic'; as I say it's just something that I am, and to be honest I have a great deal of difficulty with the term 'psychic'.

I know it alludes to the psyche and the mind, but let's just remind ourselves that it also is not that far removed from the terms 'psychiatric' and 'psycho', which, knowing what you already know about me, I am certain you will realise that this kind of terminology makes me extremely uncomfortable and nervous. Uncomfortable because it reminds me of a time when the psychiatrists were drafted in to try and give me some counselling after my mum had died. It's really ironic that; because although I didn't really respond to the psychiatrists, they have succeeded in ensuring I am no longer traumatised by the event, as all I can recall from that time is their visits, and how very odd I thought they were, and how they smelt of cigarettes, like my papa. The men gave me the creeps quite frankly, with their beards and strange jerseys, and hellish sandals worn with the thickest, scratchiest of hand-knitted woolly socks. Furthermore, as an adult I can see that any of the female 'professionals' who came round my house under the cunning guise of psychiatry or counselling, were actually wanting to win over my very lost and vulnerable dad by saving his daughter, and thereafter willing him into their beds. So from my point of view the term 'psychic' makes me nervous.

Nervous also because I can't remember the day my mum was mowed down, and to me, and you probably, that's just not right is it? As an adult now, I think I bloody well should have a memory of it. I often task myself with just trying to remember that day, and more importantly remember her. As her daughter I think I deserve that memory; even if it is to be the most hellish of memories, at least it's something. Something that means I can remember her beyond a photograph. I try to imagine that I can remember what it's like to feel her skin. If I could really do that then I would want to pull her in close and smell her hair when she has just had a bath, and just inhale her, just take in and utterly absorb everything about her. But then I have been breathing in and out for nearly thirty years now, and I just cannot remember even one of my breaths that she has been part of, not even one.

Sometimes I will sit in silence, just staring into space, not answering calls and ignoring friends, sometimes for days trying to connect with her, wherever she is out there in the ether. I know she is out there somewhere because I'm 'psychic', and I have seen ghosts. But every time I try to connect with her there's nothing, absolutely nothing there. Then I realise I am looking for something really concrete; like one day she might just sit down right in front of me and have a coffee.

Honestly, I punish myself because I can't remember any of it: 'It' being 'The crash'. That 'life changing event', when some drunken old guy went veering off the road into us. I know, it's surprising isn't it?

I remember nothing of my mum dying in front me, nothing of the fact a man was dead in an upturned car in front of me, nothing, absolutely nothing of it. What I can only imagine now as an adult, is that it must have been an incomprehensibly heart-wrenchingly chaotic scene, and the only person I feel sorry for is my dad.

More importantly to me, and I'm sorry if this seems selfish, because I don't mean it to be, I can't even remember my mum, never mind the bloke in the car. And every single part of me wishes I could remember my mum, even if it was that I could only remember her very last breath. I wish I could, I wish I could remember my mother's last despairing breath, because then, as I say, it would be a memory of something – instead all I have is a mental blank. If I spend time thinking too much about that then it just sucks the air completely out of my lungs until I am folded over. So I can't do it, and I do have to really try to avoid letting myself lapse into a hellish spiral of victim thoughts. Ultimately I try hard not to let thoughts of that day consume the luxury of time that I have here on earth, or steal any more of my very precious breaths clean away again.

About this 'psychic' thing though; what I can say is I am aware of something beyond what I physically amount to, and way beyond what I and many others can find any substantial reasoning for. For example, when I dream and it comes true, it's not just on a personal level. Some dreams materialize on a national and international level, and I can't explain that; nor could anyone else for that matter. Here's one for the record: one night in November 1999, when I was twenty-two and at college (I was nearing the completion of my teaching degree at the time, and initially put it down to the stress of making sure I got a credible honours of a pass), I dreamt I was suspended in mid-air over a ferry that was capsizing. It was very dark and I was aware I felt cold, as though I was definitely outdoors and not in my bed. I remember vividly watching in horror as Chinese-looking women, children and men tumbled helplessly from the ferry into freezing black deep water and then suddenly the ferry just disappeared, like it had been sucked under. I woke with a startle and felt incredibly sick. It was around four in the morning. I never went back to sleep, but lay in bed playing the images over and over in my head. I hadn't felt at all like I had been dreaming, it felt like I had been watching something in real life. When I got up at seven and put the radio on, reports were just starting to come in about an Indonesian ferry disaster, and I knew when I heard it on the radio I had been there. I knew because my heart was pounding, I felt faint, my guts were churning and something within me, something I have never been able to put a name to, connected me to that, whether I wanted to be connected or not. Now how can anyone explain that? It was as though I was there watching it in real time, but I had never actually left my bed.

The same thing happened when I had a dream about a group of elderly people waiting in a huge house for the pensioners from the Bristol bus crash. That was so vivid and the first time such a dream had happened to me. I can remember it clearly. It was May 1995 and again, I had been studying for exams at the time, only seventeen and terrified. I ran to my dad and tried to explain, but it just all came out like gobble-de-gook. I can remember my dad thought I was on some kind of drug! Oh my God, how that might have been easier to deal with than this.

Now for some of you reading this, this kind of stuff – hearing and seeing things when you're asleep, might screw you up, but I got used it. I also got used to seeing things around people, behind people, and moving along beside people. But there was one thing that really was weird, and that was the woman who kept visiting me in my room. As it was, she turned out to be really significant, but I would never have guessed that at the time.

What I have grown to accept now, I actually barely understand. People will say things like, 'Oh what a gift'. I don't consider it to be a gift. If it was a gift, I would have given it back a long time ago. Likewise I don't consider it a burden either, or I would have sought therapy for myself a long time ago. It's just something that happens. Sometimes it's like a reward, sometimes it isn't. To be honest I have grown to believe, after spending quite a bit of time with other like-minded individuals, that I am just a channel for energy that operates at a more divine level than we mortals can wholly appreciate.

What I do thoroughly understand now though, is the heritage behind it all, and that has helped me make some sense of it. The making sense part of it all started with an extremely important journey. Not a new age, airy fairy, spiritual journey of any sort, but a physical journey; a real journey with real sights and real smells, and real history to back everything about what it's like being me up. So to really explain what it's like to be 'psychic' I have to start by telling you as much as I can about that journey.

When I was eighteen years old my papa took me to Poland. Up to that point I had never been abroad before or even been on a plane from one end of the UK to the other. I had never spent a night away from home, or from my dad for that matter. More importantly it was not until that trip that I fully appreciated just how very special Papa was. It was strange also because, believe or not, up until then I had never really thought of Papa as coming from a foreign country. I know that might sound really stupid to you reading this, but it's true. Although I knew he had a different accent to mine, he never really spoke about where he was born or how he came to be in Scotland, so I had never given it much thought. I was a teenager; if it didn't affect me directly then I wasn't that much bothered. It wasn't that I didn't care entirely, I did. Every now and then my curiosity about my papa and where he came from would be overwhelming and I would ask him about his accent, the way he spoke and different things he ate, especially when he was chomping on his pickled cabbage, or offering me a slice of sour sausage. I would then ask Papa to tell me about where he came from. He would always answer that it wasn't important, and that I was the most important person now. It never occurred to me he might be avoiding the subject. So in the end I just stopped asking, accepting that everything about Papa's past must be a bit dull and not all that relevant.

So you can imagine it came as a bit of a surprise when he came over to the house the week before my eighteenth and told me I was going to Poland for my birthday. I remember it well. It was mid-July, and although it had been a really warm day, I had spent the afternoon indoors listening to music with a few friends. Most of whom I don't keep in touch with now, except Zoe; she was quite detached for most of the time, a bit mad, and still is. She had shaved her hair off that day, which was actually a bloody relief as it was dyed to the point of falling out of its own accord anyway. She also flirted with Dad so much it was cringe-worthy. Every time she did it I would die inside because my dad was so embarrassed. Well, if you think about it he had never had a partner as long as I could remember, and I had been the only female he had had to communicate with in any depth, so it wasn't really a surprise that he found it difficult. You have to understand my dad wasn't that sociable. He spent a lot of time reading. He was obsessed with books in an unnatural way. He would state thaty the quality of a book has little to do with how long the story is. He would say, "Take Graham Greene's *The End Of An Affair*; it could be argued that, if a book was measured on word count alone then it was paltry in comparison to Jung Chang's *Wild Swans.* But then quality," he would state, "is not bound in the number of pages, but in the economy and the integrity of the words that have been thoughtfully put down on the paper." He hated to find a book that was padded out with information that did nothing but occupy pages; he said they were simply words that had been placed like squatters, that did nothing to move the plot forward. I think he felt deceived. I think he believed that if you invested in a book then you entered into some sort of trust with the author that they will deliver every word with meaning. When the book didn't, you'd honestly think the author had stolen the money, the entire cost of the book, from him personally. He would slam it shut with the proclamation it was "… shit!"

His philosophy of authors needing to be economical with words spills out into his real life too. He has never been a chatterbox, or 'blether' as we would say in Scotland. It, whatever 'it' was, had to be worth saying. I have learned over the years that in reality it's difficult, if not impossible, to make a profound statement every time you engage with an individual, and so I can understand why most of the time in our house it was very quiet.

Unless of course he was listening to music, boy was it loud and boy was it old-fashioned stuff. He also went for very long walks, sometimes for hours. I can't ever remember him drinking alcohol, or going out with the lads or anything like that. Good God, I'm making him sound like a bit of a freak, but he wasn't at all. He was, and still is, my lovely intelligent, funny, strangely quirky dad, who I can see now that I'm an adult, was and still is a proper gentleman. There's not many of them around these days is there?

What I never fully appreciated was just how very lonely he must have been back then. Oh there were times when I was young and I indulged in fantasies about my dad falling in love with someone. I suppose I was a bit fickle but all I wanted was some sort of fairy tale thing for him, and me for that matter. I would ask him if he had ever liked anyone since Mum had died. Mostly he shunned these conversations, but there was one occasion when he did say that he had liked a girl very much when he was younger before he met my mum. He told me that her mother had died of breast cancer when she was my age (at that time), and that she mustn't ever have gotten over it as she left home as soon as she was old enough and he had never seen her again. I was a bit stunned by what he said; he had liked someone else before Mum. So then I spent some time thinking about this girl that my dad had liked, and her mum dying and I felt sorrier for her than I have ever felt for myself. As I've said I never really got to know my mum; I was too young, and I can't remember anything much about her other than what my dad has told me, and as I've said, I can't remember anything of the day she died. So I have never felt sorry for myself. I can't imagine what that day must have been like for him. It must have been absolutely, bloody horrific.

Anyhow, to get back to the day I found out about going to Poland; there were a few of us at my house, my dad was down at the shop, and we had found a collection of his old vinyls, trying a variety of tracks from them for a laugh. It wasn't till much later that I realised just how much I had invaded his space there, and I do remember he didn't seem too happy about it at the time, although he never said that. Come to think of it I can't remember my dad ever raising his voice, although he must have, because really, I was no angel.

When he came home that day he warned me Papa was going to come round to tell me about my birthday surprise. What a buzz it caused. Immediately we made a list of possible items it could be. A trip to Poland certainly wasn't one of the items to appear on this birthday list.

I used to do that for birthdays and Christmases; make lists. I would compile two lists: a need list (essential items), and a want list (luxury items). According to Papa though, the trip would be rightly placed on my *need* list – an *essential* item. Essential? I am ashamed to admit to you that I didn't even know where Poland was, other than it was in Europe. Seriously if Papa had handed me a map with names of the countries blanked out I would have struggled to put a pin in Poland. But it was strange because although he had his mind made up that we were going, regardless of what I thought, he seemed to be a bit perplexed, almost as though he didn't really want to go, or that someone was forcing him to take me. I have to say it is the first time Papa has made me feel a little bit uncomfortable. So I asked him.

"Are you sure about this Papa? You don't have to take me."

"Yes, I am. You see, Anna, I have been knowing about this flying and floating thing you do in the night time." He sat down in front of me, and I felt totally embarrassed that he had said that in front of my friends. I hadn't told any of them about all that stuff.

"Really?" Then I felt a bit stupid too, knowing that he knew about what I used to call '*the weird stuff*'.

"Yes, and I think the time is now just right for you to know about certain things that have happened, and I think to know these things will help, and to really know and understand these things you need to go to Poland."

I remember the conversation like it was yesterday, and I remember thinking it was like he was speaking in code. What things? What could have happened? And how could it help stop me from floating out my body at night? Then I wanted to tell him that it wasn't just floating around at night; there was also a curious matter of the ghostly visitors that I needed to sort out too. Would a trip to Poland help me with that? As it was, I never mentioned the ghosts to Papa, especially the woman who kept visiting me at night.

"Does my dad know?"

"Of course."

"And he's agreed?"

"Yes."

"Is he coming too?"

"No." Papa paused then added emphatically, "He does not float, does he." He was making a statement more than asking me a question.

So there it was. The big surprise was a trip to the foreign country where Papa was born; a country that I knew nothing more about except I believed that everything they ate, including puddings, smelt of garlic. I wasn't sure what to think; I didn't know whether I was disappointed or genuinely surprised. I told Papa this. Meanwhile all of my friends just sat in silence staring at him in disbelief, and I could tell they were thinking; *bloody hell did he just say she floats out of her body at night?*

"Anna," he replied. "I am petrified myself, my darling. I have not been home myself for over fifty years; I might not even know this place I call my home myself."

"You're making me nervous," I replied. I couldn't imagine why he should be petrified. I was still under the impression that the whole Poland and being Polish thing wasn't all that important. Then I thought if – or rather when, because he had booked the flights already – we get there and he doesn't know the place, we could get lost in a strange country. I could feel bile rising to the back of my throat, but I was still desperately trying to look like I had had an exciting birthday surprise and maintain some sort of composure in front of my friends. He must have been able to see how anxious I was feeling for he lent forward, took my hands and whispered, "Listen to your Papa, Anna; it will be an adventure, our wonderful adventure. It is still this beautiful country in my mind, from my memory." He told me he had read after the war that Krakow had escaped major destruction during World War II. "It cannot be changed so much. I can remember the spires of St Mary's and the bugle caller. Oh and I have read about that too – apparently there is still to this day a bugle caller, can you believe that Anna? And from what I have read he still honours the guard who was shot down during the horrific raids of the thirteenth century. He does you know, what he does is he pauses to bear honour to the guard who was shot down with an arrow, during the raids, before he takes up the bugle call again. Every hour, every single hour! My goodness, now there's a tradition." It didn't surprise me at all that my papa had been reading about this. He was a keen reader. In fact when my dad got a book order in, Papa would always skim off the cream of the books for himself. He put his healthy interest in books down to not learning to read properly until he came to Scotland. He believed he had a lot of time to make up for. As far as I could see, he had well and truly made up for it. In fact by the time he was forty he had probably read more than the average sixty-year-old Scottish person. I have always been so proud of him for that, because that wouldn't have been an easy task, would it?

"Oh Anna, my goodness, my precious Anna it's fascinating. I simply cannot imagine, or believe, that I am actually going to hear that bugle again. The last time I heard that, my darling Anna, my hand was held tight in the palm of my mother's hand… Oh… My God! The thought of that is like a hard thing punching me inside out, from right inside here." He said that punching his stomach hard, which I have to say gave me a bit of a fright. "I'm sorry I do not ever mean to startle you, it's just when I think about that day, or if even if I think about my mother… oh my God, my mother… my mother… Oh God, help me… ' It was as though he had momentarily lost his senses. It took him a few seconds and a couple of deep breaths to compose himself before he continued, "When we go, Anna, you will meet my mother, and what is more we will have a time that is good, and time to answer your mystery of your night time floating. Ha Anna! And you really will be flying! Even I have not been flying in my life!"

"I will meet your mother? My great-grandmother? But that means she must be nearly one hundred years old; I didn't know she was still alive? You've never said!"

"That's because she is not alive. When she was died, I was a boy, just a boy and I came here, that is when I came all this way to Scotland."

"So how will I meet her? I don't understand?" I found it all quite confusing, but he was calm and self-assured.

"Wait and you will see – I am so certain you will see."

"So were you a little boy, or an older boy?"

"When?"

"When you came to Scotland."

"I'm not sure of my age exactly, as I don't know when I was born, the year I was born."

"How can you not know that, Papa? Surely you know when you were born?"

"Well, it's like this; we counted my age in summers. My mother would say this is your tenth; this is your eleventh and so on. When she died it was early autumn and I had just had my nineteenth summer, so I was anywhere between nineteen and twenty years old. I know I was nearly those ages because my mother had told me that around the time I was born, Polish persons could sing their national song again. Ha! This was always her proudest thing – that I was actually Polish." He paused for a moment, puffed out his chest proudly and then continued in a slightly hushed tone as though his nationality was a secret, and he feared someone might jump out and shout, *'Actually Henryk Rosiewicz you are not and never have been Polish!'*

"From what I have since read about that time, my dear young Anna, is that it was in the spring of 1919 – that was when Poland was a country again." That puzzled me quite a bit as a hapless teenager; that a country could be a country then not be a country, then be a country again, but I never said anything and I let him continue.

"So I have since learnt that if my mother was right, I must have been born in 1919, but which day or month I will never know."

It wasn't until that point that I realised I couldn't remember Papa ever having a birthday. In fact everything about my papa started to seem a bit odd, maybe even interesting. It was as though despite being my papa all my life, I was only now just starting to actually know, or understand a little of who Mr Henryk Rosiewicz actually was. As far as I was concerned my friends had evaporated and my papa was the only important person that night. In truth they hadn't evaporated; they sat around me, staring at my papa, mesmerised.

I remember thinking it was actually quite cool that he was taking charge. In my heart though, I wanted to know more, if only to stop my head hurting with all the questions I suddenly had about him that needed immediate answers. That's what it's like when you're young isn't it? If you decide you want something then the result has to be immediate, but if someone else wants something from you, well they would most certainly have to wait.

Nonetheless, reading between the lines as I did that night, I was beginning to realise, if I knew more about him then I would eventually know more about me. However, on my quest for those immediate answers, I'm sure he must have thought my questioning to be somewhat tiring and thoroughly relentless.

"So if you've never flown before either, how did you get here?"

"Well it was not what you could say a normal journey."

"What do you mean? Did you sail here?"

"Ah, so many questions now, huh? I think, perhaps it is time to tell you some of the things about your papa. Some I will tell you now. Some you cannot know till your feet are on the soil of Poland. So it will be in two parts, like a great mystery." And with that, and with all of my friends still sitting around me, he started to tell us 'part one' of his epic tale.

He told us he had walked, actually walked, from his home near Wieliczka in southern Poland to the channel port of Boulogne in France, which must be around one thousand miles. It took him almost one year after leaving Wieliczka in September 1939 until he reached the channel coast near the port of Boulogne in June 1940. There he was bundled onto a ship, arriving in Britain with nothing more than the clothes he stood in, exhausted and malnourished. He described being quite astonished by the number of Eastern European refugees and downtrodden Polish soldiers he was surrounded by when he was herded onto the ship for the UK; all of them, like Papa, had been escaping from the German Army. Once in the UK, they were provided with shelter by way of tents in huge camps organised in any available open spaces along the English coast. He says they were not unlike refugee camps you might see even nowadays on the news on the television. With France having fallen in May 1940, Churchill feared imminent German invasion and he arranged for the exhausted refugees to be transported north to Scotland. There were various camps, including the one where Papa went, called Camp Crawford. He said that he believed Churchill was a good man, a clever man, with more wits about him than Chamberlain. He could have sent them back and watched them perish at the hands of the German Army. Instead he gave them a place to gather strength and put them to work where they were deployed in the building of the military sea defences around the south-east coast of Scotland. That was how Papa came to live in the Borders. He helped to build the sea defences around North Berwick.

It was not until Papa had finished telling me about his journey that I sat back and tried to imagine just how hellish it must have been. Starting from the point he was pulled from the stream outside the village of Warbella. He had been spotted running across the fields in the early morning by a group of peasants who had gone underground following the German occupation of Krakow. They called themselves The Ludzie Lensi, which translated means 'The Forest People'. They pulled Papa from the stream; they thought he was trying to drown himself. They had been shocked too to see him out in the dark on his own so near to Krakow, and carried him back to their undercover camp. It was from The Ludzie Lensi that Papa learnt of the German invasion and subsequent occupation of Krakow. They told him horrifying stories of persecution and mass execution. Papa told me how shocked he was to learn that the countryside he was so used to wandering aimlessly around in, was now overrun with invading forces, and was just like one huge man trap. They warned him to watch out for them speeding around in armoured trucks, hundreds of them, and that if these German soldiers were put together they would amount to a gathering of many thousands. They said there were so many of them that when they marched, their boots struck the ground collectively like lightening cracking down to earth. Most of the peasants in the group that had saved Papa from probable capture were fleeing the nearby Krakow province of Prodgórzé. There the German Army were herding all peasants and Jews into one street, cramming multiple families together into rooms meant for only one family. Then they would brick up windows and doors so the people could not see out onto the part of the city occupied by the German Army.

The Ludzie Lensi also reported seeing trains being filled with the Jews in the neighbourhood, and that once the trains had groaned off into the distance, they returned empty and the people were never seen again. All of the passengers; women, men and children, vanished. They explained how most of the important men of the city had simply disappeared amidst rumours of mass execution. The rabbi, the clergy, the bankers, the teachers, the doctors; all of them disappeared, and all such positions in the city were now occupied by Germans. Papa learnt that German soldiers were everywhere, like vermin breeding. They had closed all the synagogues, and all the important town buildings were decorated with German flags and German banners.

Papa told us that he noticed that although these men had only been underground for a few months, they already had maps, were armed, and had reliable sources of intelligence. They seemed well-organised. They gave Papa a gun and some water to drink. They instructed that he must obey their rules now if he wanted to stay alive; he must stay in the forest areas in the daytime and move out in the night time, looking for clues and information. The leader, Vladick, explained they were gathering information only just now, and planning an attack on a steel bridge to the south of the city within the week. They had been keeping tracks on a group of German soldiers who were guarding the nearby Pilsudski Bridge. They noticed that there were times in the night that the Germans were falling asleep, and leaving themselves open to attack. Vladick laughed and said, "They must think we are so stupid as to not watch them or so arrogant as to think we will not challenge them!"

Papa explained to me that he could not carry the gun; he said that perhaps he was a coward, because in the end he was too afraid to fight back and so began to plan his escape. He stayed with the group for a few nights as he had access to some water and small amounts of food. After a few days the talk was becoming more serious of attacking the Germans at the bridge. Papa said the thought of the attack gave him severe diarrhoea, and on one occasion when he left the group complaining of cramps, he went deeper into the forest than usual, and he never went back. He said they must have assumed he had been captured as they never came looking for him. It would have put themselves and their position at risk.

He had taken one of their maps with him and a knife, and had his compass in his pocket. Once he was certain they were not coming to find him he held open the map and his compass and confirmed to himself he was heading south-east. He had chosen the map of Central Europe carefully from the collection the group had. There were dark red lines and arrows that someone had drawn pointing into Poland. At this point Papa explained that he could barely read, and that there was some kind of text on the map but it was not a language that Papa understood. He had watched Vladick pointing at important places on the map, which Papa deduced must be Krakow, and was certainly Poland. He said Vladick would often slam his fist down hard on the map, and bare his teeth. Papa said if it wasn't so serious it would have been funny, and that Vladick made some terrible faces. He later learned from Vladick that the map had been stolen from the Germans, and the arrows were determining their routes of invasion, and points of planned occupation.

So Papa had picked a good map to steal. As soon as he felt he had created a safe distance between himself and the Ludzie Lenski, he stopped and opened out the map again. He held his compass open, and after careful contemplation he decided he would continue south and east towards Hungary, moving away from and ahead of the arrows. Walking by night and resting and looking for food during the day, he made slow progress. The nights were getting colder and longer. Some days the sun barely scraped itself above the horizon. It grew cold, with biting north-easterly winds gnawing at him. When his shoes fell apart he walked barefooted. He told us that his feet bled beyond a point where he was able to register that he was in pain. He said the relief when he came to a stream and could plunge them into the ice-cold water was indescribable. Once he made makeshift covers for his feet from cuttings of an old tractor tyre that had been left in a field.

When he reached the coast of Slovenia, he says he remembers standing, looking out at this strange thing called the sea. He had remembered his mother telling him about these supposed wide spans of water, that she had doubted existed, but there it was in front of him, and for a moment he was in awe of it. He couldn't really tell how long it had taken him to reach Trieste; he estimated a season and a half. He knew he had left Poland at the start of autumn when there were new frosts at night. By the time he got to Trieste, the trees were bare, the ground was hard and most days now, light wisps of snow had started to billow in the wind. The nights on foot had started to become even more difficult, for he had become a thief under the cover of darkness. He said he was never proud when he stole something but he had to in order to survive. Despite stealing whatever he could, he says that by the time he got to Trieste he was so thin he could just see his bones and joints as though the skin had been peeled back, and that when he lay down he could see the outlines of his guts moving around through his skin. He said that when he saw this it made him feel physically sick.

Soon after arriving in Trieste, he realised he would probably have to somehow get himself onto a boat in order to get away, not knowing at this point where his destination would be. He said that he spent many days, maybe weeks in

Trieste, he couldn't be sure exactly how long as he slept a lot. When he was awake, he described watching the boats set sail from the harbour to destinies unknown to him. Oh how he dreamt he was on one of them, no matter where they were headed as long as it was far away from where he was. He said his mind was so full of uncertainty, and he kept checking his map and wondering if he should be taking a route by land, which would mean travelling north again, or whether he should travel east, or south by sea. In the end so much was his desire to sail away to the east or south that he spent many of his precious days watching the boats dock and then sail off, all the time wondering what he would have to do to get himself onto one of them. He noticed there were times when the captain, or certainly the man who looked like he was in charge, would meet with individuals who looked as poorly as my papa. He watched as things were exchanged and those individuals were ushered onto the boats without seemingly having a ticket. This intrigued my papa. As he watched closely he saw they were handing over items such as tobacco, cigars and cigarettes – lots of them – alcohol, and most of all, big wads of money. Knowing he could never hand over wads of money, his quest was to acquire his 'ticket' in the form of tobacco, cigars, cigarettes and alcohol. With that he embarked on the biggest thieving spree of his entire life. Whilst it was all very serious, the funniest part of this was when he described being chased for a packet of cigarettes by a woman with a huge backside, who had only one tooth, very little hair, and screamed at my papa as though he had just chopped her arm off. His exact words were, "What a bottom, my goodness, I was very jealous

189

of the fat on it! How she managed to lift those legs so fast with all that backside going on is nothing short of a miracle!"

Luckily the captain accepted his bribe of countless packets of cigarettes and cigars, and agreed to hide him under the floorboards. When he thought about it afterwards, Papa said he realised the captain must have done this before, it was so well-rehearsed, and that as far as he was concerned he had stolen so much for his 'ticket' he should have been in first class, never mind being stuffed under the floorboards.

The ship sailed the Adriatic Sea from Trieste in Slovenia, to a port in northern Italy. He has no idea how many days it took, all he can remember is he had to piss himself at least three times on the journey, when the pain of trying to hold it in became severe. He says that could have been three times in ten days, or three times in a day, he has no idea. When the ship arrived in Northern Italy, he said he couldn't believe his eyes; ahead in the distance were snow-capped mountains as far as the eye could see; he said if it wasn't for the fact he believed he might die soon, he would have waited and watched a while, the sight of them was so incredible.

In front of him, a beautiful fishing port emerged amidst the marshes of a delta. When he laid his map out flat and asked one of the local fishermen where he was, the first thing he noticed was how very different their tongue was. Neither could understand the other. So in the end he just pointed at the map and held up his hands. The fisherman pointed to Porto Viro. Papa noticed there was a river close by that opened out into the port, a river that, when he traced it with his finger, ran across the map to the west for almost the entire breadth of the country, so he decided to follow it. Although the edges of his map cut off at the French border just after Turin, Papa followed the river Po inland, beyond the marshes of the Delta, and continued on until he reached the border with France. After that, he had no map, and no idea what lay beyond the edge of the map. On his journey across Northern Italy, he says there were days where he believed he would definitely die, and there were days he wished he would die, he was so cold and hungry. The winter dusks and sunsets were, he says, the only things worth drawing breath for some days. He told us he remembers being so weak that he did no walking for days on end, but just lay on the cold ground waiting for the sunset and sun rise. Each was striking and each eventually filled him with an inner strength to get up and carry on. Despite that, the winter was harsh and sometimes the progress he made at night was barely a few steps, but as the nights were long he did sometimes have the strength to take the opportunity to try and walk a little further than the night before. He would start by counting his steps, each night trying to walk a few more. Empty farm buildings offered shelter, and if he could he would curl up inside an old building to escape the biting winds.

When he was near a large town or city, just like when he got near Turin, he says he watched for the coal trains. They offered a rare opportunity to travel and to rest at the same time. When he was near a track he would watch for the trains during the day, like a kind of surveillance. He watched which direction they came and went, how often they moved, and how many carts they had. The best ones would have at least ten carts full of coal. Papa would get into the last cart furthest away from the driver, and wait for it to go. It would mean he had to stay roughly in the same area for a couple of days, but when it worked out, it was worth the wait. If he picked the right train he could be transported further in a day than he could have walked in a month. The trickiest part was trying to guess when the train had reached its destination, and was not just stopping at junctions. He said he had to jump quickly from the cart and run fast. Papa asked us to imagine just how difficult it would be to run fast when there is no muscle on your legs, just bones like twigs. He laughed though, and said it was even harder when his pockets were filled with coal. Usually the drivers never spotted him, but one did and chased him, but he was too fat to run any distance, unlike Papa who, despite his skinny frame and pockets filled with coal, surprised even himself by taking off like a bullet that day. Other than that occasion he says never came near to being captured. In fact he told us that he never really came near to another human being for the duration of his journey. So it was a shock to him to come upon so many Polish refugees when he did eventually reach the coast of France.

This part of his journey across France he recalls as being the most terrifying. Despite an easing in the weather, shorter nights and a warmer, more comforting air, there was something different – even sinister – in the air. It was not the fact that he could hear yet another new language, or the fact that he didn't have a map to guide him that worried him. It was more to do with the feeling of something oppressing, and the constant sense of threat that he had become more aware of. Then one day he said he heard a deep penetrating rumbling in the ground. The first time this happened he thought it must be an earthquake, and he lay on the ground bracing himself for the moment the ground would crack open and swallow him up. When he looked up and saw the massive hulks of metal grinding past he recognised the motif on the tanks, and he recognised the uniforms of the soldiers that sped by in the trucks after the tanks had passed. *Oh my God*, he panicked, *the Germans are here*. He remembers being overwhelmed with a feeling of utter despair and terror when he saw them. He said he thought he was going to vomit when it dawned on him that despite months of agonising walking he was no further away from his enemies than when he had started out. He thought to himself, *all these months I have been escaping from you, and all the time you have been right behind me*. He was not scared to admit he was very afraid that day. He barely moved all of that day and night, and believed he would be better off just left to perish in the trench where he lay near the roadside. When I asked him why he went on, why he didn't just give up there and then, he replied that I would find that out when I got to Poland.

Then he told us that while he was spending all that time just lying in that ditch, there would be nights when he heard distant droning overheard, and he would keep his eyes on the sky and watch for the terrifying mass of aircrafts creeping heavily across the skyline. All in all, it made him aware of a different intensity in this country than he had been aware of when following the river Po. There, when traversing the north of Italy, for the most part, all he could see was the vastness of the river. It was in places a huge span, so much so at times he wondered if it was actually the sea in front of him. Some days the blues of the sky and blueness of the wide river were so alike it was hard to tell when one ended and the other began. Lined with spectacular forests, mountains in the distance, and peppered all along with beautiful castles and wonderful bridges, he admits it might have all been quite stunning if he had been there for the pleasure of it. In reality he described feeling confined by the river and its sloped horizons. Some days he believed he was being imprisoned by it all, and he feared he might never see a flat horizon filled with land again. Until, that is, he got to France. There the ground flattened out and opened up. So it saddened him greatly to find that in this country, where the sun shone down on the wide open spaces bathing everything in a golden glow, there was not the sense of freedom he might have expected to feel. Instead, it was like some kind of eerie omniscient force, reminding him that the German occupation was something that was palpable in the ether, even when there was no visible sign of them.

By the time Papa had finished this epic journey and had arrived in Scotland he was a man utterly downtrodden. He was emaciated, with deep infected sores on his feet and legs. What was more concerning though, and peculiar, was that he describes that for a long time after arriving in Scotland, he was rendered speechless. He says that in fact it had been so long since he held a conversation with anyone who would recognise his language, it was as though he had forgotten how to speak. He said he also found it difficult to read the expressions on other people's faces, as initially he was surrounded by so many refugees that looked the same as him, expressionless. It was as though they had all forgotten how to feel anything but despair, and for a long time, that was the only expression they and he could wear. He said he was like a mute. He would use a kind of sign language to indicate when he needed something. He says that learning to talk, to feel and recognise emotions again was like slowly emerging from the densest of fogs.

While Papa was telling us all this, we had completely lost track of time, we had become totally and utterly immersed within the throws of his escape. When he eventually said that that was all he was telling us at that point, I remember seeing the glint return to his eye, as though something was firing up within him. It looked to me as if he knew he would be in complete command of this trip, and when I saw that, I remember finally feeling okay, even excited about our trip to the country of his birth. I trusted him and knew it would be an adventure.

From that day until the day we flew to Krakow two weeks later, I bought and studied maps. I worked out on the scale measurements how many miles he must have walked. By the time we arrived in Krakow I could name every country on the map, from Latvia in the north-east, to Hungary, south of Poland, and onwards south and west to Slovenia. I had learnt his route off by heart. I spent three full days in the library looking up books on the German invasion of Poland, and World War II. From what I read, coupled with the rough time scales, I could surmise that until he got to France, Papa was always just ahead of them. Once he got to France, the occupation of France was so overwhelming that he must have spent all of his time avoiding capture until he reached the

French coast. I grew to realise that, in light of the fall of France in May 1940, how he managed to escape them is pretty unbelievable. When I said this to him, he was so modest in his reply; he said that it wasn't too hard as he had found that a lot of the French people were willing to help him and hide him. As the German army had taken over their country, Henryk and the French had common ground for grievance, and despite their language barriers they seemed to understand one another. In fact he boasts it was the one part of the journey where he had been better fed and looked after than ever. At some points he even had shoes to wear. He remembers one elderly couple that came across him in their barn when they were collecting in their hens. They fed him with cooked eggs and bread. The elderly man then gave him what appeared to be his best suit. So for a time Papa felt like the best-dressed refugee on the run.

Despite part one of Papa's story being complete, and despite the fact I was completely riveted by it, to me there were still two important questions left unanswered:

Question one: How will going to Poland help me to understand being 'psychic'? Bearing in mind that is not what I called myself back then. At that point I was simply someone who saw people who were most probably dead; I could hear people talking that were not actually humanly visible, and I dreamt of things that happened soon after. I knew I wasn't mad, but sometimes I feared it might send me mad. Whilst Papa's story was compelling I did wonder how going Poland would help me to understand *'the weird stuff'*.

Question two: If Papa lived out in the middle of nowhere, not even that close to Krakow, why did he have to escape?

Surely if he had stayed where he was they would never have found him.

It seemed to me there was a vital piece of information missing, and I asked him about this. His reply once again was I would not find that out until my feet were firmly on Polish soil.

*

A couple of days before we were due to fly, it started to happen again. I started to feel as though I was being followed. Initially I put it down to nerves of the impending journey. However, everywhere I went I felt as though there was definitely someone brushing by me, something just behind me, something always catching the corner of my eye. It didn't matter how fast I turned to look, when I looked, it (or who, or what) would vanish. Sometimes it was so vivid, I would turn swiftly to say hello. Once I said hello right out loud but there was no-one there to answer me when I looked round; but there had been a person there, I could definitely see her in the corner of my eye. She was around my height, 5ft 5-ish, she seemed to be smiling a lot, and it was her hair that kept catching my attention. It was really dark and wild, a bit like it had never been brushed, but not in an unkempt or scruffy way, just curly and untamed. It happened so often in the couple of days before we left that I started to pause and stand still, delaying turning round, just so I could try and get a proper image of her from the corner of my eye. In my head I was saying *please stand still when I look at you. Who are you?*

It was funny because when the other woman had appeared in my room I wondered if she was my mum, because she just looked a bit more modern I suppose. But this woman looked different from my usual visitor, and I knew she was from longer ago. Don't ask me how I reached that conclusion, I suppose it's just the feeling I got from her. She never spoke to me; perhaps if she had I would have realised then before I went to Poland who she was.

The night before we flew I had one of those dreams, where I was more alive and awake than asleep, and was I was aware I was being sucked from my body and being lifted out into the air. It's a very strange and scary sensation. I felt as though my skin was being peeled away from my face, but I knew in my head I was fast asleep and couldn't fight this thing. So off I floated. I was taken outside to a path that led deep into a forest. When I looked up I was surrounded by rows of tall silver birches. Row upon row of silver birches stretched ahead of me like long white fingers reaching up to the sky. I didn't feel scared at all. I stood still and waited. I looked ahead and watched as smoke began to rise from the trees deep in this forest of silver birches. The ground was thick with a carpet of copper leaves, which made me think it must be autumn in my 'dream'. Then out of nowhere, two men came towards me. They looked like travellers, or gypsies. They had dark curly hair and vivid blue eyes. It looked like their trousers were made from some kind of animal hide and I could hear the rub of the leather as the legs of their trousers rubbed together when they walked towards me. They held out their hands and gestured I was to follow them. I noticed how weathered they looked, as though they spent lots of time outdoors. I followed them into the wood. As soon as I stepped into the wood, the damp smell of fern and dead leaves from the ground seeped into my skin and hair. When the trees cleared, there in front of me was a group of people all sitting around a fire. They looked a bit like nomads. They spoke in a completely different language to anything I had heard before or could understand. They asked me to sit beside an old woman, which I did. In my sleeping state I realised I was able to understand what they were saying. At the same time my logical mortal mind was in disbelief. I was thinking *wait a minute you know what they are saying to you!*

The old woman held open two halves of an empty coconut shell and filled them with a fruity red substance that was quite watery. She handed it to me and said I should drink it all. I did. I can still remember the fruity taste, and remember wiping the warm dribbles from the sides of my mouth with the end of my sleeve. If I shut my eyes now I can still smell their wood fire, it smelt like a damp garden fire burning leaves on a cold autumn day. The old woman leaned over and spoke to me as though she was telling me every secret of the universe. It was as if she was sharing her entire life knowledge with me. What was even stranger was that I nodded as though I understood every word. Then we stared at each other, and something silent seemed to pass between our minds. I genuinely felt as though I understood what was required of me now that I was in possession of her secrets.

When she was finished the two men led me back out to the path. When I returned to the path I noticed a barn in front of me. It was just walls of stones that were falling down really.

There was nothing in it, no roof or windows, just a pile of stones, but I could tell it had once been a building of some sort. As I stood in front of the barn, I saw the woman I often see during the day when I'm awake; I was aware she was standing to my right-hand side. In the corner of my eye I could see she was facing me, whilst I watched the old barn. Then she turned, walked into the barn and evaporated. Before disappearing, her image was so clear I could see exactly what she was wearing. She wore a skirt that was almost to her ankles. It looked like one that overlaps and is tied around at the waist. It didn't look like it fitted her slim frame too well, like it was too big and it didn't belong to her. She had a warm, dark red jersey on. That too hung from her sides like she had borrowed it from a man. She had tied her hair up into a rough knot at the back of her head. It looked like she had tried to wrestle it into some form of tidiness, rather than a kind of finished style. As she went into the old barn building she walked with ease, as though she was floating, and it struck me then that she was quite young as she didn't stoop or carry herself as though her bones were grinding. As soon she evaporated I felt such a hard thump, I thought I had actually been punched hard in my chest. I woke with a startle, my heart racing, my throat tight. When I sat up over my bed I could hardly breathe. It was as though getting back into my body had nearly killed me. I still worry about that to this day. One of these nights, when I'm taken off somewhere, it'll finish me off when I come back. I'll be found dead in my bed. No-one will ever know I've been away, or that I've been trying to get back.

II

Our whole adventure to Poland actually started the week before we were due to fly when we travelled to Glasgow for our passports. I remember Papa took with him an important-looking folder that he clutched to his chest for the duration of our journey from Galashiels to the Glasgow passport office. The folder looked like it had quite a bit of paperwork in it. He told me it contained everything that provided proof of his identity, and then added, "according to the state that is." Then he tapped the side of his forehead and said, "But this is where my identity as I know it is." I didn't really fully appreciate what he was telling me then. Even now I didn't quite know how it all works if you haven't got a birth certificate. Then I think of his reply when I asked him about that and it still makes me smile. He said, "What other proof do you need that I was born other than I am standing in front of you here? Do I really need a piece of paper to prove I am here? My goodness I think it should be obvious to them I was born, don't you?" I found that I couldn't disagree, could I?

We flew to Poland from Edinburgh on a Wednesday morning. A Wednesday didn't seem like a day to be starting a holiday. I imagined it should be a Friday or a Saturday. But there it was, Wednesday. When my dad dropped us off at Edinburgh airport in the set down only lane – the lane that dictates you have only enough time to grab your luggage and hastily kiss goodbye – I felt totally paralysed.

We all stood at the drop-off point. It was patrolled with men that looked to me like the mafia, and whilst I felt as though I was being rushed, at the same time everything around me was in slow motion. I wondered if my legs had been cut off when I got out of the car, as I could not move from the side of the car I had gotten out of, around to the boot where my case was. I suppose I must have been a bit dumbstruck with the fear of leaving my dad. I absolutely hated saying goodbye to him. When I actually did, it made me feel physically sick. I hated that desperately clenching hug. I could tell he felt the same. He was all dewy-eyed and taking huge breaths as though the air had turned to cement in his lungs. Then I watched as Papa took a really firm hold of him, pulled him in close and said something in his ear that I never heard. I watched them as they peeled apart and something in the way their eyes locked completely reassured me.

Off I went with Papa, slightly distracted from the early morning chill by the loud humming of airplane engines. As soon as we entered the terminal building we were both a bit overwhelmed by all the buzz. People with cases trundling, shooting off in one direction and another, tannoy announcements, screens flickering and queues upon queues of travellers that looked to me like a small, displaced and quite fractious proportion of the population. In one long queue, it looked like all the angry and tired people had been summoned to stand together. Luckily that wasn't the queue we would be joining. Papa showed me how to scan the screens for the check-in desk we should go to. Looking at my questioning expression, he assured me he had asked one of his friends who does travel, how to go about these things. Thank goodness for that, I thought, because for a moment I feared we would never find our way beyond the airport entrance. All went according to Papa's grand plan and within a couple of hours we were strapped into our seats on the plane.

We flew out in the morning. Early mornings in Edinburgh can be blighted by the haar from the sea. That morning was no exception. I remember asking Papa how the pilot would be able to see and find his way out of the fog. When the plane lifted into the air I thought I had left my stomach back on the ground. It made me lurch to feel so out of control of the whole thing and the speed, well that was quite a surprise. I had no idea it would travel as fast as that along the runway before lift-off. When I looked at Papa, he was sitting with his eyes tightly shut, gripping onto the arm of the chair as though he was waiting to be ejected from his seat and propelled out into the clouds. When he eventually opened his eyes and we looked out, we were both amazed to see clear blue sky with the cloud level well below us. I had never been on this side of the clouds. I was amazed. I couldn't believe that something so beautiful from above can cause us so much miserable weather below. It was incredible, I will never forget that. Papa was speechless, which was unusual. When I asked if he was all right, he replied he was fine, he was just listening. When I listened all could hear was a babble. It was a foreign babble. I watched Papa as he listened and watched. He nodded to himself at some points, and smiled to himself every now and then. It became apparent to me he understood the language of the other passengers. That was when it dawned on me that the majority of the passengers were Polish, and I realised I wasn't just going on a holiday, I was travelling with a plane load of individuals who for whatever their reasons, were returning home. That included my papa.

Only two and a half hours' later we were in Poland. It seemed very weird, to be in Scotland at one end of the morning, and in Poland at the other. It made the world seem very small to me. When we arrived in Krakow, it was a sunny early afternoon. We caught a taxi and made our way to the apartment that Papa had booked. It was in a street called SW Filipe. It never occurred to me before that point that Papa might never have actually seen the centre of Krakow.

He explained this was so as when he was around eleven years old, he and his mother had walked to Krakow, but when he got there he couldn't see anything for the hordes of people. He remembers he was jostled and squashed in the crowds as they moved along narrow winding streets, lined by tall, ornate buildings. He remembers that some of the buildings had coloured render and that he thought they looked really quite beautiful.

The crowds were mostly peasants like himself and his mother. The only place he could look without looking into the belly of one or the armpit of another, was up, so the only memory he has of Krakow is that the buildings looked as though they might topple over if they leaned over any more, and beyond the rooftops there was a blue sky, it was noisy, and it smelt like sweating, rotting flesh. That was when he heard the bugle from the tower of St Mary's Basilica, and because he was being forced to look up, he swears he saw the man playing the bugle wave at him. He also describes that day as all being a bit frantic. People were shouting names and numbers, arms reaching, people stretching and pushing, all the while his mother's grip tightening on his arm keeping him close to her. For it would have been easy to have been swept off his feet and washed away in the tide of the crowd, down the narrow ravines of side streets packed with people, that stretched out like pulsating tentacles from the main market square.

He said that when they were moved to the front of the crowd, he remembers his mother shouting at a man who was sitting at a table in front of them. The man was writing furiously and arguing with her. Papa told me that the only time his mother let go of his hand was to wave her hands in the air in an act of defiance at this man at the table. He wasn't sure why she was making such a fuss. Papa had wished she would just stop shouting at the man so they could go back home. Papa told me it was a few years later before he realised the importance of the census carried out on that day and that thanks to his mother's insistence, from that day he had been recorded as a Polish national, and he was immensely proud of that, and prouder still of his mother. I realised that that was the first time since we had left Scotland that my Papa had mentioned his mother, my great grandmother. It occurred to me too that that was the first time I had ever really thought of Papa's mother. I was such an unbelievably blinkered teenager;

it was as though he had existed as an entirely independent entity.

So we stayed in a room in a hostel (I learned that that's what apartments are called in Krakow) on SW Filipa Street near the main square. The hostel wasn't like what I imagined. It was more like a room in someone's house. It wasn't a long, cold dormitory with a toilet for everyone to share and we didn't have to carry out housekeeping tasks to pay our way. No, it was more like a self-contained apartment, and it was very comfortable. Papa was especially pleased with the accommodation as I'm sure he had expected to be sleeping in a dormitory with a group of young worldly-wise backpackers. I slept soundly, despite dreaming of that barn again. It was still looking like a wreck, but this time there were no people waiting for me, it was just an isolated shell of a thing, without its roof, windows and its doors. In my dream I could hear a chorus of birds singing overhead in the trees.

Papa awoke early our first morning. He produced a notebook and went on to explain that he had organised for a few outings during our stay.

On our first day he planned for us to go the Market Square. Our little tourist guide book told us that it was just a short walk to the centre of Krakow from where we were. On route I was initially struck by two things; graffiti everywhere and the frantic, disorganised way the traffic moved – it seemed to have no order at all. We also came across a large, wooden-hutted market near the Planc Jana Matejki, which was very close to our apartment. It was absolutely packed, not just with people, but with fresh produce, the likes of which I had never seen before. I remember I was amazed at just how colourful the displays of fresh food actually were. I came to realise too at that point, just how much these people, exactly like Papa, enjoy their food, their fresh ingredients and most of all, their sausages. Stall after stall seemed to have every type of sausage I could imagine. I looked at Papa and laughed. Seriously, he was just grinning from ear to ear. The next surprise for me were the trams and when I looked up it was like the entire length of the main road was hemmed in by a giant hairnet that seemed to cling to the immense buildings on either side of the road, as though it was tying them all together. As we stood on the corner of the main road waiting to cross, I was trying to fathom out what on earth was going on with the traffic, in that there were cars and cyclists zooming along the tram lines.

I became aware of an elderly man dressed in a suit and tie standing entirely on his own in the middle of all this buzz. He was holding out a large bunch of fresh herbs of some sort, and with his wide apologising eyes, I could tell he was simply hoping that someone, anyone, would buy some. When I looked again I could see there was also an elderly woman perched on a stool selling pieces of lace from an old leather bag. I could see they weren't part of the official market, but maybe they were hoping, or rather, needing to get the passing trade anyway. It was like nothing I had seen before. I wondered then if Papa had stayed in Poland, would that be him now: a peasant on a street corner trying to make ends meet by selling something he had plucked from the ground earlier in the day?

Once the trams, cars, cyclists and any other random mode of transport that was hurtling along the road were signalled to stop, we took our life in our hands and crossed the main road. As we reached the other side, the loud trill of the tram bell rang out as it trundled slowly onwards surrounded by all the other chaotic traffic.

As we walked along the mostly buckled and uneven pavements to the Market Square, we passed numerous little shops that would still sell you a single button, or a short length of ribbon, or little shops that had everything you could imagine packed into their window displays, from wire brushes to budgie cages.

I have to say, I could smell that square before I saw it. It was slightly overcast that day and although it wasn't cold, there was a slight breeze that was wafting the smell of grilled food in our direction. As we got to the end of Sławkowska Street, the market square in all its glory opened out before us. It took my breath away. I looked at Papa in disbelief. With his head held high, he was looking to his left toward St Mary's Basilica. When I had previously tried to imagine the market square, I had imagined a small kind of squalid place filled with screeching, toothless, scruffy traders. I couldn't have been more wrong. To an eighteen-year-old that had never yet left home, it was quite simply something awesome.

The parameters of this massive square were lined with huge, beautifully ornate buildings and straight down the centre was the Cloth Hall, a long, incredibly beautiful building with huge, carved archways. Horses and carts were transporting tourists around and the cafés and pubs that lined the square were buzzing. In the middle of the square I could see and hear where the smell had been coming from. There, stretching ahead of us were row upon row of wooden huts selling freshly grilled food. The smell that filled the air was a strange mixture of grilled spiced meat and garlic, suffused with the scent of the fresh cinnamon topping the frothy coffees being served outside the countless cafés that tourists were flocking to.

"What are you thinking, Papa?"

"Oh my goodness, I am just full in my head with the thoughts of my mother, but not worrying, I am not sad, I am happy, so happy to be here, and so very happy to be bringing you, my little angel, here. You like?"

"Yeah, it's amazing."

"Oh my goodness it certainly smells better than what I remember!"

"Smells great, it's making me hungry."

"You want to sit somewhere for a coffee or a juice, and something to eat?"

"Yeah okay, you?"

"Yes. Can we sit where I can see St Mary's?"

"Papa I'll sit wherever you want." It struck me that the towers of St Mary's were so high that we would be able to see them wherever we sat in the square.

"Okay then, we will go over here I think, unless you want a grilled sausage?" he asked, coyly pointing towards the huts with their sizzling grills, whilst walking in the opposite direction towards St Mary's.

"No, Papa, I don't want a sausage." Although, to be honest I could tell he probably did.

When we sat down, something really amazing happened. Papa launched into our order in Polish. Then, he and the waiter had something of an animated conversation, none of which I could understand. Whilst I was slightly ill at ease, as I had never heard him speak in Polish before, I watched my papa and he was so comfortable with it. You could just tell he was at home. At that point I did begin to wonder why he had waited so long to come back and just what had made him leave in the first place, make that hellish journey and then keep him away all this time from a place he so clearly belonged to.

"Look at this, Anna, my word!" He held the menu open. On one page there was a list of at least fifteen types of vodka.

"We're not having that, are we?"

"The great heavens above, no! I tell you though, my mother, she made a very wicked vodka. Phaw! Take off your legs right away!"

"How did she make that?"

"Potatoes."

"Potatoes?"

"Yes, and if she gave me a wee sip, oh my goodness, it was like my feet had been put on backwards! But to her no problem. It was like a cup of tea to her, honestly it was!"

Just then the clock struck eleven. Papa waited and there, to his astonishment, came the bugle call from high in the tower of St Mary's, and as he had so accurately described to me, it stopped for a few seconds and then started again.

"Oh my goodness, that has made my day! Hah! Would you believe it, after all this time?" He was so pleased, it was as though a long yearning curiosity of his had at last been satisfied. He couldn't imagine it did and still does happen.

In the afternoon, we walked down to the Wawwel Castle. As castles go, I thought it was okay. Well what can I say; I was eighteen and at that point was completely unenlightened with regard to Polish history. Papa on the other hand, was obviously more excited than me about it. There he went on about all its medieval grandeur and evidence that Poland was once a mighty kingdom. It's all history, you see, and it's all important in some shape or form, and as he reminded me that afternoon, it's important to always remember and never to forget.

On the second day, we went to the salt mines in Wieliczka. This day was like a personal crusade of Papa's. Finally getting to go to the place where his father had once stood and worked as a musician in the town band that met the tourists when they started to come to the mines. He explained to me that his mother had always forbidden him to come to such a dangerous place, where so many of the miners died that they actually greeted you with the words 'God bless you' when you arrived at the mines, instead of the regular 'Good morning'.

On our way there, he was amazed to be traveling along a three-lane motorway. He said that whenever he and his mother had gone to Wieliczka, which they rarely had, they tramped their way through the surrounding trees. The three lanes really did tickle him.

The day we visited the salt mines they were boasting about having newly completed works on the air conditioning, so we were assured we would find it all very comfortable. Comfortable and fascinating it might have been, but I could not forget that I was over four hundred feet underground at one point and that scared me. It was strange too, because it was quite humid and if I licked my lips I could taste the salt in the air. The biggest surprise though, was that the salt looked black until a light was placed behind it. Really, it was black.

At the lowest point that we were taken to in the mines, the mine opened out to reveal a spectacular chapel, all carved out of salt. It was absolutely breath-taking.

"I wish my mother could see this."

"It's amazing."

"Look at the altar." We both stepped forward and just gazed ahead at the altar, with its intricate carvings and even a pulpit carved from salt.

"Look up, Anna." Even the huge chandeliers were made of salt crystals. It really is a place I will never forget visiting, for one other important reason too. When we reached the surface again and were outside waiting on the rest of the group we had gone down with, Papa went over to one of the guides and asked him something, again in Polish, so at the time I didn't know what he had asked. Anyhow, he returned to me and said we must go over to the other side of the car park and stand there.

"Do you know why we are standing here?"

"I've no idea," I laughed.

"This is where the band would have stood many years ago. This is where my father would have stood." For a moment, he stood perfectly upright taking deep breaths with his chest all puffed out with pride. "And now, Anna, I am going to give you this." From his pocket he produced his small, brass compass. When I held it and looked at it, it was smaller than I had imagined and it had the words *Clement Clarke Ltd. London VI 1918* engraved on it. I thought, imagine that; he was given it in Poland, it came from the UK and it guided him back to the UK.

"This was my father's. It has always shown me the right way. It has kept me alive. For you now."

"Papa… are you sure, I have to have this?"

"Never been surer. Keep it with you for all of the journeys you make in your lifetime. Whether they be journeys in your head, or with your feet, this will keep you safe."

"I don't know what to say. I'm afraid I'll lose it."

You won't."

"Thank you."

"Most welcome." With that, he kissed the top of my head, and I gave him such a hug that he stumbled slightly.

On our fourth and penultimate day, as we were due to fly home on Sunday, Papa took me to the place where he spent his childhood. I had imagined him growing up in a village, so when the taxi dropped us at the end of a dirt track that led off along the side of a field stretching for about ten acres ahead, I was a bit puzzled. So was the driver. He asked Papa twice if he was sure this was where we wanted to be dropped off, stating there was nothing out here. He looked at me with concern. I think he wondered if I was being abducted. "It's okay, he's my papa," I said. I don't think he was reassured by that, I think he thought we must be mad. Papa nodded with certainty and instructed the driver to return in two hours as we stepped from the car. I watched the taxi speed off and I felt my insides leap;

two hours? What on earth were we going to do out here for two hours other than end up completely lost? Papa, however, was defiant and strode off. He waved for me to follow him along the dirt path.

It was a warm day and I do remember being surprised by just how warm it was in Poland in August. I had had this naive image that eastern European countries were forever concealed under a blanket of ice and snow. Not this day, it was positively hot. When I caught up with him, I was sweating. Papa explained to me that I was about to visit the place where he spent his childhood. He was talking in whispers, and I wondered if we were about to approach an ancient and fragile landmark. When we had walked for half a mile around the outskirts of the field, I could see we were heading towards a large woodland area of mostly tall, silver birches. Immediately it started to look familiar to me. So much so that when I saw the forest I started to feel very strange, weak almost, as though I hadn't eaten or drank for hours. My legs became heavy and I felt as if I was being followed, but it was only Papa that was ahead of me, and there was no-one behind me when I looked around. I could hear birds in the trees as we approached, but it was as though they were muffled. My heart began to race and the hairs on my neck started to rise as we got closer. Papa's stride quickened as he took a right turn and made his way along the path that was now running along the edge of the forest. It was as though he had forgotten I was there. His pace picked up to a jog and I had to run to keep up with him. And then there it was, in front of us; the shell of the barn that I had been dreaming about. I felt my knees weaken at the sight of it.

I have no idea why, as I didn't at that point understand the significance of this building, but I had started to cry. Tears were rolling uncontrollably down my cheeks as I watched my papa fall to the ground at the side of the barn. He started to make a strange, wailing kind of noise, he was saying something, but it was in Polish. "*Mama. Mama, I am here, I am your son, and I have not left you. Can you hear me, Mama? I am here, I have come back Mama. Mama?*" I could only understand the word Mama, nothing else. I stood utterly motionless as he started to pound his fists hard into the sun-baked soil. As he did so he wept loudly. It sounded like nothing I have heard before. He was wailing. I remember it was like an animal hurting and he was like a boy again, not a seventy-six-year-old man. He was just like a little boy, crying for his mother.

I stepped forward and was just about to kneel down beside him when something flashed up and started to take form in front me. It was as though a small, isolated mist was lifting. I remember I had to shake my head, I thought I couldn't possibly be seeing what I was seeing. As this mist cleared, there was the woman I had dreamt about, with the wild hair and clothes that looked like they had never belonged to her. She was standing behind my papa, and she was speaking in Polish, I could hear her. I remember saying, "*Bloody hell,*" out loud and feeling like some kind of vacuum was opening up around me and sucking the breath straight out of my lungs. It was like I couldn't get the air into myself quick enough and I started to feel faint. I kept shaking my head. I thought it would make her disappear, but it didn't. I watched as she bent down and placed a hand on Papa's head and said something in Polish that I didn't understand. *"My son, my beautiful son, I am with you always. I have not forgotten you, nor you forgotten me, I will wait for you, for you must understand you have never been and will never be motherless."* She never looked up at me and for a moment it was as though neither of them knew I was there. Then Papa started to speak and I wondered if he had heard her too. It sounded like he was replying. *"I know Mama, wait for me, wait for me; I will be with you soon."* At that, Papa stood up and saw that I was crying too. I was sobbing like I might never stop. He said this was what I needed to know about. That this was the most important place for me to know about and that under the soil was the body of my Great Grandmother, Rosa, that he himself had buried her there nearly sixty years ago after she was murdered by three German soldiers. He took both my hands in his and explained that she was a woman who could perform miracles; she could speak to the dead and could heal the ill and infirm by laying her hands on them. He said it was because of her that I am now floating out of my body at night. He said I had the gift of Rosalia and now I was blessed. I have to say at that point I wasn't feeling like I had been blessed. I felt more like I had been hit sideways by a ten ton truck.

When I walked over to the spot where Papa said my great grandmother was buried it was like the soil began to shift under my feet. I could feel it. It was like some kind of writhing, almost tumultuous energy, was seeping into the soles of my shoes and punching great holes into the bones of my legs. I thought I was going to fall over, my legs had gone so weak. I remember I started to feel physically sick as I began to realise then that something terrible had happened here. I knelt down and touched the soil with the palms of my hands.

"She's under there?"

"Yes. I put her there myself."

"Why did you need to bury her here? What happened here, Papa?"

"They came here, it was dusk and I was over there;" he pointed to a cluster of bushes amongst the undergrowth. "I had been out most of the afternoon, watching birds and trying to find new ones; I was always doing that, reporting back any new creatures of the wildlife to her. When I was on my way back I heard her screaming and started to run towards the house. Just at that they appeared and I had to crouch down to hide. I watched as three men in uniform dragged her out to here." He walked over to the middle of the path and knelt down. "Her knees were bleeding; they pulled her out of our little house by the hair. Then they held her head back and pointed a gun to her head and shot her square between the eyes."

"Oh my God! What about you, Papa, did they try and shoot you?"

"They never saw me, I was out of sight … I was a coward."

He hung his head and fell silent. We sat for a while in silence.

Something still didn't make sense to me.

"How did they find her away out here, I mean it really is the middle of nowhere?"

"Well I have given that a lot of thought also and I have had a theory for some time."

"You have?"

"Yes. You see it was very strange for someone to come to our house unless they had been told about my mother and her way of healing the sick."

"So you think someone told them where you were living?"

"Yes, I think I know just who that person would be, because, you see, and now what I am going to tell you might shock you, but you are an adult now, and I was not much older than you when it happened here. A woman came to the house and she was young. She was bleeding. Oh my goodness the blood was everywhere. My mother shouted to me to help her husband lift her into the house. My mother was frantic, there was blood on everything. We lifted her onto the table so my mother could look, it was between her legs, and her baba was dying, too soon to be born. My mother worked so hard to stop all the blood coming, but it was no use, there was already too much bleeding before she came to my mother. The young woman died in our kitchen."

"Oh my God!" I had put my hands up to cover my gaping mouth, but my eyes must have looked like they had come out on stoppers.

"Her husband was screaming at my mother, and banging his head hard off the stone wall. So hard I thought he would crack his head wide open. My mother was crying; she was exhausted. Everything was a mess, so much blood on everything. Then the man, he lifted his dead wife and took her out to the horse and cart and went, shouting that my mother was a murderer."

"So you think he told them, he told the Germans?"

"When I was in the forest, Vladick told me about people who were living in Krakow pretending to be Polish but who were actually Germans. He called them the German Minority; they were tricking the people into getting information. Information about people they didn't want to be in Krakow. People they wanted to get rid of so they could take power. So they found out where people like the bankers, the lawyers and the teachers lived and they went and murdered them. I think that man told the German Minority about my mother." Then he turned to me and said, "I wonder now knowing everything I know, and everything the world knows, if she was lucky, and I was luckier still. If she wasn't shot, I wouldn't be here and neither would you; my mother and I would undoubtedly have been taken to Auschwitz, and been worked and starved to death."

"I thought they just took Jewish people."

"No! Bah! They took anyone they didn't like. Second to Jews came gypsies. Oh my goodness I have read about this, and there were a lot of gypsies in Auschwitz."

"I didn't know that."

"I know this. But no to worry, you are not the only one."

"So your mum was a proper gypsy then?"

"Roma. That is what they were, and still are – The Roma."

"Roma? So there must have been more than just you and your mum?'

"Well now, there was, but my mother, well she had given birth to me and was not married, so they just cut her off. Just like that! Phew!"

"Was she from a big family?"

"I don't know. She didn't ever talk about them much. I think sometimes she was very lonely though." He let out a huge sigh. "She had to pay a big price for me, huh?"

"She was brave, wasn't she?" I laid the palms of my hands on the soil again.

"She was. She was the bravest of any woman I have known, or man for that matter."

"Did my mum know about all this?"

"I used to fear for your mother and her cards and her dreams and her stories of seeing ghosts and shadows. I worried she was cursed too, like my mother, like this *thing* is a curse and so I never told her the truth. I am ashamed of myself."

He looked so vulnerable, not like my strong papa that yesterday felt like he had conquered the world when he arrived at the salt mines. "Now I see you, Anna, and I cannot avoid it anymore. I have been running from it since the day I laid my mother down here in the ground and now I see that I can't escape it; first my mother, then my daughter, now you."

"Do you think I must be cursed?"

"No, no, no! My goodness no!"

"How can you be sure that something hellish isn't going to happen to me now?"

"I just am. I think I had to stop running away from it. We all have to stop running away from it."

"Did my mum try to run away from it?"

"No, but I made her turn away from it."

I was starting to see the parallels and I didn't like it. From what I could understand, my great-grandmother and my mother were both 'psychic', if we must use that term, and they both died, or moreover were killed by someone else. You will understand these were not the most comforting of thoughts for an eighteen-year-old. I began to wonder if I too was 'cursed', to use Papa's word for it.

"I'm scared I'll be next," I blurted out.

"Don't be Anna, if we were all cursed then I wouldn't be here, would I?"

"But you're not like us."

"Who says I am not?"

"What do you mean?"

"What do you think I mean?"

"I think you mean that you are saying that you are like us... I mean, like me and my mum, and your mum?"

"Yes." There was a slow exhalation of air from him and then slowly he drew himself up onto his knees and then to his feet and stood in front of me. "Yes, that is exactly what I am saying to you." I remember there was an eerie silence and it seemed as though all the birds that had been singing had stopped as though they were waiting high on their leafy branches to hear better what he was about to say.

"What are you saying, Papa? That you can see these ghosts?"

"Yes... sort of". He moved his head to the side slightly as though he had a pain in his neck and needed to stretch it out.

"Do you have dreams and come out of your body and stuff like that?" I was still sitting, screwing my eyes up against the sun as I looked up towards him. He looked up into the trees, not really making eye contact with me. Although I couldn't say he was avoiding eye contact, he was deliberating. It was apparent he was trying to choose his words carefully.

"Yes… yes I suppose I do, but not in the same way you do."

For a moment I didn't believe him. I thought he was just trying to placate me. Then he told me something that left me stunned.

"My dear Anna, I have been watching the shadows follow your every move since you were a baba. I have been listening to their guidance, I can hear their talk of you; sometimes it's clear, sometimes it's like a distant babbling as though I am overhearing a private conversation. Not a day goes by that I am not listening to the words of someone who I can't see, and no, no I am not mad, no I have not lost my mind, for like you they can tell me of forthcoming events, that I have learned to simply sit and wait for." He sighed as though defeated. "Well, I cannot change them, these events, can I – look at your mother. If knowing of that, meant I could have changed that, then of course I would have. That is not why I am told of such things. To be honest I don't know why I am told; for there is nothing I can do except wait. So all my life since my mother was killed I sit, I listen, I wait. This is how I survive my journey to Scotland."

"You knew about my mum, I mean what was going to happen to her?" This was a staggering revelation. Suddenly I wasn't interested in the journey to Scotland anymore. I can remember deliberating over what I had just been told, and thinking to myself – *If I understand him correctly, he has just revealed that he had a premonition my mum would die.*

"I knew something terrible was coming." He hung his head.

I was so confused that initially I wanted to beat him hard for not doing something, anything, to stop the accident and save her and then I looked at him and I could see the pain etched on his face and I began to feel truly sorry for him. Imagine knowing that something like that was about to happen and not be able to stop it. At that point it was like I could feel the cogs turning in my head; something was starting to click into place about just what exactly it might mean to be 'psychic'.

I fell silent for a time, just staring at the ground. The ground was covered in a thick bed of dried out dark copper leaves left from the previous autumn. When I looked up, there ahead of me stood row upon row of tall silver birches that I hadn't really taken notice of until then, because I had been concentrating on what had happened here, but it was just like my dream. I knew then that I was meant to be here. This was not an accident. I was meant to be here and I had to listen to Papa. This was important. I was aware Papa had turned away from me and was standing, staring into the woods. When I looked up, she was there again, the woman with the wild hair and eyes like deep pools. She was standing behind Papa, facing the woods too.

"*My son, my son, I am with you always.*" Again she spoke in Polish so I could not understand what she was saying to him. Papa didn't look round but replied in hushed tones, again he replied in Polish.

'Mama, forgive me, I am not as strong as you. And Martha, my beautiful girl, please stay with us. Stay and help us. Help Anna.'

Although I didn't know what he had said I could make out my mum's name somewhere in the middle of it and my name at the end. Then the woman lifted her hand and stroked the back of his head gently, as though he was her infant son again. The hairs on my back began to stiffen and the skin across my body began to tighten as though it was shrinking. I watched as something began to take form beside my papa. It was not as clear as the woman, it was blurred and without definite outline. I couldn't tell if it was something or someone. The air seemed to change too. It seemed to be becoming thicker and I was aware of a strange smell. After a few seconds I realised it was the smell of freshly cut grass. I looked around and no-one was around us, and there was certainly no-one cutting grass anywhere near us. Instinctively I closed my eyes and as I inhaled this smell, it triggered something like a flicker in the front of my brain, as an image of a lopsided car flashed in front of me. It was as though the inside of my head had turned into a slide show, with the front of my head acting like the projector screen. This image of an upside-down car popped up in the front of my head like it would if it were on a television screen. The instant I opened my eyes, it all disappeared. I shut my eyes again and it was gone; nothing there at all. When I opened my eyes again, Papa had turned and was watching me. I noticed his eyes were wet, as though he might have been crying again.

"Can you smell that, Papa?"

"What is it?" He knelt down in front of me, as though he could smell it and was searching himself for the source.

"It's like grass that has just been cut, can you smell it?"

"No, Anna, I cannot".

"I can smell it, it's stronger when my eyes are closed and for a moment there when my eyes were closed I saw a car, on its roof, all buckled over, leaning onto its side."

"Have you seen this car before?"

"No, and when I opened my eyes and then shut them again, it had gone. That was weird."

"Not as weird as you might think, Anna."

"Not as weird as that woman either?"

"Woman?"

"There was a woman beside you when you were standing over there." I pointed in the direction of the trees.

"I know."

"You do?"

"Yes."

"Can you see her too?"

"No, but I can feel her nearby and if I keep really, really quiet I can hear her."

"I heard her too."

"You did?"

"I did. I swear, and I saw her as clear as ever."

"Well then, my precious Anna, you are truly blessed as you have now seen and heard your Great-Grandmother Rosalia."

"Really?" I got up to my feet and brushed the dry soil from my backside. There were so many thoughts at that point that were tumbling around in my head. Mainly *What the bloody hell is happening to me? What is this thing, this bloody weird thing, this 'psychic' thing?* I would say I was in a state of persistent disbelief. As far as I was concerned, whatever this *thing* was, it was starting to seem more like a curse than any kind of gift. And having watched Papa that afternoon, I wasn't feeling all that 'blessed' as he had put it. So I just stood there, perfectly still in front of him, waiting for him to explain things a bit further. As I did so, he just smiled and nodded as though something along the way that afternoon had met with his approval.

"So you see you have seen your great-grandmother just as I told you you would".

"Not exactly though."

"No… not exactly."

Then, with his hands in his pockets he turned towards the dirt track and began to make his way back to the main road. As I followed him I thought of my dad. When I did I felt a sense of heaviness in my chest. I realised that for the first time since we had arrived in Poland I was really missing him. At that point I thought that nothing else could surprise or shock me again in my life-time. I was gob-smacked, it was as though all the events of that week, and that day especially, had turned the world as I knew it onto its head.

Part Three

I

Honestly, whenever Anna tells that story of her trip to Poland it's always completely compelling. Each time she makes everyone laugh, makes everyone cry, and then laugh again. It's a fascinating story. Not least the tales of her own travels she now takes in Poland, but those of her papa and his incredibly heroic escape from the Nazis; although Henryk will always testify he was a coward. It was ironic then that just as this journey was changing everything for Anna, there was also a dramatic change unfolding simultaneously one thousand miles away back home in Galashiels.

Ruth had accepted an invitation from Mick to meet with her for dinner on the Saturday night before Anna and her papa were due to return home. If Ruth were able to recall it I'm sure she would tell you it had really been quite a strange day: strange in that nothing quite turned out as she had planned, or thought it would be when she had woken up that morning. Literally every turn that she took that day either delivered a surprise or an almighty shock. Having read through the letters she had written to her mum yet again, Ruth was bracing herself for a date with Mick. It was her first date in over a decade, so it seemed timely therefore that on that day she found a poem she had written many years ago. It was a poem she had originally written in an attempt to express what she felt about Mick all those years ago.

There's something quite spookily prophetic about this little poem I wrote a long time ago. I found it amongst the letters to my mum. I can remember dabbling in poetry, thinking I was really intellectual because I could make things rhyme. What a laugh. Seriously though, what an idiot I was. Anyhow this is one that I still think of as important, as I wrote this when I was still sixteen but almost seventeen years old. At the time I believed that 'almost being seventeen' gave me a license to broaden my horizons. It was a 'broadening' which occurred on a daily basis, and really just meant I pushed every one of the boundaries my dad set until he eventually became exhausted with me and gave up. Mick had walked home with me from the town one afternoon. He said he had been meaning to come and see me for a while. He told me he'd been thinking about me a lot. He was having a party for his twenty-first, and asked me if I wanted to go. I remember thinking, *'Oh my God, oh my God, I can't believe my luck,'* and feeling as though the sheer excitement might just strangle the life right out of me. It was like the inside of my head had turned to candyfloss, being whipped around on a long stick that kept my head detached from my body for quite some time; years really, even now.

Anyhow, when I went to the party, he wasn't there. I felt like a fool. Like the stupid wee tart my dad had called me years earlier. Then, as I vividly remember it, I met Mick on my way home; he was walking Martha Rosiewicz home. I felt utterly betrayed. I remember having actual pain in my chest when I saw her with him. He looked right at me. I thought my knotted insides were going to spew out onto the pavement. Now when I read this poem, 'Lovesick', although it's a bit contrived and self-indulgent, I realise I never sorted out what happened there. Why on earth did he ask me, not turn up, and then walk someone else home? Although I wasn't quite seventeen, the pain I felt after passing them that night has been a defining moment in my life. To be honest I have made a lot of hasty decisions based on how I was left feeling that night. Not once did I ever suspect it might be somehow linked to the hurt I tried desperately not to feel at losing my mum.

I suppose that's what is commonly termed 'denial'.

LOVESICK

Is this love
Stabbing into my heart?
Do I feel love's blunt blade
Twisting my insides apart?
Is love the vacuum
That sucks out my brain
Feeds my psychosis
And drives me insane?
Is that love that gnaws
At the seams of my life?
That plunders my days
And lengthens my nights?
Is it love that silently steals
Away with my breath?
Quashing my words,
And tightening this noose
Around my neck?

By her own admission, Ruth would state that the memories she has of growing up are a confusing mixture of times when she felt unconditionally loved, punctuated by brief periods of hunger, when money was tight and food was short, with longer periods of extreme loneliness, with confusion and anguish sifting through everything. She wondered once, that if she were to describe her growing-up years as some kind of life recipe with all of the above as her ingredients, then her mother's illness would have been the one ingredient that was slowly and methodically folded in along with everything else, binding all the crap together – with a stiff glue-like mixture of anger, resentment, disappointment and grief. When the finished product was 'turned out' at seventeen it, or rather she, had all the elements of being completely screwed up already. So it probably comes as little surprise that she is prone to hasty decisions, like walking out on her job, leaving her home and uprooting herself. It's a pattern she's tried before.

Now, having been back in Galashiels for nearly two full months, she was trying to convince herself that she had no regrets, that her impulsive move was instinctive and definitely the right thing to do, despite the fact that she hadn't realised, or even made an indent into, all of the hopes and desires she had deemed as integral reasons for returning home. For example, she hoped she could at some point decide what she would like to do as a career. Whilst she had no regrets at leaving her job, she was becoming frustrated at not being able to find another one. It had never been her intention not to work and the 'holiday phase' of not working had long passed. She had lost count of the books she had read. She wasn't a television fan and had long tired of the radio. She made endless lists of alternative jobs she might possibly pursue after considering transferable skills. The most interesting list of skills was the one which included her unique ability to make her thumbs bend backwards as though they were made of elastic. She could also juggle up to four random objects, her current record being for two minutes and ten seconds. That record was proudly held for juggling a small toy car, an orange, a tennis ball and a little ring box. The most surprising item on this particular list was that she had perfected the art of eating jalapeno peppers without her eyes watering. (Although when they came out the other end it was a different matter entirely.) According to this list, Ruth deduced she had only to brush up her trapeze and fire-eating skills and she could then run off with the Bangkok Circus when it next pitched up in the Edinburgh Meadows for the festival season.

Rob's reaction to this list was just to stick to reality. He often worried about Ruth and the way she would let her mind wander off on tangents, almost delusional at times, which have resulted in a few close shaves in the past. He was never a risk-taker himself, which is surprising when you consider he was a gay man living in an area of the world ruled by the game of rugby: a world which is often overrun with blatant misogynists, and punctuated with frequent displays of rampant, and at times aggressive, homophobic testosterone. To be honest it was probably the single most prevalent part of living in the Borders which has always made Ruth cringe. Her scathing opinion on Rugby however was definitely a minority view, but it was a fixed and unfaltering one. In fact it was almost like she had a phobia of men in general. It was also becoming apparent that after two months of being back home it was unlikely she was going to suddenly bang into the imaginary love of her life, and what, she wondered, would she do if she did? She was beginning to realise that she had formed an opinion of the elusive Mr Munroe in her mind that, whilst it was based on a distant memory, it was a reality that was entirely constructed thereafter within the confines of her fertile imagination. If she submitted herself entirely to the truth, she could feel the panic of uncertainty rising within her. So she clung to her daydreams like she was suspended from some kind of emotional cliff edge, waiting to be wrenched to the surface by Mick, the hero. It was all but driving her around the proverbial bend when she received a call on a Friday night about a book she had ordered.

She went to collect the book on a Saturday morning. It was August and there was a light drizzle in the air. A drizzle the sun would burn a hole in later in the morning, making way for a good few hours of unbroken sunshine and nippy, painfully burnt shoulders; for some reason sunshine accompanied with heat always seems to come as a complete surprise to Scots.

To make her way to the book shop, Ruth took a short walk along Bank Street. She remembers that although it was early, maybe nine, there were already people dotted about the gardens of Bank Street, watching their world go by. Everything, absolutely everything, moved slower than it did in the city; indeed that morning she too ambled along, taking her time. It was a relatively short walk and on route Ruth thought about all her other little walks she had been treating herself to lately in and around Galashiels. The Beechy Woods were her favourite. These woods spanned a mile and a half in their length, occupying the margins of the full length of the north-east of the Langlee housing scheme where she grew up. The woods grew behind the scheme, whilst also spanning a divide between the scheme and the 'posh' houses that lined the route into the town along 'The Melrose Road'.

At this time of year the huge hedges of brier in those woods were in full bloom and were full of bees buzzing so loudly they sounded like high-energy electric fences.

Once under the canopy of the trees in The Beechy Woods she would also stand completely still and listen for the fevered tapping of the invisible woodpeckers.

Often at this time of year, when there had been frequent very heavy rainfalls – 'thunder plumps' as the older residents would refer to them – she was acutely aware she could actually smell and taste the greenery awash with rain; the ferns, the hollies, the rhododendrons and the sodden clay-like mud squelching underfoot – it all had a distinct smell and taste when it had rained.

On one of her walks the week before, the atmosphere was so heavy, humid and electrically charged that the air seemed to attract and trap grit up from the soil, and mould from the old bark that littered the pathways. When she was strolling in the woods that day, she believed she could roll the taste of The Beechy Woods over on her tongue.

They were really old woods and some of the tree trunks were twisted and gnarled to the point that they looked like they wore the faces of very, very old men. When she was a young child and was taken for walks in these woods with her mum, she always noticed the old men in the trees. When she was little she felt like she was being watched by them, and it gave her the creeps. While her mum was happy wandering around noticing everything and trying to show her things, Ruth couldn't wait to get out of the woods. Now when she returned to the woods as an adult, she felt as though she wanted to say 'hello' to the old men in the trees as though they might have been old friends. Old friends that were still there, waiting for her to return, friends that hadn't changed: friends that had just waited faithfully for her.

It often occurred to her that in reality, friends like that were rare indeed. In fact it would be true to say that Ruth was becoming fairly suspicious of people who were not just friendly, but polite or courteous towards her. This paranoia was seeping quietly into her subconscious state and day by day was gathering momentum. It was becoming more apparent in her lack of ability to trust, really trust people, or trust anything that could not be controlled by her.

Walking filled Ruth with a sense of freedom. Freedom she could control. She could let her mind wander into territory way beyond the boundaries of her reality. It didn't really matter what time of day or night it was either. If she decided that was what she needed, then off she went for a walk in her alternative world. Only last week she was out walking in the Beechy Woods early. It was really early – four in the morning. Luckily it was a nice morning. I suppose you could say summer's a good time of year for a breakdown. Problem was, Ruth hadn't fully realised that that what was happening to her yet. When she chose to walk these woods, she believed it was time to think, time to reflect and time to plan. She didn't see it as a wander into a fantasy world. She believed that every one of these walks had purpose.

Recently she had taken a walk just like this, really early, just before five, after yet another sleepless night. Off she went to connect with the countryside, like some kind of Mother Earth, believing this would keep her sane, level-headed.

The walk was a few miles from Galashiels. She wanted to have a look at a new housing development that had sprung up like a mushroom from the ruins of the old Peel Hospital, an old military hospital tucked away in the valley of steep pine-filled woodland outside the village of Clovenfords.

Ruth had parked at the little-known picnic spot of Peel Burn. It was a small, secluded area with a little stream, completely protected by surrounding trees. From there it was a very short uphill walk to the Peel Hospital site. It had been over twenty years since she had been on the single track tarmac road that leads to the old hospital site. She found it was largely unchanged; still lined with huge, drooping rhododendrons on the left, with the river Tweed on the right beyond a long, flat green haugh. As she walked up towards the hospital site, she imagined she could smell the disinfectant, and she worried for a moment that she might be met by the straight-backed nurses in their stark uniforms with their hats firmly attached to their heads like starched napkins; then she remembered the last time she saw her mum.

She had kissed her goodbye after what had seemed like a normal Friday evening visit, but this time whilst she hugged her mum, one of the nurses pulled Ruth away, telling her that she needed to rest. She remembers the skin on her mum's cheek felt cold, wet, and altogether a bit strange when she had pressed her lips to it. That is the last memory Ruth has of her mum: the smell of disinfectant, the starch, the upright defiant nature of the nurse, her mum's cold clammy skin, and how she felt her own skin smart across her shoulders from the tight grip the nurse had on her. She can't remember where her dad and brother were. Try as she might she cannot remember if her mum smiled or not, or if she looked happy, sad, worried, or indifferent. In fact she only imagines what she might have looked like. She imagined then that her mum smiled at her and might have cried, but she wasn't sure about the crying part. It was at this point on her way to the old hospital site that Ruth realised she had never actually considered what her mum might have been feeling, or her dad; instead, always, always, she had only ever considered what she had been left feeling like. She began to quietly berate herself – *what the hell have I been like? For God's sake.* She began to feel a sense of urgency to try and sort out some of this, she decided the first thing she would have to do was to go back and see her dad.

Some of the thoughts about her mum did make her laugh at herself though. Especially the one when she thought that our glands must be another part of our bodies that have teeth. She thought this because she had heard people saying the cancer was in her glands, and that it was eating away at her. For a child this was a fairly graphic description and it left Ruth with a disturbing image that parts of her mum's body were actually chewing into herself.

The thought of it all, and more specifically her memories of the last night she ever saw her mother at this hospital, made her chest seem like it had been placed in a vice, and for a moment she felt her breathing stall. Feeling quite giddy, she reached over and clutched onto a stone from the dyke that lined her path, pausing for a second to steady her nerves. When she caught her breath and turned into the old Peel Hospital site, she was astonished to see the housing development almost finished. It was a development that was akin to a Hollywood street set. At that point she thought to herself – *someday soon, someone will buy one of these houses and will live and sleep on the spot where my mum died.*

Seeing some of the older women sitting in Bank Street Gardens, the morning she ambled along to the book shop, had made her think of that day she had walked to the old Hospital site, and of the fact that she believed her mother had been robbed of a life, dying at thirty-five years old. She was preoccupied with this thought when she arrived at the book shop. As the door to the shop opened, it triggered a little bell that sounded like an old-fashioned phone ringing. She couldn't remember hearing that the last time she visited.

Initially there was no-one there, no-one at the front where Ruth remembered handing her phone number to the girl who had struck a chord with her. She was just wondering if she would see her again today, and maybe unravel the mystery of why she seemed to be familiar, when her attention was drawn to movement and some muffled, half-choked coughing to the rear of the shop. When she looked around it was as though the world as she knew it had tilted off its axis. It was not what or who she was expecting at all. There, emerging sheepishly from a room at the rear of the shop was Mick Munroe. She remembers thinking as she gasped for breath that his face was so red he looked liked he must have been slapped.

Mick was surprised at just how shocked he was. He could feel his face burn. He thought he had prepared himself for the possibility that the woman who had ordered *Sappho* might be *the* Ruth Nairn.

Anna and Henryk had been in Poland for three days when Mick decided that he would eventually call the number Anna had handed him. It had been some time since she had enquired of the small book of poetry. In fact he had taken so long to pluck up the courage, he believed she would almost certainly have acquired the book elsewhere.

Since Anna left for her birthday trip, Mick had been for a few extremely long walks, and when he had been at home he had played music so loud the old single pane windows in the house had been rattling. He had never realised just how quiet the house would be if Anna wasn't around. If he was being honest with himself he would admit he was struggling with the separation, even though it was fairly brief – a total of only five days. You see Mick and Anna had never been apart since the accident for that length of time. She had never gone on lengthy school excursions, or stayed over friends' for more than one night. Whilst he had always believed he was doing the right thing, he was now realising he had only made it harder for himself in the long run.

Take the day she and Henryk had left for Poland, for example; he was overwhelmed with a feeling of nausea, and feared he would cry in front of them. After dropping them at the airport he tormented himself almost masochistically, with the thoughts that should their plane go down, he would never see her again, and for a time it almost drove him mad.

He had spoken to her each day in the morning before they set off for their activities for that day, as meticulously planned by Henryk. He did wonder how his daughter would be coping with his kind of disciplined organisation; organisation that demanded at the very least that she leave her bed each morning before nine. He also wondered how she would cope with the planned visit to the countryside area where Henryk had been born. It was something Henryk had discussed at length with Mick. Henryk's reasons for needing to go were fairly obvious. Initially Mick struggled to agree that this exposure to the terrible events of the past would be beneficial for Anna, because that was just how he was, protective, but Henryk persisted and eventually it was added to the official schedule. Henryk's fine detailed planning of the visit had been so precise that Mick would often laugh and comment that it was as though he was planning a Papal visit.

Despite his reservations of what Anna might or might not be able to cope with, he heard nothing in the tone of her voice to suggest that she was not actually enjoying herself. So much so he felt a small seedling of hurt begin to grow in his gut at the thought that she might actually be able to manage without him, and he thought to himself, *'If she doesn't need me then what's the point in being here?'* It was precisely this kind of deliberation that gave him a push, until finally he plucked up the courage to call the number on the scrap of paper that he had been carrying around. Mick had held onto the scrap of paper for such a long time that the name and the contact number were almost illegible. All the while having convinced himself it would definitely not be *The*, with a capital T, Ruth Nairn, as he believed he could never be so lucky. Could he?

He dialled the number. After only a couple of rings a woman answered. Mick did not say who he was, merely that he was calling from the book shop in Galashiels that she had visited recently, and that the book she had enquired of, 'Sappho, The Everyman Collection Of Poetry' was in stock, should she wish to call in and collect it.

He had purposefully chosen a cool, collected approach: 'Approach A', as opposed to 'Approach B', a gushing 'is it really you?' approach, which he was certain would have ended in a mutual form of heightened embarrassment. She replied courteously that she would and was grateful that he had taken the trouble to call back. When he hung up, he felt exhausted. He had built himself up so much prior to the call, and expended so much emotional energy on preparing himself for it, that it had left him drained. What he found more frustrating was that despite repeating her reply over and over in his head, he couldn't tell for sure from the brief reply if it was The Ruth Nairn. When he hung up, he immediately wished he had chosen approach 'B'. At least it might have gotten the whole gushy mushy dewy-eyed bit out of the way before he actually met her face to face. As it turned out, neither of his official approaches would have made any difference. Much to his astonishment he had melted into a wobbling, blushing mess that could have been mistaken for drooling, as soon as he saw her.

When the shop door had opened and rung with its familiar trill he remembers he stood up to come out to the shop front, when he saw her standing at the desk. She had her back to him, and although her petite frame had filled out a little, in his mind there was absolutely no mistaking that hair. It was as though he became almost spellbound as he registered the sight of that unmistakable deep copper hair falling across her shoulders in long ringlets. It is fair to say it left him badly weakened, so much so he feared he might collapse in a heap as his legs seemed to lose all muscular control of themselves. There was no mistaking it was *The* Ruth Nairn; he knew he had never seen anyone since she left the town with such perfectly formed ringlets. So perfect, they hung from her head like bedsprings. As the realisation of this smashed into him like a huge wave of warm water, he became aware of his heart racing. You have to realise this was a man whose heart had never leapt past sixty beats a minute in over a decade, so it all came as bit of a surprise to him. Deafened by the pounding in his neck and staggered by the lack of strength in his legs he caught sight of himself in a window pane, only then to see the deep red glow that was slowly rising up over his neck and across his face.

When she turned round and looked him in the eye it was as though everything else around him had completely evaporated, and they were the only two living people left in the world. Something, somewhere clicked as Mick began to feel something other than self pity. Something so different and unusual that he didn't really know what was happening to him. He became aware that some form of paralysis had swept over him. Was he really floating, or were his feet still firmly on the ground? Why could he not speak? Why did his tongue suddenly seem too big for his mouth? It was like the wiring in his brain had short-circuited, and every muscle and nerve in his body had stopped receiving all signals other than the ones that the sight of *The* Ruth Nairn standing in front of him, in his shop, were triggering.

As the front door of the shop closed behind her, it was as though the draft had pushed a soft pillow of scented air into his face. He stood with his mouth agape at the sight of her, and actually wondered for a moment if he could taste her. Nothing like this had ever happened to him.

Ruth smiled, not in a giggly coy way. No, it was simply a smile of quiet achievement, perhaps of closure. If she was utterly astounded and surprised to see Mick standing in front of her, she never showed it. She held herself in a dignified but almost steely composure. If she had the chance to recall that moment, she would probably say it was really just that she was dumbfounded and in disbelief. She was quite literally rooted to the spot.

Mick smiled back and could almost feel his pupils dilate to the point he feared he might be suffering a major brain haemorrhage. Ruth would tell you if she could that she can't really remember what she looked at, if she looked at his face, his eyes or his body; her mind, indeed everything of her consciousness had seemed to dissolve.

The silence seemed to last for an eternity before Mick eventually spoke.

"Ruth?"

"Mick?"

"I wondered if it was you. You know the note, the *Sappho*."

Ruth smiled. She could feel the colour rising in her cheeks as the feeling began to return to her legs. But it was as though they didn't belong to her. She steadied herself, placing one hand on the large old table by the door. Mick was starting to lose control of his tongue as it raced ahead of his brain.

"I wondered, and then I thought well it can't be, and what if it is, huh? My God, Ruth? 'N I wondered what if it was, but I never thought it actually would be. Shit. Ruth?"

"Well, it's me. Who'd have thought it, huh?" Ruth shrugged her shoulders. "You work here?"

"Yeah, you could say that."

"Didn't expect to find you here, you never liked books that much."

"No I didn't, funny eh?" It didn't occur to him that she might even have been looking for him.

"Music?"

"Oh still into my music, yeah, absolutely!"

"Still play guitar?"

"No. I was shit at that. No, I listen to music mainly, 'n read, believe it or not. I read a lot, when I get peace to that is. Anna, you know." He nodded as though she would understand what life with a teenager was like, and half wanted to explain that reading was his No. 1 'Escape'. He decided not to expand, as that would beg the question *'escape from what?'*, and he couldn't bear having to explain away the last fourteen years if she hadn't already heard. Although he presumed she must have. Edinburgh's not exactly the other side of the world. It's just up the road. In truth though, she had no idea who Anna was, or what his life had been like since she left.

"Yeah. That's good," she answered as though she had understood the troubles of single parenting, without actually knowing that that was what he was referring to. In fact, she thought Anna must be his wife, or partner. At that moment her insides seemed to turn to rock, and she felt heavy. The emptiness of everything she felt at that second walloped into her. There was an awkward pause, before Mick turned to go to his office to collect her book, emerging seconds later with the *Everyman Collection Of Sappho's Poetry* in his outstretched hand.

"You haven't changed." He watched as she reached for the book. He found himself checking for a ring, there wasn't one.

"Funnily enough, neither have you." She smiled, and when she did, it was as though she had swallowed him whole. He felt like she had snared him with some kind of invisible undercurrent. If you were to ask him about this moment at any later date, all he would probably say on the matter is that *'it felt good'*.

"Haven't seen you in town for a long time – years?" Ruth simply nodded in agreement at the statement, as something huge and tangible inside her began to lessen and loosen its grip on her.

"Thank you for the book." She reached into her bag. He raised his hand to indicate she needn't pay.

"No, I insist." She paid and left. The shop door closed, triggering the trill of the bell, and as it did so it was as though an alarm had just gone off in his head. He ran from the shop to try and catch her, but she had gone. "Shit, shit, shit!" If that was what being swept off your feet is like, or bowled over by someone, then Mick realised that that was what had happened there. It was something that he had never experienced before. You see his relationship with Martha was a relationship of default. Yes he did, in time fall in love with her, deeply in love for that matter. But at the start there was no bowling over, no blown away, no swept off his feet back then. Quite simply, Martha had turned up at his twenty-first and Ruth hadn't.

When Ruth left the shop, book in hand and heart in mouth, she was confused and perplexed by how she had been left feeling after seeing Mick. It had been the moment she had long dreamt of, but it had not gone according to the plan she had formulated and visualised. After just a few short minutes in his company she realised she didn't actually know him. For instance, he didn't play guitar. How could this be? She had imagined he sat cross-legged of an evening writing his own songs, strumming along to his favourite music. Then there's the matter of the books. She had never remembered him as a person with his nose firmly embedded between the covers of a good novel. In fact she couldn't remember ever seeing him with a book. Then the hair or lack of it now, all the tousled locks had gone. She found his scalp on view a bit strange, uncomfortable even, especially when accompanied by a bright red blushing face. Then there was this Anna woman. Was that his wife or partner? Ruth realised that as she had been waiting for the time she would meet him again, stupidly she had constructed this reality where somehow he would be single, as if waiting on her to return. But he clearly hadn't, no, because he mentioned Anna. As she strode along Bank Street, there was the recollection of what her brother had said about getting the 'wee polish girl pregnant'. Up until the reality check that was a visit to a book shop, she had conveniently stored that piece of information as irrelevant. Now having met Mick, it came flooding back. There was something about the way that Robert had said it: 'Got her pregnant'. It was a statement that doesn't conjure images of a love affair, more of a mechanical insemination, which wasn't all that endearing. Regardless of the matter of the conception, Ruth now wondered if Mick was a father too, and it was at that point on her way home, quite literally only minutes away from the encounter of her dreams, that she felt everything that she had returned for had amounted to nothing. It was time for closure, and she really felt as though she could quite literally hear the door to what she had dreamt was the rest of her life, slamming shut in her face. "What a bloody fool," she actually said out loud as she went along the street. She was starting to talk to herself.

*

Just over an hour had passed and Mick hadn't thought of Anna and Henryk once. It was only ten o'clock and he was locking up for the morning; turning the key in the lock, checking the alarm had activated, checking his watch, it was only ten o'clock. He was checking the road was safe to cross, checking the weather, checking the street for familiar pedestrians, but he was aware of nothing. It was only ten o'clock and not only had he been on automatic pilot since those glossy spirals of red locks had swept out beyond his shop door, he had in fact become utterly consumed with Ruth and everything about her. He went over and over every gesture, every mannerism, the smile, the teeth, that bloody fantastic hair, and most inviting of all, no ring on her finger. Arriving at his front door he had no recollection of how he got there. He had completely forgotten about the shop and the fact that it was Saturday, his busiest day normally. He was completely distracted. He could hear the phone ringing from the other side of his front door. Could it be Ruth? Already? *Shit where are my bloody keys, shit. Keys for Christ's sake. Shit, it's gonna ring off, it's gonna ring off, shit!*

II

When Anna hung up, she sensed something was different. Something in his voice had changed. She couldn't put her finger on it, but it was as though her dad was anxious to end the call. This was very unusual. Anna knew it was always she who had to force his hand to end their calls.

"How is he?" Henryk was studying the tourist's guide to Wawwel Castle and planning their last day in Krakow. They were due to fly home early the next day. This was his final day of their trip, and he knew he would most likely never be back. He acknowledged that Anna was young enough to return if she desired to do so. He envied the thought of that; that she had time and that time allowed her the freedom of choice. However, he made bargains with each day; if I am still alive at the end of the day I will do this, or I will do that, I will apologise to him, I will make sure I sort that. On this occasion he felt he had kept his side of the bargain: i.e. *if you* (his God, as he believed it to be) *allow me to live long enough to gather the strength I need, I would agree to go back. As soon as I am strong enough in my head I will go back and see my mother.*

It had taken most of sixty years to be 'strong enough'. Now with that done, he felt it in his bones that he was making his plans to say goodbye that day. Goodbye to his beloved country, goodbye to his beloved mother. The difference was that this time it was on his terms.

Anna watched him study the tourist guide of Wawwel, his pen in hand, his list for the day being carefully put to paper.

"Don't know if my dad's all right today. Do you think he will be okay, Papa?"

"Well Anna, he is most likely missing you with a heavy heart."

"And you too."

"What? Me? I don't think so. I am not his beautiful daughter!"

Whenever her papa spoke of her in such endearing terms her heart filled with enormous pride. He wasn't looking right at her though, like he would normally when making such observations, he was studying his map again.

"Today we will walk along the banks of the Vistula. When I am looking at this there is a path for us, all the way along from here," he pointed to the map, "to here." He laid his glasses down on the end point of what would be their journey that day. "It will take us past Wawwel and along past the Prodgórzé district. From there we can go to the old Jewish quarters for a walk around." He nodded in agreement with himself. Anna sensed his walk around the old Jewish district would be more of an inspection than a visit.

"My dad was a bit quiet."

"What way?" Henryk poured himself a little cup of his tar-like coffee.

"Like he didn't want to speak." As she said this she felt a tight belt was being pulled into its buckle around her chest. "It was like he was in a hurry to get off the phone."

"Well maybe he had a customer". Henryk was aware that all the events of the previous day at his childhood home had been especially exhausting for her, and that to have stood on the site of his mother's murder, and his revelation of being psychic must have worn her out. He noticed the way she carried her shoulders lower that morning, the way she held her gaze downward, and how she blew out slow, wistful sighs without realising he was listening. It was evidence he believed, that she had become quite homesick. She wasn't just missing her dad, she realised she needed him. Needed his wise words and peculiarities, which were now more of a source of comfort to her than a burden.

"But I phoned him at home."

"Well maybe he was going to work and was worried he was going to be late, you know what he is like, always checking his watch and keeping good time for everything. He is a man who will never be late. No."

"Well he is late. He is, because it's half past ten and he's still at home. I just had this feeling to phone him at home. I knew he wasn't at the shop. It's Saturday, isn't it? Something's wrong, Papa, I can tell." She clasped her hand around the little brass compass in her pocket, praying for it to give her comfort by providing an imaginary route to her dad, as if to provide some form of mental link-up with him. She was rubbing it, willing it to do exactly as her papa had promised when he gave it to her. That it would always look after her, keep her safe and always guide her home. On this occasion she took the last part of this pledge quite literally, and imagined that all her thoughts and mental messages for her dad were being spirited across the planes of Northern Europe to Galashiels, by simply concentrating and rubbing her fingers across the lettering engraved upon the brass case of the compass.

"C'mon Anna. We shall go for a wee walk down to the square. Huh? And then along by the Vistula, it will be good. 'N you will see when you phone your dad later that he will be needing your chat, and he will be okay."

"It was just that he wasn't really listening, I don't think he was even listening to me."

"Well, tonight you can tell him all about the very tasty wee grilled sausage we will have, mm? And he will listen. Tell him about our wee, grilled tasty treat, huh?" He bent down, putting his arms gently around Anna trying to get her look to up at him. "Hah, c'mon, we can listen to the bugle caller for one last time, huh? Let me see you." He lifted her chin up with his index finger. Tears were welling like huge raindrops in the corners of her eyes. Slowly they crept down her cheeks. "Hah, now my angel, c'mon we will soon be home. Not long now. You will see he will be waiting for you. Maybe he too is very quiet with missing you. That's all. There will not be much wrong that you arriving home will not sort, and soon, very soon you will be home again." Hugging her, he kissed her forehead.

"Sorry, Papa."

"What on this earth can you be so sorry for?'

"I'm sorry for being upset."

"Will you stop saying this sorry word all these times?"

"I am though. I didn't mean to be upset. I didn't mean for you to think I'm not happy being here." The end of her sleeve glistened as she wiped aside the tears and mucus dripping from the end of her nose.

"Well let me tell you this – there was so much for you to pack into your little head from yesterday. From being where I was when I was same age as you, and from knowing now what I had to run from. When I think about it, all that I know, and what is going on in your head this minute, I think I could guess you will be having emotions that you are confused to."

Anna stared to giggle and cry at the same time, sending tears and huge bubbles of spit, and dribbles of snot spurting out onto her papa's shoulders.

"What? What is it that I say, is so funny, huh?"

Sniffing and continuing to wipe the end her nose on her sleeve, Anna replied, "It's just the way you say things."

"What? What?"

"Nothing, it's just you, Papa. You are just, just… well, different."

"Well, that's okay then. Now c'mon, let's go. I think your strange little papa is just a wee bit hungry. And what's more, with all this slavering you are spoiling my jacket.'

By the time they left their apartment and made their way towards the market square to find a prime spot to listen to the bugle caller for the last time, Anna had lifted her shoulders. With her eyes raised she was searching the skyline for the golden topped spires of St Mary's. There was a low mist hanging over the roof tops that lined their route to the square.

The mist seemed heavy, heavy enough to lock in the atmosphere around her. It hemmed in the sound of trams trundling along some way behind her. It muffled the sounds of the traffic heading down towards the square. It seeped into her hair, dragging with it the smell of the grills they were heading towards. She couldn't see the rooftops. She couldn't see the spires of St Mary's. It was as though Krakow had started to close in on her. She was looking forward to going home in the morning.

III

It was only a matter of ten hours ago that she had drifted into his shop after almost twenty years, and now he was sitting in front of her awaiting the menu and drinks. He could smell her across the table. It was a light, sweet scent, with a little hint of something spicy too, that wasn't evident as a constant or overpowering aroma. No, it was delicate and it seemed to drift gently across the table towards him in small wisps like invisible floss in the air. It was nothing he had ever been close enough to smell before. He felt as though he needed to nip himself.

It had all come about after he had grabbed the proverbial bull by the horns and called her back on the number he still had on the small corner of torn paper that she had plucked from her bag a few weeks' before and had given to Anna. To his complete surprise she had agreed to meet him that night. He could hardly believe it. His call had taken Ruth by surprise. She wasn't long home and had resigned herself to closing this particular door in her imagination behind her. She did find the conversation quite funny though. Funny strange – not funny ha ha.

"Ruth?"

"Uhuh?"

"Good morning. It's Mick Munroe here." He spoke in his business voice, it was habit. It was what he used when he spoke to anyone other than Henryk or Anna. It was a bit harsher in tone, with each word carefully clipped off at the end, keeping it all neat and tidy. Controlled. It was an approach he had developed over the years that kept the outside world outside. So you would hardly believe this was the same man who had gone all gooey and speechless only an hour before when she had stood in front of him in the shop. But that's the thing with real chemistry isn't it? When it happens, really happens, it's like a test tube melt-down. That's proper chemistry.

Funnily enough, despite her life plan, and her determination to seek out what she believed to be her future, she hadn't had the same meltdown as him. It was nowhere near the meltdown she had expected or dreamt it would be. So when she heard him on the phone, all she wanted to say was *I know it is. What do you want?* But there was something that seemed a bit curious as to why he would be phoning her; she only left the shop less than an hour ago, she had the book she had ordered in her hand and she had paid for it. To her surprise she became slightly coy, and perhaps a bit smug. *He's phoning me. Unusual, but good, perhaps.*

"How can I help you, Mick?"

"Well now, Ruth, I am just, I am just, just… wondering how you are."

"Well, Mick, thank you for asking. Funnily enough I'm just about the same as I was when I saw you about an hour ago."

"Good, good. That's good."

"I think so, I think that's good."

"I think so too. It's all good, isn't it?"

"I think it is."

"So, would it be okay if I asked you if you were free, maybe tonight?" He was completely overwhelmed by a sense of urgency.

"It would."

"Huh?"

"It would be okay if you asked me." Ruth hadn't decided at this point how she would answer that question though. She was wondering about this Anna, and who she was.

"Oh right. Right I see. Okay then. Are you free tonight?" *Shit what am I saying? I've just asked her out, oh shit, say no, say no, bloody hell, say yes, say yes.* It seemed like an eternity until she answered.

"Tonight?"

"Tonight."

"Well, I'm not sure if I'm free."

"Oh, okay then". Mick dissolved, gave in and gave up.

"Are you free?" She turned the question around, trying to get him to talk about this Anna woman.

"Me?" *Bloody hell, what does she think, of course I'm free! My whole bloody life's been so free it's empty, it's like a bloody mineshaft. Jesus.* It hadn't crossed his mind that she might know very little of his circumstances.

"You?" She was trying to get him to mention his commitments, what arrangement he might have to make.

"Of course I'm free, wouldn't have asked otherwise." He felt that sounded a bit petulant, and was starting to get a bit wary of this whole dating thing. He was starting to remind himself why he had stayed away from it for so long. There were so many bloody mind games. *Just answer my question; do you want to come out or not? It's easy. Straightforward really, either you do or you don't.*

"Then so am I." Ruth gave in.

"Good." He sighed with relief.

"Good," she agreed.

"What about Herge's, do you know where that is?"

"I do. Yes."

"Half seven?"

"Half seven," she echoed. It all seemed a bit like making an appointment at the dentists.

The whole day thereafter was torture for Mick. He thought it was like an eternity from half ten in the morning until half seven that night. The shop, his beloved shop, having been prematurely locked up, had remained closed and had been firmly put on the back burner for the day. It was really quite unheard of. It had never been closed on a Saturday since it opened. Even when he went to watch Anna play hockey, especially when she was paying in a cup game, Henryk always opened the shop. Closing up like this on a Saturday would be noticed and would certainly invite questions amongst the residents in the town. Although what anyone thought of him that day couldn't have been further from Mick's whirling mind. In the end, anyone who felt it their business to comment (and there's always one in any town) would probably put it down to Anna and Henryk being away and that Mick must be having difficulty managing without them.

They would never suspect he had been distracted from his shop by Ruth Nairn. Ruth Nairn, that poor wee soul that had lost her mother, only then to up sticks and abandon her father in his hour of need. What's more they would never suspect that what Mick was really having difficulty with was how to control his blatant, overwhelming, no bones about it, desire for her.

To prepare for his date, he didn't plan a shower, lay out his clothes or choose his cologne. No, he did what he knew best. He put on some music. Clothes, shower and all that dressing up to go out crap, as he would see it, could wait 'til later. Mick then spent the best part of the day preparing his opening line. He had practised several options, which were as follows:

Option 1: "You look stunning. It's so lovely to see you." *Oh fuck, that's far too cheesy.*

Option 2: "I just knew it was you, although you've put a bit of weight on." Whilst he wanted her to know he had been appreciating her figure, he deemed this one to be a bit risky.

Option 3: "How old are you now?" A huge risk.

He lay back and listened to his music, searching for inspiration, just as the opening bars of Whitesnake's *Lie Down* burst to life. "Oh, shit, that's no good!" He was talking to himself again.

It took some time for him to choose the right song. Indeed what should really have been something quite straightforward became an enormous task. He was aware he didn't want to choose one that would make him think of Anna, because he was really missing her, or worse still remind him of Martha. That would have thrown the whole idea of dating out the window. In fact, the very thought that he might be trying to avoid thinking about Martha turned his head like a corkscrew and brought him to a standstill. *I can't do this, I can't do it. I can't go.*

At the other side of the town, Ruth had gone to visit her dad as planned earlier in the day, to try again, just this one more time to build a bridge between them. On her way there, she wondered if she should have called Robert to ask him about Mick and get some background information before their date/appointment that evening, little knowing she was about to get it from her dad whether she liked it or not. It's worth noting too, that her dad wasn't about to deliver this information in the compassionate way Robert might have filled in the gaps.

Getting to her dad's was a walk of just over a mile from the town centre. It took her past a few old landmarks. She passed Our Lady and St. Andrew's Church, the one she went to as a child, before making her way up the Station Brae and past the F.E. college. She thought about how many times she and her dad had walked this route to and from church. She looked back and considered that the church really did occupy a most majestic location at the bottom of Station Brae. The F.E. college used to be the town's Academy when her dad was a youngster. Back then there were two high schools – The Academy, and the 'Roxy'. The Roxy was the secondary school for those that were not quite as bright, but better with their hands, whilst The Academy was reserved for the academic achievers. Her dad went to the Roxy. He was, before shattered by the loss of his wife, a hardworking man. He had had a good job as a foreman telephone engineer.

It took roughly twenty minutes to get to her dad's. When she got there she knocked and walked in, not waiting to be asked. She followed the heavy smog that hit her in the face. He was asleep in his chair. He looked for a moment like he had been gassed by the accumulation of smoke caused by his excessive smoking. Sports coverage chattered on in the background on the TV. She stood back and took a moment to look closely at him. She was unable to tell if he was sober or drunk, and what's more, predicting the mood he would wake up in was impossible. So she afforded herself a couple of seconds to brace herself for his onslaught before she gently shook his shoulder.

"Whatsehwhatsmm…" He was mumbling incomprehensibly and still seemed asleep. Just as she leant forward to give him another prod, he opened his eyes. "You?"

"Dad, how are you?"

"Fine 'til I was woken up."

"Sorry." She risked sounding a bit huffy as she hadn't really said sorry as though she meant it.

"Ee should be. What are 'ee wantin'?"

"Do I need to want something to come see you?" The conversation was beginning with all the trademarks of an impending argument before it had even really got started.

"Look dinnae be smart, hen. I'm watchin' the fitbaw; what are 'ee wantin'?" He strained his neck to look past her to the television.

She took a deep breath, stood up and, praying her jelly legs would carry her just a few steps, she walked over to the television and switched it off.

"What the bloody hell are 'ee dain? Put that back on!"

"No." She stared at him and thought she was going to faint with the terror of what he might unleash upon her.

Sucking air in through clenched teeth, he made to get up out of his chair. She held her breath, but despite his best fury-filled efforts he didn't get past pressing down on the arms of the chair. It became apparent then that he had also been sleeping off the morning's alcohol intake. She heaved a sigh of relief that he couldn't get himself out of the armchair. It meant he couldn't get to her.

"Dad… Dad, listen, we all miss Mum. We have all been heartbroken. It's not just you. You don't have to be sitting here on your own."

"Think yer so smart, eh? When are you buggering off going to yer ponsy city?"

"I'm not. I'm staying here."

"Eh! There's not a hope in hell yer movin' in here, madam."

"I'm not. I mean I'm staying in Gala."

"Whae wi? Yer queero brother? Have 'ee no heard he prefers tae live wi' men, no women?" He had never allowed himself to come terms with Robert's homosexuality.

"He lives with one man, one man only and has done so for a very long time." She utterly detested hearing him talk of Robert and Michael like this. It made her blood rise to the boil in her veins.

"Shite that is. That type are aye skulkin' aboot looking for arse."

"Sometimes, Dad, you're pathetic."

"Is that so?"

"Well why don't you try and get to know Robert a bit better, get to know Michael?" There was a moment's silence. Despite her dismay at his comments about Robert, Ruth was determined to retrieve this, to break some ground today, if only for her own sake, her own sanity. "You, me and Robert, we are all we have got. What would Mum think if she saw us? If she saw you and me like this? We need each other now. I need you, Dad." She was risking sounding as though she was pleading.

"I. Need. Nobody. Got it!" It was the only moment so far he looked her right in the eye. It was a look that said *'who do you think you are? Don't you ever mention your mother to me as though I don't understand.'* But she just didn't get it. She didn't read that look well, because it was all about her, you see. It was always, always going to be about her. It always had been, and that's okay when you are thirteen years old, but at thirty-five that kind of self-centred stuff was never going to work here.

"I don't believe you, Dad. You know why? Because despite everything I still know I need you. It's just so bloody sad it's taken me nearly twenty years to realise it. I need you, Dad."

He sat quiet, staring straight ahead. Ruth was forced to sit it out. She was used to sitting on her own, in silence. She steadied herself for what could be a lengthy battle of wills. Then her dad took a deep breath and said, "You'd think after awe these years you'd wake up hen. Bloody well wake up and see it's no just awe aboot you." He sighed a heavy, disappointed, long, exhausted sigh, "Now will ye switch that back on." He pointed to the television. Ruth got up and

263

switched it on. Suddenly she thought of Mick. She had agreed to meet him; it had all but escaped her mind. She should be going home now and getting ready for her date, but she worried if she got up and left now without explaining then he would think she had walked out on him again. Whilst she was feeling a bit uncomfortable with what he was saying to her, at least they were talking. He wasn't shouting, so there had been an important, if small breakthrough. Considering this, she knew she couldn't just get up and leave without explaining why.

"I'm meeting a chap for dinner tonight." He did not look at her or answer. She continued, unrelenting. "He works in the bookshop, Mick Munroe."

"Would ye just have a wee listen tae yersel, for Christ sake, you, you and more you." He shook his head, dismissing her. Surely he must have been wondering, when is she ever going ask me how I am, how I've been for the last decade?

"It was just that he's someone I remember from years ago. I met him today and he seems like a really nice person." She was trying to justify herself.

"He owns it." Three words, no eye contact.

"Mm? He what?"

"He owns it."

"Owns what?"

"It."

"It?"

"The shop, he owns the shop."

"What?" She sounded as though she found that hard to believe. As though he hadn't looked like a shop owner, if there's a look a shop owner's supposed to have.

"Huh you'll be fine there, hen. He'll be bloody loaded, him."

"Who? What are you talking about?" She was thinking, *what is he inferring: 'I'll be fine there?' It's a date, one date.*

"Dead money there, hen. Oh you just get in there, 'n look efter yersel." Loaded with sarcasm, his comments were by no means a form of encouragement.

"What d'you mean?"

"Payoot."

"What?'

"His wuman was run ower."

"His what?"

"Oh aye, 'n wee bairn saw it awe, she did, mother croakin' oot her last. That bairn saw it awe. Just a wee bloody lassie. Aye, saw whole bloody lot, nae choice, poor wee bugger."

"Wait, wait, no, what?" She could sense his emphasis on that girl watching her mother die.

"Aye, he got money when his wumen deed." He was matter of fact and in an absurd way it was as if he was inferring that the money somehow made up for it, made up for a mother dying, made up for a child bearing witness to it, made the tragedy acceptable. Though it was impossible too, not to detect a hint of bitterness in his voice. "Seems if somebody else kills 'ee, ye get money. If 'ee happen tae dee yersel, o' yer own accord, 'ee get fuck all." For a second occasion he made and held stony cold eye contact with her. She could feel her eyes

265

sting as she tried to meet and hold his glare, but she felt as though her throat had collapsed completely. She rose quickly to leave, stunned by that curve ball and the realisation she was not the only one with a heap load of baggage.

It was not how she had imagined Mick had spent the last however many years, not at all. As she left, she noticed her dad seemed smug, in fact he appeared to be quite satisfied with that conversation and how it had hit her hard, squarely, in the gut, and what's more it was as though he was proud at having delivered that punch himself. In reality he was hoping it might shock her out her constant state of self-possession. All it did though, was tighten her screws up a little.

*

It's me Mum, Ruth, I'm still here. Still here. I might have moved away and back physically, but in here, in my head, I'm still in the same place I was when I was thirteen. I know it's been a long time since I've written to you – years in fact. And just lately I've read through all those letters that I wrote to you. Every time, I thought you would come down and read them as if by magic, and that one day, just once, there would be a reply, just a small note written by you and left on my bed. I know now though. I know that was just a wee girl's dream. But I'm still that wee girl and I have to write to you today to get this out of my system. He, A.K.A. your husband, my father, is driving me mad; I just can't make any headway with him. Honestly sometimes I just want to take hold of him and squeeze the bloody breath right out of him. Sometimes I wonder if I've been stupid to think I could build a bridge between us. Honestly, the bloody bridge over the Kwai would be easier to build. "Time's a healer." I don't think so. Twenty-three bloody years since you died and he hasn't moved forward one day either. Neither have I inside, neither has Robert. Not inside. But outside, to everyone else, I have to be something other than the motherless daughter, the alcoholic widower's daughter. I have to be me, Mum. I have to be somebody. Do you understand? I am not selfish. He thinks I am. He thinks I am just on about me all the time. I'm not. I'm just trying to *be* me. Whatever 'being me' actually amounts to. Truth is I don't know who 'me' is.

It's as if he hates us for just trying to do that, for just trying to live, for just trying to be us. Because this is our life too you know. Oh hell what did I come back to Galashiels for? It's like he was never my dad, and you have never been my mum. It's like he's a stranger, and so are you. I just don't recognise that sad angry old man in there, and he just won't do anything to try and even recognise me. I'm his daughter. It's like he has forgotten all about me. I know he detests Robert for being gay, but at least he remembers Robert for something. Even if his opinion's shite. Robert's a good man, and that silly old, homophobic bugger in there should be proud of him. But do you know what? It's like we have never existed as his kids, your kids. It's like he's just wiped me out. So what the hell am I doing here? What have I done? Help. Oh what the hell, you're not listening. So what if we all just forgot? Would that make it easier? What if I forgot about you? What if I just forget about everything?

267

IV

It was their last night in Krakow and Anna was finding it difficult to sleep. It wasn't just that she was excited to be going home in the morning, or that she really had had something of an information overload since she arrived in Poland. She couldn't sleep because it was happening again. Her room in their apartment seemed eerily chilled and silently charged. Whilst she was on her own, she was aware of an omniscient energy seeping into the room and she felt like she had company. She considered everything that she had learnt over the past four days about her papa and his mother, and she took a deep breath, reminding herself that she was in charge of this 'psychic' thing. That's what her papa had told her. He said, "Remember you are always in charge of it, not the other way around, so if you don't want a visit, just tell them. In a nice way of course, polite, you know, because it is a special thing, maybe even a blessing".

Now, having been armed with the background on everything that she considered odd about herself, she had become less afraid of these encounters and more curious, so rather than asking them to leave, ironically she was quietly hoping they, who or whatever 'they' were, would come back again. It was funny though, because part of her thought she would have to be in her own bedroom for it to happen, as though she thought that was where she had to be to get the best 'reception'. With her papa's advice at the forefront of her mind, she got up quietly to check on him. He was asleep in the room next door; there was no mistaking the quality of that snoring. On returning to her room she could definitely tell the atmosphere was energised. She kept her bedside light on and with her diary in hand, she started to add in her thoughts of their final day in Poland. This was a new thing for her – keeping a diary. Her papa had suggested it. She agreed, as she had also wanted to make sure she could remember absolutely everything of her visit to Poland. She wanted to make sure she forgot nothing of her heritage and especially, remember everything about his epic escape. Likewise he seemed to be very satisfied with her commitment to her diary and trusted she would make an accurate record. He was reassured by the fact that there was now a written record of everything he had stored in his brain for the best part of his lifetime. It was now there on paper before his brain and his recollection began to falter. She didn't realise at that point just how much these notes, with all his words of wisdom carefully recorded, would in time act as a guide, like a kind of handbook on how to cope with being psychic.

Despite this and the fact that she was able to log all the various places they had walked, the weather, the food they ate, how Henryk spoke in Polish to the waiters and the people who owned the apartments, she found it difficult to put into words what it was that was worrying her about her dad. He was just different when they had spoken on the phone that morning. Whilst she was contemplating this very thought, she was aware of something that looked like cigarette smoke rising up in front of her. It was like a soft film of grey moving air that was easier to see if she didn't look directly at it, but looked as though she was looking through it. She reached over to pick up the compass from the bedside drawers, wondering whether if she held onto that, it would make this thing stronger, as though the compass was some kind of antenna. She wondered what her papa would say if he thought she was encouraging it, dabbling in something she only partly understood, more than trying to control the whole thing; politely of course. But then it's a true saying, you can't put an old head on young shoulders.

Holding her compass tightly in her left hand, she began to make notes on her dad, starting with a list of words that might describe how he had been on the phone that morning. It went like this:

He had been quiet, maybe tired, slept in, not interested, maybe sad, not listening, absent, maybe late, annoyed, no he wasn't annoyed, switched off, but maybe switched on, onto something else, pre-occupied. That's it, he was pre-occupied. She started to let her thoughts ramble on a bit about what he could be pre-occupied with. Before she could get far, something caught her totally off-guard. In the corner of her eye she could see there was a woman standing at the side of her bed, right beside her. Anna felt as though she was definitely close enough to be reading what she was writing down in her diary. She held the pen still and tried to just keep looking at the page, whilst she slowly laid the compass down, fearing it might really have some kind of magical power that was beyond her control. Everything in her head was screaming at her to *look up, just look up*, but she was frozen stiff with fear and the realisation that this psychic thing isn't as easy to deal with as she was trying to believe. There was an unnerving, almost menacing stillness around her and as she focused on the rise and fall of her chest as she breathed, it became so quiet around her that it was as if she could hear the air banging into the bottom of her lungs every time she breathed in. *Look up, just look up.* Unable to wrestle any longer with the desire not to look up, she looked up, and to her complete surprise there was the same woman who came to her own bedroom standing right beside it. "What the hell? What are you doing here? How did you know I was here?" Anna blurted it all out loud. Whilst it was the first time she had actually spoken to the woman, the whole idea that she could be followed around was so overwhelming that she burst into tears with frustration more than fear. Frustration that despite everything her papa had told her, despite everything she now believed she understood, she really understood none of it. When she looked up again half expecting the woman to have gone, she was still there. She was smiling at her and held both of her hands out as if to say, take hold of these. The tears streamed down Anna's cheeks like a torrent. "Are you my mum? Are you?" The woman shook her head. Whilst she never actually spoke, it was as though Anna could hear her saying something, as though it was being sent telepathically. *'I'm Doreen, I'm Doreen, tell her she's not forgotten, please just tell her I've not forgotten her."*

271

"Tell who, who have I to tell?" Anna was frantic, and it sounded to all and sundry very much like she was rambling on to herself now. She could feel her nose run with the mucus sticking to her lips. As she wiped it away, the woman disappeared. Just simply vanished.

V

Whilst Anna was grappling with her psychic experience, Mick was one thousand miles away in Galashiels, on his first date in over a decade.

"So have you been back in Gala since you left when you were what – seventeen?" To think Mick had spent all day trying to come up with an original opener.

"No." It was easy for Ruth to answer Mick's pretty unadventurous, almost safe, but yet a little prying, question. She was still smarting from the visit to her dad that afternoon.

"Not once?" That's strange, he thought, imagine never coming back home in all that time.

"No."

"So why now, why have you come back now?" He was aware that question was a bit riskier.

"Well, you know I have given this a lot of thought." She paused. "I'm the same age now that my mum was when she died so I… "

"I'm sorry Ruth, I didn't mean… "

"No you're fine, it's a question I've asked myself a lot lately."

"Do you always have an answer?"

"No, not initially. For as long as I can remember I've been afraid of turning thirty-five in case I would be struck down." She let out a nervous chuckle, "Like it's some kind of family curse."

"Honestly, Ruth, I'm sorry to have asked."

"It's okay. It does make you paranoid though, honestly I'm forever checking." Ruth instinctively clasped both her breasts in her hands. Seeing the expression on Mick's face, his eyes firmly fixed on her breasts, she quickly removed them. "Sorry… that was a bit awkward, wasn't it?"

"No… em no… it's fine." Mick let out a sigh, admitting to himself that he was, for a moment there, completely distracted and was actually thinking – *it's been a long time since I held a breast in my hand.* Then immediately he recoiled, feeling guilty because, as he understood things, she had bravely been making reference to her breasts as a source of disease not as an object of his desires. Nevertheless, his mind kept drifting back to the fact that it had been a long time, a very long time, and far from behaving like the recluse he had been for so many years, he was starting to act like some kind of testosterone-packed homing missile that had just had its 'all systems activated' button pressed. He watched as she raised a single questioning eyebrow at him, and then he remembered she was the only person he knew that could do that, raising one eyebrow almost to her hairline if something intrigued her. He remembers that expression well, as she did that when he asked her to his twenty-first.

"Why didn't you come to my twenty-first?" He blurted it out. She sat back in her seat as though he had delivered a right hook at her. It struck him then that this whole social skill thing was pretty unmanageable for him; perhaps that question could have waited.

"I was there, you never turned up. I even had Babychams to drink while I was waiting, honestly I did".

"Forgot about them, Babychams".

"Oh, I thought that was the height of sophistication," she answered defiantly.

"You probably were," he laughed, remembering some of the misfits that had turned up at his party.

"Until I got drunk waiting on you."

"I did turn up though, I was there, and I waited on you."

"You were not."

"I was, it was my party, and of course I was there. Then I got tired of waiting on you, I knew you wouldn't take me seriously."

"Not take you seriously! Are you kidding? I hung on your every word. I nearly died when you asked me. I thought I had actually stopped breathing, honestly."

"It took me months to pluck up the courage to ask you out."

"Why on Earth?"

"Well you were a lot younger back then."

"Still am, though five years doesn't seem such a big deal now does it?"

"No, it's nothing, but back then it was, and what with your Mum not being around, I didn't want people to think… "

"What? Think what? That I was some kind of easy date?"

"No, no, it wasn't that at all. Oh I don't know what I wanted people to think, I suppose I knew you were a bit vulnerable and I didn't want folk to think I was an ass."

'I did go though, and you weren't an ass, and I did take you seriously. I even had to steal some of my brother's after shave so I didn't smell of carbolic soap."

"I know."

"You know?"

"I could smell the *Brut* when you passed me."

"Really? Oh my God." Even today she could feel herself blush with the humiliation of that.

"I just thought you must've ended up going out with someone else."

"Well, you did," she quickly retorted. "You were with Martha Rosiewizck."

"I know."

"I cried."

"I know."

There was a momentary pause as they both remember that event. It was clear it was still vivid for both of them.

"What do you mean, somewhere else, that I'd been somewhere else?" Ruth started the examination of the events again.

"Well, it's just that when I saw you, you were heading home."

"Yeah I was."

"It wasn't that late though."

"Where were you and Martha going?"

"Trying to shake off her dad."

"I got fed up waiting on you to turn up at your own… "

"Wait a minute, where did you go?" Mick interrupted, responding to a flash of insight.

"Langhaugh like you said."

"Terrace or Gardens?"

"Terrace."

"Gardens, Ruth I lived at Langhaugh Gardens."

"What?"

"Gardens. Shit."

"Whose party was I at then?"

"God knows. That's unbelievable."

"Bloody hell, whose house was I in then?"

Their drinks arrived, providing a well-timed pause. They were both genuinely perplexed. She had gone to the wrong house. You could tell they were both thinking *'What if?'*

"I went to see my dad today". Ruth wanted to somehow gently engineer the conversation around to him, and ultimately who the 'Anna' woman might be that he referred to. Altogether she had had a difficult day, and was feeling very uncomfortable with the thought that she might now be dining out with someone who was already spoken for.

"Oh, your dad. How is he? I haven't seen him in town for a while." That took her by surprise.

"You remember my dad?"

"Yeah, of course I do." He wondered why she was talking as though he had died. "Is he okay?"

Ruth realised this conversation was not moving quite in the direction she had hoped.

"Yeah he's okay, I suppose, in his own way."

"Nice guy."

"What?"

"Your Dad, nice guy."

She wondered if they were talking about the same man.

"Nice guy?" Her reply sounded unmistakably bitter.

"I'm sorry, think I've missed something? Your dad, yeah?"

"Yeah."

"Same guy who used to come round for books every week. Would take two maybe three, he reads a lot he does, although I haven't seen him for a few weeks."

"My Dad reads?"

"Well, he buys books every week."

"What kind of books?"

'Mmm?'

"What kind of books, genre, does he buy, read?"

There was a newfound intensity in her questioning that made Mick feel like he was being subjected to some kind of undercover surveillance. He was starting to remember everything he dreaded about dating women.

"I'm not sure. He read, or rather, he bought a lot of poetry." He was aware he had started to choose his words very carefully.

"My dad? Poetry?"

Mick began to feel as though he had broken a confidence. He looked across the table at her but never spoke. There was an uncomfortable moment where Ruth was being slowly consumed by a wave of envy that this man might know her dad better than she did and there was a slow realisation that this envy might be born of guilt.

Mick was watching her, he watched as her determined, inquisitive expression dissolved into something almost reproachful. Although he was a man who was used to his own company and his own silence, he found this silence unbearable.

"Sometimes he would just pop in for a chat, nothing special."

"What'd he chat about?" Part of her was hoping Mick would say *'you and your brother.'*

"Mostly how I was getting on, you know after everything."

"That's nice." There was coldness in her reply; to be honest she felt as if referring to her dad as *nice* would just about tear her tongue out.

"It was actually. Not many people asked. When something like that happens, people avoid you."

"I can't imagine him being that bothered, to be honest." She couldn't hold it in any longer. There was a steely shard of venom in her retort that Mick felt was as much directed at him as it was at her dad. He was really conscious of feeling as though he was wandering unarmed into unknown and almost certainly dangerous territory. So he decided to change the subject.

"My daughter's over in Poland just now."

Ruth thought she might actually faint. *Bloody hell he is a dad. Oh my God, what if he's married again too?* She suddenly realised her brother had told her. Her dad had told her. She hadn't listened though. She hadn't really taken that information in, until now.

"Your daughter?"

"Anna, it's for her eighteenth birthday. Her papa's idea."

"Eighteen? You're never old enough."

"You think?" He enjoyed that compliment though.

She smiled at him whilst politely excusing herself to go to the ladies, and allow herself time out to consider all this. *Anna's not his wife, it's his daughter, his bloody daughter, you bloody idiot.* Then she did some quick mental arithmetic that lead her to the conclusion that Anna was born when he was twenty-two, the year after his ill-fated party. At that point all of her brother's words came flooding back to her. *'He got the wee Polish lassie pregnant.' Right now his daughter's in Poland with her papa, so Martha Rosiewicz must be Anna's mum.* Then she remembered what her dad had said that afternoon and started to feel overwhelmed with nausea. *Oh hell, oh God, Martha must be the one that's dead. Oh my God almighty. Bloody hell. That can't be right. Martha? All these years I've been envious of her over a walk home, all this time she's been dead.* The enormity of what Mick had actually come through slammed into her like a two-ton truck. *Oh Jesus Christ, just what kind of person am I?* She was losing her composure as quickly as she was losing her appetite. *Martha's dead, why did I not know that? I have only been thirty-two miles up the road, but where the fuck have I actually been in here, in my head? Why, why, why have I never come back home? What have I done, what the hell have I done?* She started slapping her forehead, just as another diner entered the ladies.

"Oh it's hot in here, isn't it?" she said, trying to cover up the fact that she was having something of a major meltdown. It was indeed a defining moment for Ruth, as images of her dad spending day after day, year upon year on his own railroaded into her consciousness, along with the realisation that Mick, at the very least, still had his daughter. I suppose you could say it was crucially a moment of insight. She wasn't sure if she liked what she was seeing. In fact it was making her boak.

When she returned to the table, Mick noticed right away that something wasn't quite right with her. She was altogether much paler than when she had gone to the ladies, and the sparkle in her eyes that he had found very appealing, had all but disappeared.

"Are you okay, Ruth?"

"Not sure." She couldn't look up. She felt as though everything inside her had started to gnaw at her. She felt as though the lights were being dimmed around her.

"Can I get you anything?"

"I don't think so. I think I'll have to go." With no apology and no explanation, Ruth got up and left. They hadn't even started their meal yet.

Mick sat in silence for a few minutes, slowly finishing his drink, aware that all eyes were fixed upon him, waiting for his response. He had no idea what the response should be. This was a whole new experience for him, both being out on a date, and being jilted the very same night. To say he might be confused and disappointed would be an understatement. He felt a complete fool. *Knew I shouldn't have bothered with this shit. I liked her though and that's a first. I actually liked someone.* Half of him wanted to celebrate that sentiment, whilst the other half wanted to crawl back into a hole and hide away from the world again for the next few years.

VI

If the trip to Poland was supposed to help Anna come to terms with being psychic, then it did go some way to achieving that, but by no means did it enable her to embrace it. After the visit from Doreen, she lay awake the whole night, trying to think who the message was for. She felt the woman had told her as if Anna should already know who the message was for. In the morning she could barely keep her eyes open over breakfast. Henryk had noticed she was tired, but he wasn't surprised, she had a lot of new information to absorb. Whilst our brains are clever little things, he knew that sometimes it takes a bit of time to sort all the new stuff out, sorting it into manageable little bites of detail. He figured that was what Anna was up against right now, and that it was best if he just gave her a little space to let this happen. So he went off to get a newspaper – a Polish one.

Not only had he been speaking Polish since arriving in Krakow, he was trying to read his native tongue too, which was a bit of an achievement in itself, when you consider he was illiterate when he arrived in Scotland. He always pays tribute to Martha for being able to read English. He learnt to read along with Martha using her school books, and it's true to say he had never taken being able to read for granted, in fact he firmly believed that reading was a privilege. He would often tell Anna that when her mum went shopping, he would ask her when she got back, "What did you buy – anything nice?" expecting she might say, yes, a new dress, or new shoes, or some make-up. But she never did. She would simply reply, "Books, just books." He says that's why he and Mick decided to call the shop 'Books'. Anna can remember thinking as she grew up: *books, just books, what a stupid name for a shop*. Now of course, on a day such as this, when she sees her papa attempting to read a Polish newspaper, she thinks differently. When you consider it, 'Books', well, it kind of speaks for itself, in just one word, doesn't it?

Mick and Henryk had opened the shop after Henryk received a compensation award following Martha's accident, because it had been a drunk driver. At first they thought he had had a heart attack, but it wasn't that – he was blind drunk in the middle of the day. Henryk can still recall the outrage in town after it happened.

They both agreed at the time that the book shop would be a fitting tribute to her. It was a far cry from Henryk's first proper job that he got in the local tannery when the war finished. It was his job to separate the skins when they arrived. He would often say it wasn't a pleasant job; it was heavy work, little machinery, and that he "… was stinking to the high heavens every day." He has always had a way with words that made Mick laugh.

Despite the unpleasantness of his work, he said he was lucky and grateful just to have a job, as after the war there was a fairly ferocious 'Poles Go Home' campaign, as the returning troops began to demand their jobs back. Thankfully he survived that campaign too.

It would seem he's a born survivor, even now, as after their trip to Poland he can add his fear of flying to the list of demons he has overcome. Even so there was no mistaking his relief as they touched down in Edinburgh on a misty Sunday morning.

Mick had been in arrivals for at least an hour; he had never quite experienced the excitement he was feeling whilst waiting for them to appear through arrivals. He hadn't anticipated the feelings that were whipping up inside him. On top of that, he hadn't slept very well. He was confused about Ruth. He couldn't understand why she had just left. He went over and over everything he might have said that might have caused offence. The only thing he could come up with was the reference he had made to her dad. She hadn't seemed pleased at all at that. In fact, she had gone quite pale when he had said that he was a nice guy. But then that's what Mick thought. After the accident, Ruth's dad had been only one of a few who didn't cross to the other side of street when Mick approached. He was one of the few who actively sought Mick out to check how he was doing. He had been telling the truth when he said her dad had come regularly to the shop. Sometimes just for a chat, sometimes he did buy a book. Mostly he bought non-fiction, a lot of historical books and autobiographies. He did buy poetry though, that wasn't a lie. Whether he read any of the stuff he bought, Mick couldn't say. I suppose it was just a presumption that if someone bought a book, then they most likely had the intention of reading it, unless of course they were gifts. Mick thought that he must have given a lot of gifts if that was the case. So that would make him a generous guy as well as a nice guy. He imagined Ruth might have actually fainted if he had expanded any further on her dad's interest in books and whether or not this deemed him to be a decent and generous man or not.

Just as he was wondering what kind of night Ruth might have had, and how she might be that morning, the automatic doors parted and the arrivals from Krakow started to stream through. All thoughts of Ruth evaporated as he strained his neck and sprung from foot to foot to try and see Anna emerging from the bustling crowd.

VI

After rebuffing Mick and almost running all the way home, Ruth burst into her flat gasping for air as though someone was physically choking her. It had little to do with the humid air that night. No, having just walked out on Mick, for no apparent reason to him, her head had spun so much that it was almost as if she had uncorked herself, and all the emotional pressure that had been stored up over the last eighteen years came spewing out uncontrollably. She was quite literally blowing a gasket.

Without taking off her coat or putting on the light, she scrambled into her kitchen and in the dark she started to pull at the kitchen drawers, throwing things out onto the floor; it would have been hard to tell if she was randomly trashing the room, or genuinely looking for something. Tripping over a selection of cutlery, a few batteries and a couple of place mats, she made her way into the living room, where she pulled out the papers and magazines from under her coffee table and hauled the books out of the bookcase. She was grunting and wheezing, as though she was struggling for breath. On finding a pen and her notebook that had been stuffed down the side of her chair cushion, she dropped to her knees, ripping out the pages of the book in the dark.

"You never answer me, you never answer me!" she was shouting out in the dark, ripping pages out and throwing them out across the floor. "Look at these, look at them!" She was holding aloft a collection of torn papers; "Come and read them!" she demanded fiercely, but no-one was there. No-one was going to answer. There was no-one there, and despite her desperate, frantic pleas no-one was coming to read her notes or letters. There were no tears, just angry rants and boiling frustration, as page by page she tore at the paper until the notebook was emptied and tattered pages were strewn around the room.

On her knees she scrambled around the room, pulling over photographs and hauling down plants and anything remotely ornamental onto the floor. She was like a tight knot unravelling, until the ends that were once all cleverly joined and tightly secured were all loosened up and dangerously detached.

Having walked out on her job, and leaving the flat that had been her home for eighteen years, returning on the whim of an unresolved teenage crush, she had finally crashed at the vulnerability of it all. Nothing, absolutely nothing was how she had hoped it would be, from the very real relationship she hoped to claw back with her father to the imaginary relationship she had hoped to exploit with Mick. It was as if a small atom had exploded in the centre of her brain.

When she did eventually put on a light, she was met with a scene that looked as if she had been burgled, ransacked.

Slowly and methodically she walked around the living room replacing what she could and throwing into the bin anything she had broken. Scooping up the pages torn from her notebook, she sat down and carefully arranged them in chronological order; some of the notes she had dated from as far back as the 1970s. In the kitchen she returned the cutlery she had hauled out back to the drawers and items from the cupboard were tidied and returned. Quietly and with a focused determination, she restored an unsettled order of some sort to her home.

Then, with a deep breath, she reached into the cupboard for her brandy and poured herself what could be best described as an extremely generous measure, which was swiftly followed by large measure two and larger measure three.

She was moving around the place less frantically now, gathering and moving items purposefully. She took her brandy bottle through to the sitting room with her glass and sat on the floor beside her notes. There she sat for more than an hour reading through every letter, every note, and every poem she had written, from the year her mum died to the notes she had made after returning to Galashiels. When she had finished, she calmly reached into her bag for two small packets. One contained her anti-depressants, the other her sedatives. She normally takes two of these sedatives at around this time. She had been taking sedatives for most of her adult life. She often wondered if they were still actually working, as she often lay awake considering what direction her life should be moving in, whilst despairing often at the stagnation of it all.

She had had a good career working in a job she seemed devoted to, she had had a nice home, and good health. To onlookers this might simply mean 'being settled'. To Ruth it was as though she had become captive to ordinariness. Returning to Galashiels wasn't so much instinctive as impulsive. It was more of an escape than a directive.

It was a determined Ruth, however, that pressed out the tablets from both packs of medication, and it was a determined Ruth that refilled her glass so that she would have enough liquid with which to swallow them.

Ruth was quick to succumb to the effects of the alcohol, antidepressants and sedatives she had taken, descending into a deep, dark ravine of unconsciousness. As she did, she really did imagine that she might just, at long last, be drifting along in the right direction.

Part Four

I

Anna's Story II

My papa's hands are starting to go cold. I've been holding onto them for a while now, rubbing them, trying to warm them up and force the life back into them. When I look at them I can tell they were a hardworking pair of hands, and clever hands too. In saying that, he hasn't got brutish, manly hands like shovels, no, his have a delicacy about them. I've had time today to quietly trace along the lines on his hands. His life line so deeply etched and unbroken around the ball of his thumb, you'd think he should actually live forever. His heart line though, that's a different matter. As soon as it leaves his index fingers it breaks, and breaks again several times across the top of his palm. I can see his one child deeply etched on the outer aspect of his hand below his pinkie. Then I can see that his heart line doesn't even reach that length. His heart predestined to be broken several times. I feel sick when I look at this. My poor papa, hardly a day must have gone by that his heart mustn't have ached; ached for the loss of his mother, the loss of his daughter and the mysterious departure of his wife. We don't even know if my grandmother is still alive or not. If alive we don't even know where she lives for that matter.

I turn his hands over and run my hands gently over each of his veins; all of them look flat, thin and cold, like they are all already empty. When he was well he always kept his nails trimmed, but yesterday when he was restless I noticed he was scratching himself when he was thrashing around, so I clipped them for him this morning. Funny that; he's been here for nearly a week now and they hadn't cleaned or trimmed his nails. You'd think that would be part and parcel of washing his hands. I could never have been a nurse. The smell of this place is bad enough. Don't hospitals smell strange? I've never been a fan I have to say, but we have had to get used to being in them recently as Papa's been fighting his illness for a few years now. Recently he's become very weak, and been coming in periodically to get built up. But it's never done much good coming in here to get built up; in fact now you can almost see the cancer consuming him on a daily basis. His little arms have virtually no muscle left at all. To think he was once as strong as an ox.

Last Sunday, nearly a week ago now, Papa phoned my dad, but he couldn't speak, so Dad knew something was wrong immediately. Usually when Papa phoned he didn't even bother with a 'hello', or wait for the 'hello,' for that matter, he just started up where he had left off when on his previous call. Bearing in mind that call might have been three or four days ago.

That day though, Dad says all he could hear were strange sounds, a bit like Papa might have been sleeping when he called and was snoring, or sort of rasping down the phone. Dad had one of these phones that displayed the number thankfully, or he would have hung up thinking it was a rogue caller of some sort. So when he saw the number and heard the noise Papa was making, he dropped the phone and dashed over. It's been really cold this January, and that morning the frost hadn't lifted yet. Dad said that he ran from the house in his shirt sleeves and his slippers, and nearly broke his neck falling on ice on the stairs down to the car park. When he got to Papa's he found him kneeling on the floor, crouched over beside the phone, drooling onto the floor. He still had the receiver in his hand.

It's Friday now, and Papa hasn't eaten or been able to drink anything since he came into hospital. At first he opened his eyes when we were by the bed, but now his eyes are closed. Dad said a funny thing yesterday before he gave in and left the room; he said, "This is not how I expected him to die." I couldn't quite figure out if he was angry or surprised. I suppose we had prepared ourselves for Papa's death by cancer, not by a stroke. You see we knew everything about his cancer, as Dad went with him to all his checks and treatment. Then I thought about what my dad had said. I reckoned that he coped best if he knew all the information, and with regard to Papa's cancer he did. He knew what to expect, as the Macmillan nurses had spent a great deal of time with them explaining all the ins and outs of everything. But they never mentioned stroke. That had never been on the agenda. When I thought about it I realised that my dad doesn't handle anything to do with death well at the best of times, but the combination of surprise and death were just unbearable for him. He told me that Papa dying of cancer was something he was managing to get his head around, and that he would do everything he could to help Papa as he knew what was happening, and what was about to happen. Then it all went pear-shaped last Sunday. Suddenly Dad hadn't a clue what was going on. It was the nurses and doctors that were in charge now, and not him. Yesterday when Papa was restless and agitated my dad just couldn't stay. I suppose as he says, it just wasn't how he had imagined it was going to be, or how he wanted it to be.

II

I should say that if you've reached this part then you'll know a little of what happened. But we were all in for the biggest shock of our lives when we heard that Ruth had been found dead.

My poor dad, I still can't believe what happened. He was completely stunned by it all; talk about being knocked sideways. He really was, and has never really recovered.

For a long time after Ruth died he shunned people, more than he had ever done. He employed a girl to run the shop, said his heart just wasn't in it. I saw that lost, maybe even broken, heart in his eyes. It was in the way he stood, in the way he walked. I think he felt as though the events that surrounded Ruth dying weighed entirely on his shoulders. So much so that sometimes when I looked at him it was actually as though he was suddenly three inches shorter. Do you know that for a long time he never read a book? Not one. The same book, *Nick Hornby's High Fidelity* sat beside his chair for nearly nine months. It was the book he was reading when Robert, Ruth's brother, came knocking at our door on the Sunday night. At the point that my dad had been laughing out loud reading this book that had arrived amongst the latest stock order. I remember him telling me it was new out and had had great reviews, and 'for once.' he declared, he was 'going to read something with the single intention of having a bloody good laugh'.

I had been away in Poland for only five days, and I noticed there was something different about him. Just as I had noticed when we spoke on the phone the day before Papa and I returned from Poland. It was like there had been a shift, for whatever reason yet unknown to me, in his consciousness, from deep and dark to light.

Then, within a matter of minutes of letting Robert into our house it was like he had completely blown a fuse. Oh my God, even now, when I think about that night now, it brings me out into a cold sweat. I didn't know who this guy was when I answered the door, but my dad did. He didn't introduce him to me though; they just went straight into the kitchen together. I could tell there was something wrong, but had no idea what, as we had only been back for one night and my dad hadn't told me about going out with Ruth on the Saturday night. He must have been waiting on the 'right time'. Unfortunately he wasn't ever going to get a chance to find the 'right time'. It was a shame really because neither I nor Papa knew what was going on; we didn't know why Dad was so agitated and upset. We thought it had something to do with us being away. Then he sat us down, and as much as it was really tragic for him to tell us about this woman dying from a suspected overdose, it seemed he was equally devastated that he'd gone out on a date with a woman without us knowing. Even though, as he explained, the whole date had gone pear-shaped, at least he had gone, and more importantly, he had wanted to go. He had wanted badly to go. He was like a little boy, making a confession whilst berating himself at the same time. When he spoke he was rambling on and on, a bit like a verbal machine gun, and he just kept firing out all this random information. Jumping back and forward from situation to situation, person to person. It was hard to keep track:

She had arrived for her book. Her hair was beautiful. They went for dinner. He closed the shop all day. She went pale. Imagine closing the shop. He upset her when he mentioned her dad; shit, it was his fault. He should never have gone out. He should never have closed the shop. It's Martha's shop. Ruth had left letters behind, lots of them. He won't do it again. There were letters to her mum, letters to him, lots of them all around her, where they found her. That's why Robert came to me, she had written countless letters to me, but never posted them.

Then came the most crucial piece of information; he mentioned Doreen and that Ruth had never gotten over losing her mother, and that in the end she must have lost her mind. As soon as he said this I felt like I had been thumped hard on the head. Doreen was Ruth's mum. My ghostly night visitor had been Ruth's mum, not mine.

So I suppose you can understand that over the years I have come to realise that being psychic is not a gift, or a blessing, it's just something that happens. I'm not special and I'm not chosen. I'm just a bit like an aerial, a receiver of some sort. The clever bit is figuring out what to do with the information. That's what makes the difference between maintaining my sanity and steering off the threat that it might drive me mad.

For instance, I often wonder what might have happened if I had been able to work out who Doreen was, and if I could have saved Ruth from taking her own life. If only she had known her mum had come looking for her. If only I had known who she was. That's a hell of a thought for me. That's where my papa has been so important to me, when he said I had to learn to control it. He had been so afraid of it after my great grandmother was murdered that he defiantly controlled it to the point that he virtually ignored it.

But that event and indeed everything about Ruth Nairn epitomises what it's like to be psychic. For some time I blamed myself for Ruth doing what she did, as I thought that if I had just been able to figure out who my ghostly visitor was, and that I was meant to pass her message onto Ruth, then she would have known her mother was with her, and that she hadn't forgotten about her. I felt really really bad for a long time afterwards, especially when I saw my dad. I cannot remember him crying when my mum died, I suppose I was too young. But when we heard about Ruth he just folded up. It was like all those years' worth of grief came pouring out. I have never heard a noise like it. It was horrific. I was absolutely terrified. He cried like I've never seen anyone cry before, with his whole body shaking, and huge wailing sobs.

III

Despite Papa's encouragement to get control of this psychic thing, I found it almost impossible, as it was unrelenting and exhausting. It just kept coming at me; dreams, voices, people appearing and disappearing, people who just kept arriving at the end of my bed most nights. A funny thing though, Doreen stopped visiting when Ruth had gone. I like to think that they must have been able to meet up somewhere, because I know there's an 'out there'. In fact some days it felt as though I was so tuned into the 'out there' that it was like I was trying to live on two different ethereal planes; my feet being firmly on the ground, while at the same time my mind was being flown like a giant balloon way above the mortal world.

My poor papa, we hadn't been back from our trip to Poland for long when he began to complain of back ache. We all put it down to too much walking whilst we had been away, and then sitting for a long time in the plane and the car. But over the next few weeks it never eased off as it should have. A couple of visits to the GP and a couple of scans later and we had the news, the 'diagnosis'; prostate cancer, a silent killer for men, apparently. It was true though because without much ado, it had actually gone right into the bones of his back. They started him on drugs, really strong ones, chemotherapy. It worked for a good long while, but it was back now and back with a vengeance. To think this man escaped the German army. It's hard to believe, looking at him now, that he would have the stamina, and the wherewithal to make that journey and make a new life for himself, with all that pain and fear in his heart. It's such a shame he wasn't going to escape the enemy this time.

I don't think it will be long now; his breathing has changed. It's not regular like it should be anymore. Every time there's a long pause I think, that was the last one, then a gasp and he has another one or two. One of these will be his last though, and I wish my dad would come back in, but he just can't do this part. I know he wishes he could, but he just can't. Let's face it, after Papa dies my dad will have been unfortunate enough to have had to get himself over the three main ways there are to die – accidental, suicidal and now natural. I'm sitting here wondering, morbidly I suppose, which is easier to get over, if any? I am wondering too about death and how it seems as though the aftermath and grief is like glue, emotional glue that pulls all the elements of your life in together, makes you consider what's important and what's not, what should stay and be glued into your consciousness, and what doesn't fit anymore and needs to be discarded.

However, if being psychic has taught me nothing else, it has taught me that everyone handles death differently. Which is really a strange thing when you consider it is the one thing absolutely everyone on this planet has in common: we will all die. There's no right or wrong way to handle it though. You just have to get through it and out the other side. That goes for both the dying and the living that are left. Strange that, isn't it, that dying is like a race to get to the other side of this living hell, the hell that is parting.

I do believe that those given warning that they are dying, have to go through the same grief, if not worse than those that are left. After all, they have to say goodbye to everyone they know. While us, the ones left, well we just have to say goodbye to one person. Sometimes I think it's a bit like we are pitched against each other on a running track. We are in the living lane; they are in the dying lane. The finishing line is peacefulness. We are all running hard towards the same line. It's just that as with any race, some of us get there quicker than others. And whilst peacefulness for me seems a long way off right now, I can look at my papa and tell he's there already. He is now. He's got there before me, and before my dad.

The nurse that came in to check him earlier told me that I need to tell him it's all right to go. She said he is hanging on until he knows we will be okay. I couldn't answer her. After she'd finished her tasks and left, I thought to myself, I don't know if it's all right for him to go. What on Earth will I do without him?